"Cold, Liv?"

She gasped and whirled. She hadn't heard the terrace doors open, or Thorpe's steps. The moonlight shone directly on her face, while his was in shadow. She felt at a disadvantage.

He moved closer and laid his hands on her arms. "You're chilled. Nobody wants a newscaster with the sniffles." Then he pulled her against him and silenced her with a kiss. She felt the pull of desire just before his mouth lifted from hers.

"Maybe you didn't need that," he said "but I did."

"You must be crazy." The words were scathing, yet husky with passion.

"I must be," he agreed easily. "Otherwise I wouldn't have walked out of your apartment the other night.

Dear Reader:

There is an electricity between two people in love that makes everything they do magic, larger than life. This is what we bring you in SILHOUETTE INTIMATE MOMENTS.

SILHOUETTE INTIMATE MOMENTS are longer, more sensuous romance novels filled with adventure, suspense, glamor or melodrama. These books have an element no one else has tapped: excitement.

We are proud to present the very best romance has to offer from the very best romance writers. In the coming months look for some of your favorite authors such as Elizabeth Lowell, Nora Roberts, Erin St. Claire and Brooke Hastings.

SILHOUETTE INTIMATE MOMENTS are for the woman who wants more than she has ever had before. These books are for you.

Karen Solem
Editor-in-Chief
Silhouette Books

Endings and Beginnings

Nora Roberts

Published by Silhouette Books New York
America's Publisher of Contemporary Romance

For my father, whose press badge read:
Bernard E. Robertson, Sr.

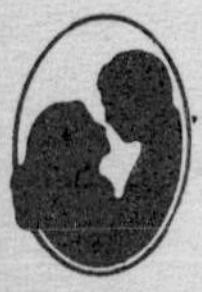

SILHOUETTE BOOKS, a Division of Simon & Schuster, Inc.
1230 Avenue of the Americas, New York, N.Y. 10020

Distributed by Pocket Books

ISBN: 0-671-46157-5

First Silhouette Books printing January, 1984

10 9 8 7 6 5 4 3 2 1

America's Publisher of Contemporary Romance

Printed in the U.S.A.

Books by Nora Roberts

Silhouette Romance

Irish Throughbred #81
Blithe Images #127
Song of the West #143
Search for Love #163
Island of Flowers #180
From This Day #199
Her Mother's Keeper #215
Untamed #252
Storm Warning #274

Silhouette Special Edition

The Heart's Victory #59
Reflections #100
Dance of Dreams #116

Silhouette Intimate Moments

Once More With Feeling #2
Tonight and Always #12
This Magic Moment #25
Endings and Beginnings #33

Chapter 1

"A WHITE HOUSE SOURCE HAS CONFIRMED THE IMMINENT retirement of Secretary of State George Larkin. Secretary Larkin underwent extensive cardiac surgery last week and is currently recovering at Bethesda Naval Hospital. His health is given as the reason for his midterm retirement. Stan Richardson has an on-the-scene report from Bethesda Naval."

Liv watched the monitor switch to the location shot before she turned to her co-anchor. "Brian, this could be the biggest thing to hit since the Malloy scandal last October. There must be five viable replacements for Larkin. The scrambling's going to start."

Brian Jones flipped through his notes, running over his timing. He was a thirty-five-year-old black with a flare for clothes and ten years of television news experience. Though he had grown up in Queens, he considered himself a Washingtonian. "Nothing you love better than a good scramble."

"Nothing," Liv agreed, and turned back to the camera as control gave her her cue.

"The president had no comment today on Secretary Larkin's replacement. Speculation from a high official lists Beaumont Dell, former ambassador to France, and General Robert J. Fitzhugh as top candidates. Neither could be reached for comment."

"A twenty-five-year-old man was found slain in his apartment in Northeast Washington this afternoon." Brian took over his first segment of their anchor partnership.

Liv listened with half an ear while her mind raced with possibilities. Beaumont Dell was her choice. His aides had given her the classic runaround that afternoon, but she was determined to be parked on his doorstep the next morning. As a reporter, she was accustomed to runarounds, waiting, and having doors shut in her face. Nothing, absolutely nothing, she told herself, was going to stop her from interviewing Dell.

Hearing her next cue, Liv turned to camera three and began her lead-in. In their homes, viewers saw the head and shoulders of an elegant brunette. Her voice was low-key, her pace unhurried. They would have no idea how carefully the minute and fifteen seconds had been timed and edited. They saw sincerity and beauty. In the television news game one was often as important as the other. Liv's hair was short and sculptured around a finely boned face. Her eyes were cool blue, serious and direct. A viewer could easily believe she spoke especially for him.

Her television audience found her classy, a little remote, and accurate. Liv was satisfied with the consensus on her role as co-anchor of the local evening news. As a reporter, she wanted more, much more.

A colleague had once described her as having "that wealthy, Connecticut look." Indeed, she had come from a well-off New England family, and her degree in journalism was from Harvard. However, she had worked her way up through the ranks of television reporting.

She had started at base pay at a tiny independent station in New Jersey, reading weather and doing quick consumer spots. She had played the usual game of hopscotching from station to station, city to city—a little more money, a little more air time. She had landed a position at a CNC affiliate in Austin, working her way up in her two-year stay to an anchoring position. When she had been offered the co-anchor spot at WWBW, the CNC affiliate in Washington, D.C., Liv had jumped at it. There were no firm ties in Austin, nor, for years, anywhere else.

She had wanted to make her name in television journalism. Washington, she felt, was a perfect place to do it. She didn't mind dirty work, though her smooth, narrow hands looked as if they were accustomed to only the silks and satins of life. She had a seeking, eager, shrewd brain under the ivory skin and patrician features. She thrived on the fast, close to impossible pace of visual news, while on the surface, she was cool, remote and seemingly untouchable. For the past five years, Liv had been working hard to convince herself that the image was fact.

At twenty-eight, she told herself she was through with personal upheavals. The only roller coaster she wanted to ride on was a professional one. What friends she had made during her sixteen months in D.C. were allowed only a glimpse of her past. Liv kept a lock on her private life.

"This is Olivia Carmichael," she told the camera. "And Brian Jones. Stay tuned for 'CNC World News.' "

The quick throb of theme music took over; then the red light on the camera facing her blinked out. Liv unclipped her mike and pushed away from the semicircular desk used by the news team.

"Tight show," the man behind camera one commented as she started past. Overhead, the hot, bright lights shut down. Liv shifted her thoughts and focused on him. She smiled. The smile transformed her cool polished beauty. She only used that particular smile when she meant it.

"Thanks, Ed. How's your girl?"

"Cramming for exams." He shrugged and pulled off his headset. "Doesn't have much time for me."

"You'll be proud of her when she gets that degree in education."

"Yeah. Ah—Liv." He stopped her again, and she lifted a brow in acknowledgment. "She wanted me to ask you . . ." He looked uncomfortable as he hesitated.

"What?"

"Who does your hair?" he blurted out, then shook his head and fiddled with his camera. "Women."

Laughing, Liv patted his arm. "Armond's on Wisconsin. Tell her to use my name."

She moved briskly from the studio, up the steps and through the winding corridors that led to the newsroom. It was noisy with the transition from day to evening shift.

Reporters sat on the corners of desks, drank coffee or typed furiously to meet the deadline for the eleven o'clock broadcast. There was a scent of tobacco, light sweat and old coffee in the air. One wall was lined with television screens, which gave the action but not the sound of every station in the metropolitan area. Already on screen one was the intro for "CNC World News." Liv headed straight through the confusion to the glass-walled office of the news director.

"Carl?" She stuck her head in his door. "Do you have a minute?"

Carl Pearson was slouched over his desk, hands folded, as he stared at a TV screen. The glasses he should have been wearing were under a pile of papers. He had a cup of cold coffee balanced on a stack of files, and a cigarette burned down between his fingers. He grunted. Liv entered, knowing the grunt was affirmative.

"Good show tonight." His eyes never left the twelve-inch screen.

Liv took a seat and waited for the commercial break. She could hear the crisp, hard-line tones of Harris McDowell, New York anchor for "CNC World News," coming from the set at her side. It was fruitless to talk to Carl when the big guns were out. Harris McDowell was a big gun.

She knew he and Carl had worked together in their early days as reporters at the same station in Kansas City, Missouri. But it had been Harris McDowell who had been assigned to cover a presidential cavalcade in Dallas in 1963. The assassination of a president, and his on-the-scene reports had rocketed McDowell from relative obscurity to national prominence. Carl Pearson had remained a big fish in a sea of little fishes in Missouri and a handful of other states until he had hung up his notebook in exchange for a desk in Washington.

He was a tough news director, exacting, excitable. If

he was bitter about the different path his career had taken, he was careful not to show it. Liv respected him, and had grown steadily fonder of him during her stint at WWBW. She'd had her own share of disappointments.

"What?" It was Carl's way of telling her to speak her piece once the break had come.

"I want to follow up on Beaumont Dell," Liv began. "I've done a lot of legwork on this already, and when he's appointed secretary of state, I want to put it on the air first."

Carl sat back and folded his hands over his paunch. He blamed too much sitting at a desk for the extra fifteen pounds he carried around. The look he aimed at Liv was as direct and uncompromising as the look he had aimed at the television screen.

"A little ahead of the game." His voice was roughened by years of chain-smoking. As she watched, he lit another, though a cigarette still smoldered in his overfilled ashtray. "What about Fitzhugh? And Davis and Albertson? They might question your appointment of Dell. Officially, Larkin hasn't resigned."

"It's a matter of days, probably hours. You heard the doctor's statement. The acting secretary won't be appointed permanently; Boswell's not the president's favorite boy. It's going to be Dell. I know it."

Carl sniffed and rubbed a hand over his nose. He liked Carmichael's instincts. She was sharp and savvy despite the born-to-the-manor looks. And she was thorough. But he was understaffed and the budget was tight. He couldn't afford to send one of his top reporters out on a hunch when he could assign someone he could spare more. Still . . . He hesitated a moment, then leaned over the desk again.

"Might be worth it," he mumbled. "Let's hear what Thorpe has to say. His report's coming up."

Liv shifted in her chair in automatic protest, then subsided. It was pride that had her ready to object to having her assignment hinge on the words of T.C. Thorpe. But pride didn't cut weight with Carl. Instead, she rose to sit on the corner of his desk and watch.

The Washington anchor was broadcasting from the studio above her head. It was a much more stylized set than the one she had just left. But that was the difference between the local and national news—and the local and national news budgets. After his brief lead-in, the screen switched to the location shot and T.C. Thorpe's stand-up. With a frown, Liv watched him.

Though it was no more than thirty degrees with a wicked windchill factor, he wore his coat unbuttoned and had no hat. It was typical.

He had a rugged, weather-tanned face Liv associated with a mountain climber, and the streamlined body of a long-distance runner. Both professions required endurance. So did reporting. T.C. Thorpe was all reporter. His eyes were dark and intense, locking on the viewers and holding them. His dark hair blew furiously around his face, giving his report an air of urgency. Yet his voice was clean and unhurried. The contrast worked for him more successfully than flash or gimmicks worked for others.

Liv knew his visual appeal was tremendous. He had the athletic, just-short-of-handsome looks that appealed to both men and women. His eyes were intelligent and instilled trust, as did the deep, well-pitched voice. He was accessible. She knew reporters were put into slots: remote, mystical, omnipotent, accessible. Thorpe was flesh and blood, and viewers could welcome him into their living rooms comfortably and accept his word. And there was the feeling that if the world began to collapse, T.C. Thorpe would report it without missing a beat.

In his five years as senior Washington correspondent, he had built an enviable reputation. He had the two things most essential to a reporter: credibility and sources. If T.C. Thorpe said it, it was believed. If T.C. Thorpe needed information, he knew which numbers to call.

Liv's resentment against him was instinctive. She specialized in the political beat for the local broadcast. Thorpe was her nemesis. He guarded his turf with the ferocity of a dog in a junkyard. He was rooted in Washington; she was still the new kid on the block. And he wasn't giving her any room. It seemed inevitable that when she had a hot lead, he had been there first.

Liv had spent months looking for a viable criticism of him. It wasn't accurate to call him flashy. Thorpe dressed down on the job, wearing nothing to distract the viewer's attention from his reporting. His style was straightforward. His reports had depth and bite, while he remained objective. There was no fault to find in the way he worked. All Liv could criticize him for was arrogance.

She watched him now as he stood with the White House lit in the background. He was recapping the Larkin story. It was obvious he had spoken to Larkin personally, something she had been unable to do though she had pulled all the strings available to her. That alone grated. Thorpe, too, listed prospective candidates for the position. He named Dell first.

Carl nodded behind her back as Liv scowled at the screen. He felt it put a bit more power into her hunch.

"This is T.C. Thorpe, at the White House."

"Tell the desk you have an assignment," Cal announced, and drew hard on the butt of his cigarette. Liv turned to him, but his eyes were still on the screen. "Take crew two."

"Fine." She swallowed the annoyance that it was Thorpe's influence more than her own that had gained her what she wanted. "I'll make the arrangements."

"Bring me something for the noon news," he called after her, and squinted to focus on the next segment.

Liv looked over her shoulder as she opened the door. "You'll have it."

It was eight A.M. and freezing when Liv and her two-man crew arrived at the iron gates of Beaumont Dell's home in Alexandria, Virginia. Liv had been up since five, preparing her questions. After half a dozen phone calls the evening before, she had elicited a promise from one of Dell's aides that she would be granted a ten-minute interview that morning. A good reporter could learn quite a bit in ten minutes. Sliding out of the crew van, Liv approached the guard at the gate.

"Olivia Carmichael with WWBW." She flashed her press pass. "Mr. Dell is expecting me."

The guard examined Liv's credentials, then his clip board, before nodding. Without a word, he pressed the button to open the gates.

Friendly sort, she decided as she climbed back into the van. "Okay, be ready to set up fast; we're not going to have much time." She was reaching in her purse to take out her notes for a final check as the van wound up the drive. "Bob, I'd like a pan of the house, and one of the gates when we leave."

"Already got one of the gates." He gave her a grin as she smiled back at him. "And of your legs. You've got some great legs, Liv."

"Think so?" She crossed them and gave them a critical stare. "You're probably right."

She enjoyed his good-natured flirting. Bob was harmless, happily married with two growing children. A serious flirtation would have frozen her. She separated men into two catagories: safe and dangerous. Bob was safe. She could relax with him.

"All right," she said as the van stopped in front of the three-story brick house. "Try to look like respectable members of the working press."

Grinning, Bob muttered a short expletive and climbed out of the back of the van.

At the front door, Liv was once again the cool, aloof newswoman; no one would dare to comment on her legs. Not out loud. She knocked briskly, leaving the crew to follow with their equipment.

"Olivia Carmichael," she announced to the maid who opened the door. "To see Mr. Dell."

"Yes." The maid glanced past her with the slightest moue of disapproval at the blue-jeaned crew hauling equipment up the front steps. "This way, Ms. Carmichael. Mr. Dell will be right with you."

Liv recognized the maid's disapproval. She thought little of it. Her own family and many of her childhood friends felt the same way about her profession.

The hall was an elegant, refined entrance to a wealthy home. Liv had seen the same hall in a dozen homes in a dozen styles when she was growing up. There had been hundreds of teas, stiff little parties and carefully organized outings, all of which had bored her to distraction. She never cast a glance at the Matisse on the wall on her left. She heard Bob's low whistle as he entered behind her.

"Some place," he commented as his sneakers moved soundlessly over the parquet floor.

Liv made a distracted sound of agreement as she went back over her strategy. She had grown up in a home not so very much different from this one. Her mother had preferred Chippendale to Louis XIV, but it was all the same. Even the scent was the same—lemon oil and fresh flowers. It stirred old memories.

Before Liv had taken two steps behind the maid, she heard the sound of male laughter.

"I'll swear, T.C., you know how to tell a story. I'll have to make sure the first lady's not around when I repeat that one." Dell came lightly down the stairs, trim, handsomely sixtyish and beside Thorpe.

Liv felt her stomach muscles tighten. *Always one step ahead of me,* she thought on a swift rush of fury. *Damn!*

Briefly, potently, she met Thorpe's eyes. He smiled, but it wasn't the same smile he had given to Dell as they had begun their descent.

"Ah, Ms. Carmichael." Spotting her, Dell extended his hand as he crossed the hall. His voice was as smooth as his palm. His eyes were shrewd. "Very prompt. I hope I haven't kept you waiting."

"No, Mr. Dell. I appreciate the time." Liv let her eyes pass over Thorpe. "Mr. Thorpe."

"Ms. Carmichael."

"I know you're a busy man, Ambassador," Liv turned her eyes back to him with a smile. "I won't take much of your time." An unobtrusive move put the mike in her hand. "Would you be comfortable talking to me here?" she asked, to give the soundman a voice level.

"Fine." He made an expansive gesture and gave a generous smile. The smile was the stock-in-trade of the diplomat. From the corner of her eye, Liv watched Thorpe move out of camera range to stand by the door.

The eyes she felt on the back of her neck made her uncomfortable. Turning to Dell, she started her interview.

He continued to be expansive, cooperative, genial. Liv felt like a dentist trying to pull a tooth from a patient who smiled with his mouth firmly shut.

Of course he was aware that his name was being linked with the position to be vacated by Larkin. Naturally, he was flattered to be considered—by the press. Liv noted he was careful not to mention the president's name. She was being led in circles, gently, expertly. Just as gently, she backtracked and probed from different angles. She was getting the tone she wanted, if not the firm words.

"Mr. Dell, has the president spoken to you directly about the appointment of a new secretary of state?" She knew better than to expect a yes or no answer.

"The president and I haven't met to discuss an appointment."

"But you have met with him?" she persisted.

"I have occasion to meet with the president from time to time." At his subtle signal, the maid appeared at his elbow with his coat and hat. "I'm sorry I can't give you more time, Ms. Carmichael." He was shrugging into his coat. Liv knew she was losing him. She moved with him to the door.

"Are you seeing the president this morning, Mr. Dell?" It was a blunt question, but it wasn't the verbal answer Liv looked for as much as the reaction in the eyes of the man she asked. She saw it—the faint flicker, the briefest hesitation.

"Possibly." Dell extended his hand. "A pleasure talking to you, Ms. Carmichael. I'm afraid I have to run. Traffic is so heavy at this time of the morning."

Liv lifted a hand to signal Bob to stop the tape.

"Thank you for seeing me, Mr. Dell." After passing the mike to the soundman, Liv followed Dell and Thorpe outside.

"Always a pleasure." He patted her hand and smiled with his old-world southern charm. "Now you be sure to call Anna, T.C." He turned to Thorpe and gave him a friendly slap on the shoulder. "She wants to hear from you."

"I'll do that."

Dell walked down the steps to the discreet black limo where his driver waited.

"Not bad, Carmichael," Thorpe commented as the limo pulled away. "You do a tough interview. Of course . . ." He looked down at her and smiled. "Dell's been dancing his way around tough interviews for years."

Liv gave him a cool stare. "What were you doing here?"

"Having breakfast," he answered easily. "I'm an old family friend."

She would have liked to knock the smile from his face with a good swift punch. Instead, she meticulously pulled on her gloves. "Dell's going to get that appointment."

Thorpe lifted a brow. "Is that a statement, Olivia, or a question?"

"I wouldn't ask you for the time of day, Thorpe," she retorted. "And you wouldn't give it to me if I did."

"I've always said you were a sharp lady."

Good God, she's beautiful, he thought. When he saw her on the air, it was easy to attribute the nearly impossible beauty to lighting, makeup, camera angles. But standing face to face in harsh morning light, she was quite simply the most physically beautiful woman he had ever seen. The incredible bone structure; the flawless skin. Only her eyes were hot, giving away the fury she was controlling. Thorpe smiled again. He loved to watch the ice crack.

"Is that the problem, Thorpe?" Liv demanded as she stepped aside to let the crew pass. "Don't you like reporters who happen to be women?"

He laughed and shook his head. "You know better than that, Liv. 'Reporter' is a word without sex."

His eyes weren't intense now, but filled with good humor. She didn't like them any better. More accurately, she refused to like them any better. "Why won't you cooperate with me?" The wind was tossing his hair around his face as it had the night before. Thorpe seemed untouched by the cold as Liv shivered inside her coat. "We have the same job; we work for the same people."

"My turf," he said quietly. "If you want a share, Liv, you're going to have to fight for it. It took me years to establish myself here. Don't expect to do the same in months." He saw her shudder against the cold as she continued to glare at him. "You'd better get inside the van."

"I'm going to have my share, Thorpe." It was half threat, half warning. "You're going to have a hell of a fight on your hands."

Thorpe inclined his head in acknowledgment. "I'll count on it."

It was obvious to him that Liv wasn't leaving until he did. She would stand there shivering for an hour out of sheer stubbornness. Without a word, Thorpe walked down the steps to his car.

Liv stood for another moment after he'd driven off. She was aware—and annoyed by the fact—that she was able to breathe with more ease when he was no longer standing beside her. He had a strong personality; it was impossible to be indifferent to him. He demanded definite emotions. Liv decided hers were all unflattering.

He wasn't going to block her way. She wasn't going to put up with it. She walked down the steps to the van slowly.

Anna, she thought suddenly, remembering the name Dell had mentioned to Thorpe. Anna Dell Monroe—Dell's daughter and official hostess since the death of her mother. Anna Dell Monroe. Whatever was going on in her father's life, she'd know about it. Moving quickly now, Liv climbed in the van.

"We'll drop the tape at the station for editing; then we head for Georgetown."

Chapter 2

Liv typed furiously. She had given Carl the Dell interview for the noon news; but she had more, a great deal more, for the evening show. Her hunch about Anna Monroe had paid off. Anna knew the details of her father's life. Though she had been careful during the interview, she wasn't the trained diplomat her father was. Liv had enough from her half-hour interview in the parlor of Anna Monroe's Georgetown row house to give her viewers a story with touches of glamour and suspense.

The tape was good. She had already taken a quick look at it while it was still being edited. Bob had captured the stylish elegance of the room and the gentle, privileged breeding of the woman. It would be a good contrast to the compact shrewdness of her father. Anna's respect for her father came through, as well as her taste for the finer things. Liv had worked both into the interview. It was a solid piece of reporting, and it gave a glimpse of the larger-than-life world of affluent people in politics.

Liv transcribed her notes hurriedly.

"Liv, we need you for the voice-over on the tease."

She glanced up long enough to search for Brian. The look she gave him made him sigh. He pushed away from his desk and stretched his shoulders. "All right, all right, I'll do it. But you owe me one."

"You're a prince, Brian." She went back to her typing.

Ten minutes later, Liv pulled the last sheet from her typewriter. "Carl!" she called to the director as he crossed the newsroom toward his office. "Copy for the lead story."

"Bring it in."

As she rose, Liv checked the clock. She had an hour before air time.

The television was on, its volume low, when she entered Carl's office. Seated behind his desk, he checked copy and time allowances.

"Did you see the tape yet?" Liv handed him her pages.

"It's good." He lit a cigarette from the butt of another and gave a quick, hacking cough. "We'll run part of this morning's business with Dell, then lead into the interview with the daughter."

He read Liv's copy with a small furrow of concentration between his brows. It was a good, tidy story, giving quick bios on all top contenders for the cabinet post, and focusing in on Beaumont Dell. It gave the audience a full, open view before it brought them to Dell's doorstep.

Liv watched smoke curl toward the ceiling and waited.

"I want to flash pictures of the rest of them while you read the bios." He scribbled notes on her script. "We should have them on file. If not, we'll get them from upstairs." Upstairs was the term for CNC's Washington bureau. "Looks like you're going to have about three minutes to fill."

"I want three and a half." She waited until Carl looked up at her. "We don't replace many secretaries of state midterm, Carl. Our next biggest story is the possibility of a partial shutdown of the Potomac River filtration system. This is worth three and a half."

"Go argue with the time editor," he suggested, then held up his hand as she began to speak.

Liv saw immediately what had shifted his attention. The graphics for a special bulletin flashed across the screen. She obeyed his quick hand signal to turn up the volume. Even as she did, T.C. Thorpe stared directly into her eyes. Liv hadn't been prepared for the intensity of the look.

She felt a sexual pull—a quick, unexpected flash of desire. It left her stunned. She leaned back against Carl's desk. She hadn't felt anything like that in more than five years. Staring at the television image, she missed the first few words of Thorpe's report.

". . . has accepted Secretary of State Larkin's resignation as expected. Secretary Larkin resigned his cabinet post for reasons of poor health. He remains in Bethesda Naval Hospital recovering from extensive cardiac surgery performed last week. With the acceptance of Larkin's resignation, the president has appointed Beaumont Dell to fill the vacated post. Dell officially accepted an hour ago in a meeting in the Oval Office.

Press Secretary Donaldson has scheduled a press conference tomorrow at nine A.M."

Liv felt the supports fall out from under her and leaned back heavily. She heard Thorpe recap the bulletin while she closed her eyes and took a deep breath. Carl was already swearing.

Her story was dead. The guts had just been torn out of it. *And he had known it.* Liv straightened as the scheduled program flashed back on the screen. He'd known it at eight o'clock that morning.

"Do the rewrites," Carl was telling her, grabbing for his phone as it rang. "And get somebody upstairs for Thorpe's copy. We need it to fill in. The bit with the daughter is scrubbed."

Liv grabbed her papers from Carl's desk and marched to the door.

"They need you in makeup, Liv."

She ignored the statement and continued out of the newsroom. Impatient, she paced back and forth in front of the elevator, waiting for it to make the descent.

He's not going to get away with it, she fumed. He's not going to get away with this without a scratch.

She continued to pace back and forth inside the elevator on her way to the fourth floor. It had been years—she could count the years—since anything or anyone had made her this angry. She was bursting with the need to let out her temper. And there was only one man who deserved the full force of it.

"Thorpe," she demanded curtly when she entered the fourth-floor newsroom.

A reporter glanced up and cupped her hand over the mouthpiece of her phone. "In his office."

This time Liv took the stairs. She darted up them, forgetting her carefully constructed poise and control.

"Ms. Carmichael." The receptionist outside the fifth-floor offices rose as Liv dashed through. "Ms. Carmichael!" she repeated to Liv's retreating back. "Whom did you want to see? Ms. Carmichael!"

Liv burst into Thorpe's office without a knock. "You louse."

Thorpe stopped typing and turned toward the door. He watched, more intrigued than annoyed, as the unannounced visitor crossed the room. "Olivia." He leaned back, but didn't rise. "What a nice surprise." He noted the receptionist hovering in the doorway and shook his head slightly to send her away. "Have a seat," he invited with a gesture of his hand. "I don't believe you've graced my office in over a year."

"You killed my story." Liv, her copy still in her hand, remained standing and leaned over his desk.

He noted the high color in her normally pale face, the dark fury in her normally calm eyes. Her hair was mussed from her mad scramble up the steps and she was breathing hard. Thorpe was fascinated. How far, he wondered, could he push before she really let loose? He decided to find out.

"What story?"

"You know damn well." She put her palms down on the desk and leaned over farther. "You did it deliberately."

"I do most things deliberately," he agreed easily. "If you're talking about the Dell story, Liv," he continued, sweeping his eyes back to hers, "it wasn't your story. It was mine. It *is* mine."

"You broke it forty-five minutes before my broadcast." Her voice was raised in fury, something he had never witnessed before. To his knowledge, Olivia Carmichael never spoke above her carefully modulated pitch. Her anger was usually ice, not fire.

"So?" He laced his fingers together and watched her over them. "You've got a complaint about my timing?"

"You've left me holding nothing." She held out her copy, then crumpled it and let it drop. "I've worked for two weeks putting this together, since Larkin had the heart attack. You killed it in two minutes."

"I'm not responsible for protecting your story, Carmichael; you are. Better luck next time."

"Oh!" Enraged, Liv struck both fists on the mahogany desk. "You're contemptible. I poured hours into this story, hundreds of phone calls, miles of legwork. It's because of you that I have an obstacle course to run in the first place." Her eyes narrowed, and he noted that a faint New England accent was slipping through. "Do I scare you that much, Thorpe? Are you so insecure about your sanctified piece of turf and the mundane quality of your reporting?"

"Insecure?" He was up, leaning on the desk until they were nose to nose. "Worrying about you inching onto my ground doesn't keep me up at night, Carmichael. I don't concern myself with junior reporters who try to scramble up the ladder three rungs at a time. Come back when you've paid your dues."

Liv made a low sound of fury. "Don't talk to me about paying dues, Thorpe. I started paying mine eight years ago."

"Eight years ago I was in Lebanon dodging bullets while you were at Harvard dodging football players."

"I never dodged football players," Liv retorted furiously. "And that's totally irrelevant. You knew this morning; you knew what was going down."

"And what if I did?"

"You knew I'd be spinning my wheels. Don't you feel any loyalty to the local station?"

"No."

His answer was so matter-of-fact, it threw her for a moment. "You started there."

"Would you call WTRL in Jersey and give them your exclusive because you read the weather there?" he countered. "Drop the alma mater routine, Liv; it doesn't cut it."

"You're despicable." Her voice had dropped to a dangerous level. "All you had to do was tell me you were going to break the story."

"And you'd have politely folded your hands and let me break it first?" She watched the ironical lift of his brow. "You'd have slit my throat to put that story on the air."

"Gladly."

He laughed then. "You're honest when you're mad, Liv—and gorgeous." He took some papers from his desk and held them out to her. "You'll need my notes to revise your lead. You've less than thirty minutes until air."

"I know what time it is." She ignored the outstretched papers. She had an almost irresistible urge to hurl something through the plate glass window at his back. "We're going to settle this, Thorpe—if not now, soon. I'm tired of having to crawl over your back for every one of my stories." She snatched the notes, hating to accept anything from him, but knowing she was boxed in.

"Fine." He watched her retrieve her own crumpled copy. "Meet me for drinks tonight."

"Not on your life." She turned and headed for the door.

"Afraid?"

The one softly taunting word stopped her. Liv turned and glared at him. "O'Riley's, eight o'clock."

"You're on." Thorpe grinned as she slammed the door behind her.

So, he thought when he settled back in his chair. There is flesh and blood under the silk. He'd begun to have his doubts. It appears I've made my first move. He laughed a little as he swiveled to stare out at his view of the city.

Damn but she'd made him mad. All for the best, he decided; otherwise he'd still be biding his time. One of the most important qualities a reporter had to have was patience. Thorpe had been patient for more than a year. Sixteen months, he thought, to be exact.

Since the first night he'd watched her broadcast. He remembered the low, calm voice, the cool, clean beauty. His attraction had been immediate and absolute. The moment he had met her, felt that aloof gaze on him, he had wanted her. Instinct had told him to hold off, keep a distance. There was more to Olivia Carmichael than met the eye.

He could have checked her background thoroughly. He had the talent, the contacts. Yet something had curbed his reporter's drive to know. He had fallen back on patience. Having spent time cooling his heels staking out politicians, Thorpe knew all about patience. He sat back and lit a cigarette. It looked as though it were about to pay off.

At eight o'clock, Liv pulled into a parking space beside O'Riley's. For an instant she rested her brow against the steering wheel. All too clearly, she could picture herself storming through the newsrooms and into Thorpe's office. With perfect clarity, she heard herself shouting at him.

She detested losing her temper, detested more losing

it in front of Thorpe. From the first time she had met him face to face, Liv had recognized a man she would need to keep at a distance. He was too strong, too charismatic. He fell into the "dangerous" category. Headed it, in fact.

She had wanted to keep an impersonal distance, and formality was necessary for that. A few hours before, Liv had dropped all formality. You couldn't be formal with someone when you were pressed nose to nose and shouting.

"I'm not cool and unruffled," she murmured, "no matter how hard I try to be." And, she realized with a sigh, Thorpe knew it.

When she was a child, she had been the misfit. In a family of sedate, well-mannered people, she had asked too many questions, cried too many tears, laughed too lustily. Unlike her sister, she hadn't been interested in party dresses and ribbons. She had wanted a dog to run with, not the quiet little poodle her mother had babied. She had wanted a tree house, not the tidy pristine playhouse her father had hired an architect to build. She had wanted to race, and had been constantly told to walk.

Liv had escaped from the strict rules and expectations of being a Carmichael. There had been freedom in college . . . and more. Liv had thought she had found everything she could ever want. Then, she had lost it. For the last six years, she had been dealing with a new phase in her growth. The final phase, she had determined. She had only herself to think about, and her career. She hadn't lost the thirst for freedom, but she had learned caution.

Liv straightened and shook her head. This wasn't the time to think of her past. Her present—and her future—demanded her attention. I won't lose my temper again, she promised herself as she climbed from the car. I won't give him the satisfaction.

She walked into O'Riley's to meet Thorpe.

He saw her enter. He'd been watching for her. She's slipped the veil back on, he noted. Her face was composed, her eyes serene as they scanned the room in search of him. Standing in the noise and smoke, she looked like marble—cool and smooth and exquisite. Thorpe wanted to touch her, feel her skin, watch her eyes heat. Anger wasn't the only passion he wanted to bring out in her. The desire he had banked down for months was beginning to crowd him.

How long will it take to peel away those protective layers? he mused. He was willing to take his time, enjoy the challenge, because he intended to win. Thorpe wasn't accustomed to losing. He waited until her eyes settled on him. He smiled and inclined his head, but didn't rise to lead her to the table. He liked the way she walked—smooth, fluid, with undercurrents of sensuality.

"Hello, Olivia."

"Thorpe." Liv slid into the booth opposite him.

"What'll you have?"

"Wine." She glanced up at the waiter, who was already at her elbow. "White wine, Lou."

"Sure, Ms. Carmichael. Another round, Mr. Thorpe?"

"No, thanks." He lifted his scotch. He had noted the quick smile she had given the young waiter. It had warmed her face for a brief moment. Then her eyes were back on his, and the warmth was gone.

"All right, Thorpe; if we're going to clear the air, I suggest we get to it."

"Are you always all business, Liv?" He lit a cigarette, watching her face. One of his greatest assets was his ability to study directly, endlessly. More than one high-powered politician had squirmed under his dark, patient gaze.

She didn't like the quiet power, or its effect on her. "We met here to discuss—"

"Haven't you ever heard of pleasantries?" he countered. "How are you? Nice weather we're having?"

"I don't care how you are," she returned evenly. He wasn't going to get the best of her. "And the weather's terrible."

"Such a sweet voice, such a nasty tongue." He observed the flare, quickly controlled, which leaped into her eyes. "You have the most perfect face I've ever seen."

Liv stiffened—back, shoulders, arms. Thorpe noted the involuntary movement and sipped his scotch. "I didn't come here to discuss my looks."

"No, but then looks are part of the job, aren't they?" The waiter set the wine in front of her. Liv slipped her fingers around the stem, but didn't lift the glass. "Viewers would rather invite attractive people into their living rooms. It makes the news easier to swallow. You add a little class as well; it's a nice touch."

"My looks have nothing to do with the quality of my reporting." Her voice was cold and unemotional, but her eyes were beginning to heat.

"No, but they do score you points in broadcasting." He leaned back, still studying her. "You're a damned good broadcaster, Liv, and you're picking up speed as a reporter."

She frowned at him. Was he trying to unbalance her by tossing out a compliment?

"And," he added without changing rhythm, "you're a very cautious woman."

"What are you talking about?"

"If I asked you out to dinner, what would you say?"

"No."

He acknowledged this with a quick, unoffended grin. "Why?"

Deliberately, she took a sip of wine. "Because I don't like you. I don't have dinner with men I don't like."

"Which implies that you do have dinner with men you like." Thorpe took a last, thoughtful drag, then crushed out his cigarette. "But you don't go out with anyone, do you?"

"That's none of your business." Infuriated, Liv started to rise, but his hands came down firmly on hers.

"You tend to jump and run when the button's pushed. I'm curious about you, Olivia." He was speaking quietly, below the laughter and raised voices around them.

"I don't want you to be interested in me in any way. I don't like you," she repeated, and controlled the urge to fight against his hold. His palms were hard and unexpectedly rough. It was an odd sensation on her skin. "I don't like your understated machismo or your overstated arrogance."

"Understated machismo?" He grinned, enjoying himself. "I think that's a compliment."

The grin was appealing, and she steeled herself against it. She knew she had been right to term him dangerous.

"I like your style, Liv—and your face. Iced sex," he continued, then saw that he had hit a nerve, a raw one. Her hands jumped convulsively under his. Her eyes went from angry to hurt to carefully blank.

"Let go of my hands."

He had wanted to annoy her, prod her, but not to hurt her. "I'm sorry."

The apology was simple, sincere and unexpected. It killed her urge to spring up and leave. When his hands left hers, she reached for her wine again. "If we're finished with the pleasantries now, Thorpe, perhaps we can get down to business."

"All right, Liv," he agreed. "Your turn at bat."

She set down her glass. "I want you to stop road-blocking me."

"Be specific."

"WWBW is an affiliate of CNC. There's supposed to be a certain amount of cooperation. The local broadcast is just as important as the national."

"And?"

At times he was maddeningly closemouthed. She pushed her wine aside and leaned forward on the table. "I'm not asking for your help. I don't want it. But I'm tired of the sabotage."

"Sabotage?" He picked up his drink and swirled it. She was becoming animated again, forgetting her vow to remain distant and untouchable. He liked the hint of pink under her ivory-toned skin.

"You knew I was working on the Dell story. You knew every step I took. Don't try that innocent, boyish look on me, Thorpe. I know you have contacts in the woodwork at WBW. You wanted me to make an ass of myself."

He laughed, amused at the phrase coming from her. "Sure, I knew what you were doing," he admitted with an easy shrug. "But that's your problem, not mine. I gave you my copy; that's standard procedure. The local always gets feed from upstairs."

"I wouldn't have needed your copy if you hadn't held

a knife to my throat." She wasn't interested in standard procedure or the generosity of upstairs. "With the right information, I could have changed the tone of my interview with Anna Monroe and still have used it. It was a good piece of work, and it's wasted."

"Tunnel vision," he stated simply, and finished off his scotch. "A hazard in reporting. If," he continued as he lit another cigarette, "you had considered a few more possibilities, you would have asked Anna different questions, led her by the nose a bit more. Then, after I'd broken the story, the interview could have been reedited. You'd still have been able to use it. I saw the tape," he added. "It was a good piece of work; you just didn't press enough of the right buttons."

"Don't tell me how to do my job."

"Then don't tell me how to do mine." Now, he too leaned forward. "I've had the political beat for five years. I'm not handing you Capitol Hill on a platter, Carmichael. If you've got a problem with the way I work, take it up with Morrison." He tossed out the name of the head of CNC's Washington bureau.

"You're so smug." Liv had a sudden desire to choke him. "So sure of your sanctified position as keeper of the Holy Grail."

"There's nothing sanctified about the political beat in this town, Carmichael," Thorpe countered. "I'm here because I know how to play the games. Maybe you need a few lessons."

"Not from you."

"You could do worse." He paused a moment, and calculated. "Look, for the sake of professional courtesy, I'll give you this much. It takes more than a year to spread roots here. The people in this town are insecure; their jobs are always on the line. Politics is an ugly word—uglier since Watergate, Abscam. Exposing them is our job; they can't ignore us, so they try to use us the same way we use them."

"You're not telling me anything I don't know."

"Maybe not," he agreed. "But you have an advantage you're not cultivating. Your looks and your class."

"I don't see what—"

"Don't be an idiot." He cut her off with a quick, annoyed gesture. "A reporter has to use everything he can beg, borrow or steal. Your face doesn't have anything to do with your brain, but it does have something to do with the way people perceive you. Human nature." He let his words sink in.

She was digesting what he said, annoyed because she knew he was right. Charm worked for some reporters, abrasiveness for others. And class, as he put it, could work for her.

"There's an embassy party Saturday night. I'll take you."

Her attention came full circle back to him. Astonished, she stared. "You'll—"

"You want to get in the door, take the one that's most accessible." The incredulity in her eyes amused him. "A lot of interesting gossip goes on in the ladies' room after a few glasses of champagne."

"You'd know all about that, of course," Liv said dryly.

"You'd be surprised."

She was cautious, uneasy, tempted. "Why would you do this?"

He pushed her wine glass back in front of her. "There's a saying about gift horses, Liv."

"There's one about Trojan horses, too."

He laughed and sat back. "A good reporter would have opened the gates and had a scoop."

He was right, of course, but she didn't like it. She knew that if it had been anyone else but Thorpe, she wouldn't have hesitated. That gives him too much importance, she told herself, and gathered up her purse. "All right. What embassy?"

"Canadian." It had amused him to watch her work out the decision.

"What time should I meet you?"

"I'll pick you up."

She had started to rise, but now stopped. "No."

"My party, my terms. Take it or leave it."

She didn't like it. To have met him would have kept the evening professional and relatively safe. Though she doubted that a woman was ever really safe with Thorpe. He was boxing her into a corner. If she refused now, she'd look, and feel, like a fool. "All right." Liv reached for her notebook. "I'll give you my address."

"I know your address." He watched her eyes fly back to his, wary and suspicious. Thorpe smiled. "I'm a reporter, Liv; I deal in information." He slid from the booth. "I'll walk you out."

Taking her arm, he led her to the door. Liv kept silent. She wasn't certain if she had won a point or taken two steps backward. In any case, she thought it better than standing still.

"You don't have to come out," she began, as he steered her toward the parking lot. "You haven't got your coat."

"Worried about me?"

"Not in the least." Annoyed, she reached for her keys.

"Have we finished conducting business for the evening?" he asked her as she stuck the key in the door lock.

"Yes."

"Completely?"

"Completely."

"Good."

He turned her to face him, kept his hands firmly on her shoulders, and took her mouth with his. Liv was too stunned to protest. She hadn't been prepared for that kind of move from Thorpe. She hadn't expected that hard, uncompromising mouth to be soft and gentle. He drew her closer, and she was pressed against him.

His body was hard, firm and arousing. Her blood began to heat. Liv lifted her hands, not certain whether she would draw him closer or push him away. She ended by curling her fingers into the material of his shirt.

Thorpe made no attempt to deepen the kiss or seek quick intimacy. He could sense her struggle against responding, and knew he would simply wait her out. He blocked out his own needs and concentrated on hers.

Slowly, her lips softened, yielded. She could feel the world slip out of focus, as if a new lens had been placed on a camera and hadn't yet been adjusted. "No," she murmured against his mouth, and uncurled her hands to push him away. "No."

When he released her, Liv leaned back against the car. Feelings she had thought completely dead had begun to flicker into life. She didn't want them, didn't want Thorpe to be the man to revitalize them. She stared at him while he watched the emotion, the vulnerability, run over her face. He felt something more complex than desire move through him.

"That—" Liv swallowed and tried to speak again. "That was—"

"Very enjoyable, Olivia, for both of us." He kept his

voice light for himself as well as for her. "Though it would appear that you're a bit out of practice."

Her eyes flared and the cloudiness vanished. "You're insufferable."

"Be ready at eight on Saturday, Liv," he told her, and walked back into O'Riley's.

Chapter 3

She chose a plain black dress. It fit her closely from neck to hem, with no glitter, no flounces to spoil the line. Against the unrelieved black, her skin glowed like marble. Liv hesitated over jewelry, then decided on the pearl studs she had received on her twenty-first birthday.

For a moment, she only held the earrings in her hand. They brought memories, bittersweet. Twenty-one. She had thought nothing could mar her life, her happiness. Hardly more than a year later, her world had started to crumble. At twenty-three, she hadn't been able to remember what it had been like to feel happy.

She tried to recall what Doug had said when he had given her the pearls. Liv shut her eyes a moment. It had been something about their being like her skin, pale and smooth. Doug, she mused. My husband. She looked down at her ringless hands. Ex-husband. We loved each other then, I think. For the four years we were together; for at least part of them. Before . . .

Feeling the pain well up, she shut her eyes again. She couldn't think of what she had lost. It was too enormous, too irreplaceable.

Seven years had passed since he had given her the earrings. She had been a different woman then, in a different life. It was time for this woman to wear them again, in the life she had now.

Liv put the earrings on and went to find her shoes. It was nearly eight o'clock.

She was nervous, and tried to convince herself that she wasn't. She hadn't been on a date in years. It's not a date, she reminded herself. It's business. A professional courtesy. And why was Thorpe suddenly showing her courtesy of any kind?

Liv sat with one shoe on and the other in her hand. He wasn't a man she should trust, personally or professionally. On the job, he was ruthless and proprietary. She'd known that from the outset. And now . . .

The way he had kissed her. Just like that. Just as if he had the right to. She chewed on her bottom lip and stared into space. He hadn't led up to it. She would have thrown up the barricades if he had. She knew the signs to look for: the smiles, the soft, promising words. Thorpe hadn't spared any of those. It was an impulse, she decided, and shrugged it off. There hadn't been anything desperate or even particularly loverlike in the kiss. He hadn't been rough; he hadn't tried a seduction. She was making too much of it. She had wanted to kiss him. She had wanted to go on kissing him. To be held close, to be needed, desired. Why? He meant nothing to her, she told herself firmly.

"What do you want?" she whispered to herself. "And why don't you know?"

To be the best, she thought. To win. To be Olivia Carmichael without having to lose pieces of myself along the way. I want to be whole again.

The doorbell rang. Business, she reminded herself. I'm going to be the best reporter in Washington. If I have to socialize with T.C. Thorpe to do it, then I'll socialize with T.C. Thorpe.

She glanced at the perfume on her dresser, then turned away from it. There was no point in giving him any ideas. She felt sure he had enough of his own. She moved through the apartment without hurry. It gave her a small touch of satisfaction to keep him waiting. But when Liv opened the door, Thorpe didn't appear annoyed. There was approval and simple male appreciation for a woman in his eyes.

"You look lovely." Thorpe handed her a single rosebud, long-stemmed and white. "It suits you," he said, as she accepted it without a word. "Red's too obvious; pink's too sweet."

Liv stared down at the flower and forgot everything she had just told herself. She hadn't counted on being moved by him again so quickly. She lifted serious eyes to his. "Thank you."

Thorpe smiled, but his tone was as serious as hers. "You're welcome. Are you going to let me in?"

I'd be smarter not to, she thought abruptly, but stepped back. "I'll go put this in water."

Thorpe scanned the living room as she walked away. It was neat, tastefully furnished. No decorator, he thought. She had taken her time here, choosing precisely what she wanted. He noted that there were no photographs, no mementos. Liv wasn't putting any parts of herself on display. Very careful, very private.

The vague hint of secrecy had aroused his reporter's instincts.

It might be time, he considered, for a bit of gentle probing. He walked into the kitchen and leaned on the door as Liv added water to a crystal bud vase.

"Nice place," he said conversationally. "You have a good view of the city."

"Yes."

"Washington's a far cry from Connecticut. What part are you from?"

Liv raised her eyes. They were cool again, cautious. "Westport."

Westport—Carmichael. Thorpe had no trouble with the connection. "Tyler Carmichael's your father?"

Liv lifted the vase from the sink and turned to him. "Yes."

Tyler Carmichael—real estate, staunch conservative, roots straight back to the Mayflower. There had been two daughters, Thorpe remembered suddenly. He'd forgotten because one had simply slipped from notice a decade before, while the other had struck out on the debutante circuit. Five-thousand-dollar dresses and a pink Rolls. Her daddy's darling. When she had graduated from Radcliffe and snapped up her first husband, a playwright, Carmichael had given her a fifteen-acre estate as a wedding present. Melinda Carmichael Howard LeClare was now on husband number two. She was a nervous, spoiled woman with a desperate sort of beauty and a taste for the expensive.

"I've met your sister," Thorpe commented, studying Liv's face. "You're nothing like her."

"No," Liv agreed simply, and moved past him into the living room. She set the rose down on a small glass table. "I'll get my coat."

A good reporter, Thorpe mused, makes the worst

interview subject. They know how to answer questions with a yes or no, and without inflection. Olivia Carmichael was a good reporter. So was he.

"You don't get along with your family?"

"I didn't say that." Liv chose a hip-length fox fur from her closet.

"You didn't have to." Smoothly, Thorpe took the coat and held it out. Liv slipped her arms into the sleeves. She wore no scent, he noted, just the light lingering fragrance from her bath, and the clean faintly citrus scent from shampoo. The lack of artifice aroused him. He turned her so that she faced him. "Why don't you get along with them?"

Liv let out an annoyed breath. "Look, Thorpe—"

"Aren't you ever going to call me by my first name?"

She lifted a brow and waited a beat. "Terrance?"

He grinned. "Nobody calls me that and lives to tell about it."

Liv laughed. It was the first time he'd heard her laugh and mean it. She leaned down to pick up her bag.

"You never answered my question," Thorpe pointed out, and unexpectedly took her hand as she turned back to him.

"And I'm not going to. No personal questions, Thorpe, on or off the record."

"I'm a stubborn man, Liv."

"Don't brag; it's unattractive."

He laced his fingers with hers, then lifted the joined hands and studied them thoughtfully. "They fit," he decided, giving her an odd smile. "I thought they might."

She wasn't used to this. It wasn't a seduction, though she was feeling stirrings of desire. It wasn't a challenge, though she felt the need to fight. It wasn't even an assumption she could dispute. He had simply stated a fact.

"Aren't we going to be late?" Liv said a little desperately. She found it strange that though his eyes never left hers, she could feel their gaze through her coat, through her dress, on her skin. She would have sworn he knew precisely what she looked like right down to the small sickle-shaped birthmark under her left breast.

"Thorpe." There was a quick sense of panic at what she was feeling. "Don't."

Hurt. He saw it. He sensed it. She had been hurt. He reminded himself of his decision to move slowly. Keeping her hand in his, he walked to the door.

Light. Music. Elegance. Liv wondered how many parties she had been to in her life. What made this party different from hundreds of others? Politics.

It was a hard-edged, intimate little world. You were appointed or elected, but always an open target for the press, vulnerable because of their influence on the public. One group habitually accused the other of staging the news. Sometimes it was true. Whether at a social event or an official one, there were images to project. Liv understood images.

The senator nibbling pâté was a liberal; his hair was boyishly styled around an open, ingenuous face. Liv knew he was sharp as a tack and viciously ambitious. A veteran congressman told a slightly off-color story about marlin fishing. He was lobbying furiously against a pending tax proposal.

Liv spotted a reporter for an influential Washington paper drinking steadily. By her count, he had downed five bourbons without showing a flicker. But his fingers were curled around the glass as though it were a life preserver and he were drowning. She recognized the signs and felt a stir of pity. If he wasn't already drinking his breakfast, he soon would be.

"Everybody handles pressure differently," Thorpe commented, noting where Liv's gaze had focused.

"I suppose. I had a friend on a newspaper in Austin," she said, as she accepted the glass of wine Thorpe offered her, "who used to say newspapers gave information to the thinking public, while television put on a show."

He lit a cigarette. "What did you say to her?"

"I pointed out that the ads scattered through the *New York Times* weren't any different than commercials in a broadcast." She smiled, remembering her earnest fellow reporter. "I would say that television was more immediate; she'd say newspapers were more reflective. I'd say television allowed the viewer to see; she'd say print allowed a reader to think." Shrugging, she sipped the cool, dry wine. "We were both right, I suppose."

"I did some print reporting when I was in college." Thorpe watched Liv study the people, her surroundings. She was soaking it all up. Now, she looked back at him, curious.

"Why did you switch to broadcasting?"

"I liked the faster pace, the sense of reaching people on the spot."

She nodded, understanding perfectly. There was a glass of scotch in his hand. Unlike the reporter she had observed, Thorpe drank moderately . . . but smoked too much, she decided. She thought of Carl and his endless chain of cigarettes. "How do you deal with the pressure?"

He grinned, then surprised her by running a thumb over the pearl in her ear. "I row."

"What?" His touch had distracted her. Now she focused fully on his face again.

"Row," he repeated. "A boat, on the river. There's handball when it's too cold."

"Rowing," Liv mused. That would explain the calloused, worked feeling of his palms.

"Yes, you know: Go, Yale!"

She smiled at that—a quick smile that lit her eyes.

"That's the first time you've done that for me," he said. "Smiled with your whole face. I think I'm in love."

"You're tougher than that, Thorpe."

"A marshmallow," he corrected, and lifted her hand to his lips.

Carefully, she removed her hand from his. Her fingertips were tingling. "No marshmallow was responsible for that exposé on misappropriation of funds in the Interior Department last November."

"That's work." He took a step closer so that their bodies nearly touched. "The man is a pathetic romantic, weakened by candlelight, devastated by a Chopin prelude. A woman could have me for the price of an open fire and a bottle of wine."

Liv lifted her glass again. It had to be the wine that was making her feel unsteady. "And thousands have."

"You told me not to brag." He grinned. "And reporting limits your time."

Liv was having a difficult time keeping her distance. She shook her head and sighed. "I don't want to like you, Thorpe. I really don't."

"Don't rush into anything," he advised genially.

"T.C." The gentleman from Virginia clapped a hand on Thorpe's shoulder. "I knew I'd find you with an attractive woman." He ran an appreciative eye over Liv. Senator Wyatt was a few pounds overweight, pink cheeked and jovial. Liv knew he was leading a campaign to kill proposed cuts in education and welfare. She had been fighting to get past his front door for two weeks.

"Senator." Thorpe took the heavy-handed greeting genially. "Olivia Carmichael."

Liv's hand was pumped in the best senatorial style. "Well now, I don't forget faces, and I've seen this one. But I'll swear you're not one of T.C.'s regulars."

Thorpe made a sound that was somewhere between throat clearing and sighing. Liv shot him a glance. "I'm with WWBW, Senator Wyatt. Mr. Thorpe and I are . . . colleagues."

"Yes, yes, of course. I remember perfectly now. T.C. fancies a different type." He leaned closer to Liv and winked. "Lots of leg, short on brains."

"Is that so?" Liv aimed a thoughtful look at Thorpe.

"You have great legs, Liv," Thorpe commented.

"So I've been told." She turned to Wyatt. "I'd very much like to speak with you, Senator, about your stand on the proposed education cuts. Perhaps you could suggest a more appropriate time?"

Wyatt hesitated a moment, then nodded. "Call my office Monday morning. You two should be dancing," he decided, and straightened his dinner jacket with a quick tug. "I'm going to see if I can find any real food at that buffet. Fish eggs and goose liver." With a grimace, he sauntered away.

Thorpe took her hand. When Liv glanced up at him, he smiled. "Just taking the senator's advice," he explained. Keeping to the edge of the dance floor, he drew her into his arms.

It was the second time she had been held against him. The second time her body had responded despite herself. Liv went rigid.

"Don't you like to dance, Olivia?" he murmured.

"Yes." She made an effort to keep her voice cool and even. "Of course."

"Then relax." His hand was light at her waist, his mouth close to her ear. Small thrills trembled along her skin. "When we make love, it won't be with members of Washington's brass looking on. I like privacy."

Because she had been struggling with the first part of his statement, it took a moment for the second part to penetrate. Liv threw her head back so that their eyes met. "What makes you think—"

"Not think, know," he corrected. "Your heart's racing just as it did when I kissed you outside of O'Riley's."

"It is not," she denied hotly. "It wasn't then; it isn't now. I told you before, Thorpe, I don't like you."

"More recently you said you didn't want to like me—a totally different thing." She was so slender. He wanted to press her closer until she melted into him. "I could find out how you feel right now if I kissed you. The federal grapevine would be buzzing about Thorpe and Carmichael fraternizing on neutral ground."

"The lead story would be Thorpe's broken jaw when Carmichael severs diplomatic relations."

"You don't have the hands for packing much of a punch," he mused. "Anyway, I prefer reporting stories, not being featured in them."

Liv drew away when the music ended. "I'm going to check out your theory about the ladies' room," she said evenly. Her heart *was* racing. She detested him for being right.

Thorpe watched her move away. He suddenly wished the damn party were over so he could have her alone, even for a few minutes. His body still tingled from the brush of hers against it. He had never wanted a woman so badly, nor been as frustratingly certain of the uphill battle he had yet to fight. Taking out a cigarette, he flicked on his lighter and drew deeply.

He was used to pressure in his work. In truth, he thrived on it. That was his secret. He could go for days on snatches of sleep and still throb with energy. He didn't need vitamins, just a story. But this was a different sort of pressure—wanting something and knowing it was still out of reach. Not for long, he decided grimly, and drew on the cigarette again. If he had to lay siege to Olivia Carmichael, that's exactly what he'd do. She wasn't getting away from him.

"T.C., you pirate. How are you?"

Thorpe turned and clasped hands with the Canadian ambassador's press secretary. Returning the greeting, he reminded himself to relax. A successful siege took time.

Liv took her time renewing makeup which needed no renewing. She tried, as she dusted powder on her nose, to consider her response to Thorpe logically. Hadn't she termed him a charismatic man? Even attractive, she admitted reluctantly, in a purely physical, athletic way. That had nothing to do with his being difficult and frustrating.

"Of course he's a pompous old bat, but I rather like him."

Liv glanced in the glass to see the reflections of two women who entered. One was Congresswoman Amelia Thaxter, a thin, hardworking woman who had a penchant for lost causes and dowdy clothes. Her constituents loved her, proving it by electing her for a second term by a landslide.

The woman with her, who was speaking, was also fiftyish, but plumper and dressed in elegant gray silk.

There was something vaguely familiar about her. Liv took out her compact a second time and listened.

"You're more tolerant than I am, Myra." Amelia sat down and tiredly took out a comb.

"Rod's not a bad sort, Amelia." Myra sat and took out a silver case of flashy red lipstick. "If you'd use a bit of honey, you might find him a help instead of a hindrance."

"He's not concerned with the ecological problems of South Dakota," Amelia put in. She hadn't bothered to use the comb, but kept tapping it against the palm of her hand. "No matter what you or I say to him tonight, he's not going to support me when I put my proposal on the floor Monday."

"We'll see." Myra slashed on the lipstick.

Rod, Liv realized as she slipped a thin brush out of her purse, was Roderick Matte, one of the more influential men in Congress. If a vote was going to be close, he was the man to sway.

A pompous old bat, Liv thought, and suppressed a grin. Yes, he was that, as well as his party's hope for the highest office in Washington in the next election. Or so the rumors went.

The congresswoman muttered at the comb, then stuck it back in her purse. "He's a bigoted, narrow-minded pain in the—"

"My dear," Myra said sweetly, interrupting her friend's impassioned speech with a smile for Liv, "that's a perfectly stunning dress."

"Thank you."

"Didn't I see you with T.C.?" The woman took out a small vial of expensive perfume and used it lavishly.

"Yes, we came together." Liv vacillated between identifying herself and keeping silent. She decided it was both wiser and more fair to establish her credentials. "I'm Olivia Carmichael with WWBW."

Amelia made a small, unidentifiable sound, but Myra pressed on, undisturbed. "How interesting. I don't watch the local news, I'm afraid, or much news at all, except for T.C.'s reports. News tends to give Herbert indigestion."

Justice Herbert Ditmyer. Liv finally placed the face. Justice Ditmyer's wife, Myra, a woman with power and influence enough of her own to call Congressman Matte a pompous old bat without fear of repercussions.

"We're on at five-thirty, Mrs. Ditmyer," Olivia told her. "Your husband might find our broadcast easy to digest."

Myra laughed, but she was studying Liv carefully. "I know some Carmichaels. Connecticut. You wouldn't be Tyler's younger daughter, would you?"

Liv was used to the nameless term. "Yes, I am."

Myra's face split into a smile. "Isn't that something. The last time I saw you, you were seven or eight years old. Your mother was giving a proper little tea, and you came into the parlor—a scruffy thing with a rip the size of a fist in your skirt and the buckle off your shoe. I believe you got quite a scold."

"I usually did," Liv agreed, not remembering the particular incident, but others like it.

"I remember thinking you must have had a great deal more fun that afternoon than the rest of us did." She gave a gleaming smile. "Your mother gave a stuffy party."

"Myra, really." Amelia took her mind from her pending bill long enough to give a disapproving tsh-tsh.

"It's all right, Congresswoman," Liv said smoothly. "She still does, I believe."

"I must say, I would never have recognized you."

Myra rose and brushed off her skirt. "Quite an elegant young woman now. Married?"

"No."

"Are you and T.C. . . . ?" She let the sentence trail off delicately.

"No," Liv said positively.

"Do you play bridge?"

Liv lifted a brow. "Poorly. I never acquired a taste for it."

"My dear, a detestable game, but useful." She plucked a business card out of her bag and handed it to Liv. "I'm having a card party next week. Call my secretary Monday; she'll give you the details. I have a nephew I'm rather fond of."

"Mrs. Ditmyer—"

"He won't bore you—at least not too much," Myra continued smoothly. "And I think I'm going to like you. My husband will be there," she added, shrewd enough to dangle tempting bait before the reporter. "He'd love to meet you."

"Let's go back, Myra," Amelia suggested, wearily rising. "Before you're up on bribery charges. Good evening, Ms. Carmichael."

"Good evening, Congresswoman."

Alone, Liv studied the elegant little calling card for a moment, then dropped it into her purse. One didn't turn up one's nose at a direct invitation from Myra Ditmyer—even if it included bridge and a nephew.

Snapping her purse shut, Liv rejoined the party.

"I was beginning to think you were holding a press conference in there," Thorpe commented, offering her a fresh glass of wine.

She gave him an enigmatic smile. "Close."

"Want to elaborate?"

"Does accepting your invitation mean I have to

share?" Liv took a careless sip of wine. She was feeling curiously buoyant. Three unexpected contacts in one evening was well worth the trip. "Actually," she continued, "I believe I'm going to be a blind date at a bridge party."

"Date?" Thorpe frowned. He had noted the women who had come out of the powder room before Liv.

"Yes, date. You know—a man and a woman finding a common interest for a certain number of hours."

"Cute. Had enough of this place?"

"As a matter of fact, yes." Liv took a last sip, then handed him back the glass.

"We'll get your coat." He took her arm and propelled her through the room.

"I do appreciate your letting me tag along, Thorpe." Liv reached for her keys as they stepped from the elevator on her floor.

"Tag along," he repeated. "That wasn't included in your definition of a date, was it?"

"This wasn't a date."

"Still." Thorpe took the keys from her and slipped one into the lock on the door. "Good manners would buy me a cup of coffee."

"Fifty cents would buy you one down the street."

"Liv." Thorpe gave her an offended look that made her smile.

"All right, manners it is. A cup's worth."

"You're incredibly generous," he told her as he opened the door.

Liv tossed her coat on a chair as she walked to the kitchen. He eyed the coat with a small smile. Now and again, she forgot the carefully created image she had built. Olivia Carmichael would never throw down a coat—much too fastidious. Much too organized. More than ever, Thorpe wanted to know the woman behind the image. There was warmth there, humor, passion—all hidden behind a thin shield. The shield had been raised for a reason. He intended—sooner or later—to find out what it was.

She liked color, he decided. He'd noted it before in the way she dressed. Now he noted it again in the furnishings of her apartment: a brilliant blue throw pillow, a persimmon-colored bowl. Small signs of fire, he thought, like the quick flare of temper. She banked it, constantly, but it was there.

"How do you take your coffee?" she called out as he walked to the kitchen.

"Black."

He wandered to the stereo and flipped through records. "Van Cliburn to Billy Joel," he commented when Liv came back into the room. "Very eclectic."

"I like variety," she answered, and set a tray with two cups and saucers on the coffee table.

"Do you?" He smiled—a bit, she thought, as if he were enjoying a private joke. Liv began to wish she hadn't agreed to the cup of coffee. "What do you do for entertainment?" Thorpe walked over and took a seat on the sofa. Liv hesitated a moment, then sat beside him. She could hardly choose a chair across the room.

"Entertainment?" she repeated, and reached for her coffee.

"That's right." He had noticed the hesitation. It pleased him to know that she wasn't indifferent toward him. If he made her nervous, it was a beginning. "You know, bowling, stamp collecting."

"I haven't had much time for hobbies lately," Liv murmured, and sipped at her coffee. She wondered why she had been at ease when she had walked out of the kitchen and was now strung tight. Thorpe lit a cigarette and kept watching her. She struggled against an adolescent urge to move away from him.

"What have you had time for?"

"I work," she said, and moved her shoulders. Why was a simple cup of coffee and conversation making her pulse pound? "That keeps me busy enough."

"Sunday afternoons?"

"What?" She had looked up to meet his eyes before she realized the mistake. His were dark and direct and closer than she had thought.

"Sunday afternoons," he repeated. He didn't touch her. His eyes drifted slowly down to her mouth, then back. "What do you do on Sunday afternoons?"

Something was kindling inside her—something elemental and strong. Liv hadn't felt the quick tug of desire for years. But he wasn't touching her, wasn't making love to her. They were only drinking coffee and talking. She told herself she had had too much wine, and lifted her coffee again.

"I usually try to catch up on my reading." She watched a plume of smoke drift by before Thorpe crushed out his cigarette. "Murder mysteries, thrillers." Her eyes flew up again when Thorpe took the cup from her hand.

"I've always liked solving puzzles," he murmured. "Digging underneath to find something that's not on the surface. You've very thin skin." He brushed a knuckle over her cheek. "But I haven't been able to get beneath it—not yet."

She started to draw away. "I don't want you poking into my mind."

"We'll save that for later, then." He slid his arms around her. "I want to hold you. When we were dancing, I promised myself I'd hold you again when we were alone."

You don't want him to hold you, her mind insisted. But she didn't tell him, and didn't resist as he pressed her closer.

His eyes flicked briefly to her mouth. "I've wanted for days to taste you again." Lightly, his lips rubbed over hers. "Too long," he muttered.

You don't want him to kiss you, her mind insisted. But she didn't tell him, and didn't resist as he crushed her mouth with his.

Thorpe wasn't patient this time. The demand seemed to spring up—hot, almost violent. Liv was caught in it, stunned by his lightning passion and her own instant response. She had no time to think, to reason, only to react. Her arms locked around him. Her lips parted.

Where had the urgency come from? Both of them seemed trapped by it, unable to keep to their planned routes. She couldn't stop him or herself; he couldn't adhere to the easy pace he had outlined. Desperation. They both felt it. Need. Outrageous need to taste and touch and belong. He hadn't known her mouth would become so soft in passion. He wanted to rip the black dress from her and discover her. It was madness. Control was slipping from him too quickly.

Liv moaned when his mouth went to her throat. She wanted to be touched, and heard herself telling him, then pressed against him as he caressed her breast through the thin layers of silk. She pulled his mouth back to hers.

She was starving and took from him what she had so long denied herself. She craved the intimacy of his tongue against hers, the feel of his hands roaming her body. There was strength there, and need. A need for her. And he made her need him with an intensity that frightened her. She couldn't allow herself to need anyone again. The risks were too great, the punishment too severe.

"No." Liv pushed against him in sudden panic. "No," she said again, and managed to draw back, if not away. His hands stayed firm on her shoulders. She could see the raw desire in his eyes, knew it must be mirrored in her own.

"No what?" His voice was rough, half-angry, half-aroused. He hadn't expected the brutal degree of passion she had brought out in him.

"You have to go." Liv pulled out of his hold and stood. She needed distance, needed to stand on her feet. Thorpe rose more slowly.

"I want you." It was a simple statement, almost flat, as he fought against the throbbing that beat inside him. "You want me."

It would have been absurd to deny it. Liv took a deep breath. "Yes, but I don't *want* to want you." She let the breath out again. "I won't."

Thorpe felt his control snap. He grabbed her and pulled her against him. He saw her eyes widen as the pupils dilated. "The hell you won't," he said quietly. He released her again so quickly that she nearly tumbled back onto the sofa. He stuck his hands in his pockets to keep them off her.

"This isn't the end of it, Carmichael," he warned before he turned for the door. "It's just the beginning."

He let the door swing closed behind him as he headed for the elevator. He needed a drink.

Chapter 4

"THE TAPE ON THE SCHOOL BOARD MEETING'S STILL BEING edited." Liv glanced briefly at the clock before she sat down to review the script for the evening broadcast. I'd have more time, she thought fleetingly, if I hadn't had to do those teases.

"Know what the story count is tonight?" Brian stripped the wrapper from a chocolate bar and sat on Liv's desk.

"Hmm?"

"Eighteen." He took a generous bite. "We're packing them in. The general manager's frantic because we slipped a couple notches in the ratings. I heard he wants to change the tone of the weather forecast. Go for the chuckles. Maybe he'll hire a comedy writer."

"Or put on a ventriloquist and a magic act," Liv mumbled. Gimmicks annoyed her. Even as she spoke to Brian, she was running over her timing on the stories she would soon read on the air. "The next thing you know, we'll have the weather being given by a guy in a clown suit standing on one leg and juggling plates."

"Maybe we need the comic relief." Brian balled the candy wrapper and pitched it into Liv's wastebasket. "Lead story's the rape in the supermarket parking lot."

"So I see." She was skimming the copy, one eye on it, the other on the clock, with her attention divided between the script and her colleague. It was a skill most reporters developed early.

"Marilee did a spooky little stand-up out there. I just saw the tape." He swallowed the last of the chocolate. "My wife shops there. Damn."

"Everything in here tonight's grim." Liv glanced up, running a hand over the back of her neck. "Wholesale prices are up six percent; unemployment's following suit. Two robberies in Northeast and an arson in Anne Arundel County to add to the rape. Lovely."

"Like I said, maybe we need that comic relief."

"I want to see daffodils," she said suddenly. Weariness settled over her all at once. Was it the tone of the news? she wondered. Surely by now she was immune to it. Was it something else? Something had been nagging inside her for the last few days. Something she couldn't quite pinpoint. It had kept her awake long after Thorpe had left her apartment the night before.

Brian studied her a moment. He'd noticed the faint shadows under her eyes that morning. It was past five now, and they were deeper. "Is it something you'd like to talk about?"

Liv opened her mouth, surprised by the question. She shut it again. There was nothing she could say.

"I know something's been eating at you lately." He leaned a bit closer so other ears wouldn't overhear his words. "Look, why don't you come to dinner tonight? I'll call Kathy and tell her to add a can of water to the soup. Sometimes a few hours with friends helps."

Liv smiled and squeezed his hand. "That's the nicest invitation I've had in a long time."

"So don't turn it down."

"I have to. I've got something lined up tonight." The offer made her feel better, less isolated. "Can I have a rain check?"

"Sure." He rose, but Liv took his hand before he moved away.

"Brian, thanks." She tightened the grip a moment when he started to shrug it off. "I mean it."

"You're welcome." He pulled her to her feet. "It's nearly airtime. You'd better haul yourself into makeup and have them do something about those shadows under your eyes."

Liv lifted her fingers to them automatically. "That bad?"

"Bad enough."

With a quiet oath, Liv walked off to follow Brian's advice. The last thing she needed was to appear haggard on the air. It would be her luck to go on looking as if she hadn't slept, and then have Thorpe catch her broadcast.

So I haven't been sleeping well, Liv thought as she took her place on the set. It hasn't anything to do with Thorpe. I've just been a bit restless lately. And I was at the southwest gate of the White House at eight o'clock this morning waiting to catch comments from cabinet officials. I'm a bit tired. It has nothing to do with the night of the embassy party . . . or what happened later.

Liv clipped on her mike, then flipped through the

script one last time. Timing was important as story was piled on top of story.

She'd been working too hard. That's what she told herself. The last few days had been particularly hectic —that was all. T.C. Thorpe had been the last thing on her mind. There'd been the aftermath of Dell's appointment, then that mess at the school board to cover. She frowned down at the script and told herself she hadn't given a thought to her last meeting with Thorpe. It hadn't crossed her mind since it happened. Not once. Only a thousand times.

Swearing silently, she heard the thirty-second cue. She straightened in her chair and glanced up. Thorpe stood in the back of the studio. He was watching her steadily, eyes level as he leaned back against the heavy doors.

Fifteen seconds.

What is he doing here? Liv felt her throat go dry. Ridiculous, she told herself, and tore her eyes away from his to the camera.

Ten seconds.

The monitor was flashing the opening, an aerial view of the city.

Five seconds. Four, three, two, one. Cue.

"Good evening, this is Olivia Carmichael." Her voice was cool and precise. It amazed her that her palms were damp. She read off the lead story, then never glanced toward the rear of the studio as they went to tape for the reporter's stand-up on location.

The cameras switched between Liv and Brian, keeping the pace brisk. She gave her report on the school board meeting without missing a beat, though she could feel the physical pressure of Thorpe's eyes on her face.

She gave the depressing news on the wholesale price index. To her knowledge, Thorpe never came to the studio before or during a broadcast. Why wasn't he upstairs where he belonged, polishing his own words of wisdom?

There was a buildup of tension at the base of her neck, which increased when they broke for commercial. Liv knew, without glancing over, that he was coming toward her.

"Nice style, Liv," Thorpe commented. "Sharp, cool and clean."

"Thank you." The sportscaster settled into his chair at the end of the table.

"Going to the Ditmyer card party tonight?"

There was nothing he didn't know, she decided, and folded her hands over her copy. "Yes."

"Want a lift?"

Now she met his eyes directly. "Are you going?"

"I'll pick you up at seven-thirty. We'll grab some dinner first."

"No."

He leaned a bit closer. "I can arrange for you to be my partner tonight."

"You'll lose," she told him. She had never known a set of commercials to take so long.

"No," he corrected, and smiled. "I don't intend to lose." He kissed her quickly, casually, before she could prevent it, then sauntered away.

Thirty seconds.

She scowled as the doors swung behind his back. Without turning, she could feel the speculative gazes on her. Thorpe had successfully set the ball rolling. And the tongues wagging.

Ten seconds.

Fuming, she vowed to make him pay for it.

Cue.

* * *

Liv arrived at the Ditmyers' promptly at eight. Bridge wasn't the inducement. She could remember the dry, stuffy card parties her mother had given when she was growing up. Liv remembered Myra's flashy red lipstick and careless gossip from the powder room at the embassy. She pressed the doorbell and smiled. She didn't think Myra Ditmyer gave stuffy parties. And, she reminded herself, how often does a reporter get invited to the home of a justice of the Supreme Court? Unless, of course, the reporter's name was T.C. Thorpe.

Liv frowned, then quickly smoothed out her features as the door opened.

Though it was a maid who led Liv inside, Myra herself came bustling down the hall seconds later. It was obvious, Liv thought, smiling to herself, that Myra was a woman who didn't like to miss anything.

"Olivia." Myra clasped both of her hands warmly. "So glad you could come. I like having beautiful women around. I was one myself once."

As she talked, she was pulling Liv with her down the hall. "I watched your newscast. You're good."

"Thank you."

Myra propelled Liv into a large drawing room. "You must meet Herbert," she went on. "I reminded him of the tea with your parents, and your torn dress, but he didn't remember. Herbert's mind is filled with weighty matters. He often misses details."

But you don't, Liv decided as she was pulled through the room at top speed. It was spacious, accented with splashes of vivid color and ornately patterned wallpaper. Liv decided the room suited her hostess perfectly.

"Herbert." Myra snatched her husband away from a conversation without a moment's hesitation. "You must meet lovely Ms. Carmichael. She does the newscast on . . . What is the name of that station, dear?"

"WWBW." Liv extended her hand to Justice Ditmyer. "We're the Washington affiliate of CNC."

"All those initials," Myra commented with a cluck of her tongue. "It would be simpler if they just gave it a name. Isn't she beautiful, Herbert?"

"Yes, indeed." The justice smiled with the handshake. "A pleasure to meet you, Ms. Carmichael."

He was a small and, Liv thought, curiously unimposing man without the black robes of his office. His face was lean and lined. He looked like someone's grandfather rather than one of the top judiciary leaders of the country. The skin of his hand was soft and thin with age. He lacked the vitality of his wife, possessing instead a quiet stability.

"Myra tells me we met briefly, a number of years ago."

"A great number of years ago, Justice Ditmyer," Liv agreed. "I disgraced myself, I believe, so we're both to be forgiven for not remembering."

"And she hardly resembles that little wildcat who burst into tea that afternoon," Myra put in. She was eyeing Liv with her good-natured shrewdness. "How does your mother feel about your career in television?"

"She wishes I'd chosen something less public," Liv astonished herself by saying. It wasn't like her to be so frank with strangers. Myra Ditmyer, she decided, would have made a terrific interviewer.

"Ah, well, parents are so hard to please, aren't they?" Myra brushed it off with a smile and a pat on Liv's hand. "My children find me terribly difficult, don't they, Herbert?"

"So they tell me."

"All nicely married now," she continued, overlooking her husband's dry response. "So I've time to work on my nephew. Nice boy—a lawyer. He lives in Chicago. I believe I mentioned him."

"Yes, Mrs. Ditmyer." Liv heard the justice sigh, and tried not to echo with one of her own.

"He's here on business for a few days. I do want you to meet him." Myra scanned the room quickly, then her eyes lit. "Yes, there he is. Greg!" She lifted her voice, and her hand in a signal. "Greg, come over here a moment. I have a lovely girl for you to meet."

"She can't help it," Justice Ditmyer said in an aside to Liv. "A dyed-in-the-wool busybody."

"Romantic," Myra corrected. "Greg, you must meet Olivia. She's a newscaster."

Liv turned to meet the nephew, and stared. An avalanche of memories crashed down on her. If any words had formed in her brain, she wouldn't have been able to speak them.

Greg stared back, equally stunned. "Livvy?" He reached out a hand to touch hers, as if to reassure himself she was real. "Is it really you?"

She wasn't certain what she felt. Surprise, yes, but she couldn't separate pleasure from anxiety. The past, it seemed, refused to stay buried. "Greg." She hoped her face wasn't as pale as her voice.

"This is incredible!" He smiled now and pulled her against him for a hug. "Absolutely incredible. What has it been? Five years?"

"It appears you two know each other already." Myra said wryly.

"Livvy and I were in college together." Greg drew her away to take a long look. "My God, you're more beautiful than ever. It doesn't seem possible." He lifted his hand with the privilege of an old friend and touched her hair. "You've cut it." He glanced at his aunt. "It used to be down to her waist, straight as a dime. Every woman in Harvard envied Livvy her hair." He turned back to her. "Still, this suits you—very chic."

There were a hundred questions jumbled in her head, but she couldn't bring herself to ask them. He looked almost the same, hardly older, though the beard he had sported in college had been trimmed down to a moustache. It suited him, sandy blond like his hair, and gave his almost boyish face an air of experience. His eyes were as friendly as ever, and his smile as enthusiastic. Five years seemed to evaporate in an instant.

"Oh, Greg, it's good to see you again." This time it was she who hugged him. It didn't matter that college was a million years behind her. It mattered only that he was there for her to touch and hold on to—someone she had known in happier times. And in sadder ones.

"I'm going to steal her from you for a few minutes, Aunt Myra." Greg gave her a quick kiss on the cheek before taking Liv's hand. "We've got some catching up to do."

"Well, well." Myra beamed as she watched them walk away. "That worked out better than I planned." She glanced over and lifted a brow. "T.C. just came in." Myra smiled and ran her tongue over her teeth. "I think I'll have a word with him."

"Now, Myra." Justice Ditmyer laid a restraining hand on her arm. "Don't go stirring up trouble."

"Herb." She patted the hand before she drew away from it. "Don't spoil my fun."

Greg led Liv through a pair of corridors and into the solarium. "I just can't believe it. Running into you like this. It's fantastic."

"When we were in college, I didn't know you had such illustrious relatives."

"I didn't want comparisons," he told her. The moonlight was dim, and because he wanted to see her, Greg switched on a low light. "Living up to family expectations can be traumatic."

"I know what you mean." Liv wandered to one of the windows. It was an interesting semicircular room with cushioned benches and a light scent of flowers. She didn't sit. Seeing Greg again so unexpectedly had unnerved her. Liv thought better on her feet.

"How long have you been in Washington, Livvy?" She was slimmer now than he remembered, and more poised. Five years. Sweet Lord, he thought, it could have been yesterday.

"Almost a year and a half." She tried to remember the last time anyone had called her Livvy. That too, she realized, had been left in another life.

"Aunt Myra said you were a newscaster."

"Yes." She turned back to him. In the shadowed light, her beauty struck him like a blow. He'd never gotten used to it. "I'm co-anchor on the evening news at WWBW."

"It's what you always wanted. No more weather reports?"

She smiled. "No."

There were no rings on her fingers. Greg crossed to her. Her scent was different, he noticed, more sophisticated, less artless. "Are you happy?"

She kept her eyes level as she thought over the question. "I think so."

"You used to be more definite about things."

"I used to be younger." Carefully, she moved away from him. She wanted to keep it light. "So, your aunt tells me you're single."

"She would." Greg laughed and shook his head. "Whenever I'm in town, she finds an eligible female to dangle in front of me. This is the first time I've appreciated it."

"You never married, Greg? I'd always thought you would."

"You turned me down."

She faced him again and smiled gravely. "You were never serious."

"Not enough. My mistake." He took her hand between both of his. It was still fine boned and fragile, a contrast to the strength in her eyes. "And you were too crazy about Doug to see it if I had been." He saw her expression change even as she started to turn away. "Livvy." Greg stopped her. "Doug and I are partners in Chicago."

For a moment she didn't speak. She had to fight through a wave of pain for the easy words. "That's what you both had planned. I'm glad it worked out for you."

"Those first few months after . . ." He stopped, wanting to chose his words carefully. "After you left weren't easy for him."

"Neither were the last few months before." She felt cold suddenly.

"It was a bad time. The worst kind of time for both of you."

Liv drew a deep breath. She didn't often allow herself to remember. "You were a good friend to us, Greg. I don't think I ever told you just how good. It was a difficult period of my life. You made it a bit easier." Now, she returned the pressure of his hand. "I don't think I realized that until much later."

"I hated to watch you hurting, Livvy." When she turned away, he took her shoulders and rested his head on her hair. "There's nothing that makes you feel more helpless than watching people you care about in pain.

Everything that happened seemed so unjust at the time. It still does."

Liv leaned back against him. She remembered he had tried to comfort her all those years ago, but she had been beyond it then. "Doug and I didn't handle it well, did we, Greg?"

"I don't know." He hesitated a moment, wondering if he should tell her. Perhaps it was best for her to know everything. "Livvy, Doug's married again."

She said nothing at all. Somehow she had known he would be, had been all but sure of it. *Does it matter?* she asked herself. She had loved him once, but that was over. Dead. Love was long dead. Still, she felt a wave of grief for what they had had, what they had lost. A long, shuddering sigh broke from her.

"Is he happy?"

"Yes, I think so. He's put his life back together." Greg turned Liv to face him. "Have you?"

"Yes." She went into his arms, wanting to be held by someone who understood. "Yes, most of the time. My work's important. I needed something important to keep me sane. I've put all those years behind me, into their own little box. I don't open it often. Less and less as the years pass." She closed her eyes. The grief was still there, only dulled by time. "Don't tell him you saw me." She lifted her face so that she met Greg's eyes. "He shouldn't open the box either."

"You always were strong, Livvy, stronger than Doug. I think he had a hard time accepting that."

"So did I." She sighed again and rested against him. "I wanted too much from him; he didn't want enough from me." Suddenly, she clung to him. "When the one thing that bound us together was gone, we fell apart. Picking up the pieces is hell, Greg. I'm still missing some, and I don't even know where to look for them."

"You'll find them, Livvy." She felt him kiss her hair, then lifted her face to smile at him.

"I'm awfully glad I was the female your aunt chose to dangle in front of you this trip. I've missed you."

He would like to have kissed her, as a man kisses a woman who has always held a special place in his heart. But he knew her too well. He touched her lips lightly with his.

"Excuse me."

Liv's eyes flew to the doorway. Even in the shadows, she could make out Thorpe's silhouette. Carefully, she drew out of Greg's arms, angry that Thorpe had discovered her in a weak, unguarded moment.

"Myra needs to fill in a table."

"Bridge." Greg grimaced and took Liv's arm. "This is my punishment for not making it down last Christmas. You'll have to tolerate being my partner for old times' sake, Livvy."

"You couldn't do much worse." She knew Thorpe's eyes were fastened on her face, and felt absurdly guilty. To compensate, she smiled at Greg. "If you fix me a drink, I'll try not to trump your ace."

Thorpe stepped aside as they walked through the doorway.

He stood in the shadows another moment, watching them walk away. Jealousy was a new emotion. He found he didn't care for it. Olivia Carmichael belonged in a man's arms. He was going to make damn sure they were his.

"Two clubs." Liv bid on a poor excuse for a hand. She and Greg had as opponents the head of thoracic surgery at a Baltimore hospital and his wife. They were being badly beaten. Neither of them played the game with much skill. After a particularly humiliating hand,

Greg jokingly challenged the surgeon and his wife to a tennis match. He remembered well Liv's energy on the court. With a grin, the surgeon marked down the scoring.

The three other tables in the room included two senators, a five-star general and the widow of a former secretary of the treasury. Liv kept her ears tuned to the light political talk and gossip. She wouldn't learn any state secrets, but she had made contacts. A reporter couldn't afford to ignore the smallest scrap of information. You could never tell what could lead to bigger things. Liv found it ironic that a torn dress and scuffed shoes had brought her to the drawing room of a Supreme Court justice.

"Five spades." Greg took the bid, and Liv spread her cards on the table and rose.

"Sorry," she said when he gave a small sigh at what she had to offer him.

"Tennis," he muttered, and played his first ace.

"I'm going to get some air."

"Coward," he said, and shot her a grin.

With a laugh, Liv slipped out to the terrace.

It was still cool. Spring was fighting its way into Washington like a dark horse candidate. After the heat of the drawing room, Liv found the chill refreshing. There was little light as clouds drifted over a half-moon. And it was quiet. The rear of the house was shielded from the street sounds and hum of city traffic. She heard Myra's boom of a laugh as she won game point.

How strange it was, Liv thought, to meet Greg again like this—to have those bittersweet years of her life brought back. Extremes, she mused. I lived on extremes. Staggeringly happy, unbearably sad. It's better this way, without all those peaks and valleys of emotion. Safer. I've had enough of risks and failures. Smarter.

Wrapping her arms around herself, she walked to the edge of the terrace. Safer and smarter. You can't be hurt if you don't take chances.

"No wrap, Liv?"

She gasped and whirled. She hadn't heard the terrace doors open, or Thorpe's steps on the stone. What moonlight there was shone directly on her face, while his was in shadows. She felt at a disadvantage.

"It's warm enough." Her answer was stiff. She hadn't forgiven him for embarrassing her in the studio.

Thorpe moved closer and laid his hands on her arms. "You're chilled. Nobody wants to listen to a newscaster with the sniffles." He stripped off his jacket and slipped it over her shoulders.

"I don't need—"

Keeping his hands on the lapels, Thorpe pulled her against him and silenced her with a bruising kiss. Her arms were pinned between his body and her own, her mouth quickly and expertly conquered. Liv's thoughts seemed to explode, then spiral down to a small, unintelligible buzz in her head. She felt the unwanted pull of desire begin to take over just before his mouth lifted from hers.

"Maybe you didn't need that." He kept her close, still gripping the lapels of his own jacket. "But I did."

"You must be crazy." The words were strong and scathing, but husky with awakened passion.

"I must be," he agreed easily enough. "Otherwise I wouldn't have walked out of your apartment the other night."

Liv let that pass. The memories of her response to him were too uncomfortable. "You had no right pulling that business in the studio this evening."

"Kissing you?" She watched his grin flash. "I intend to make a habit of that. You have a fantastic mouth."

"Listen, Thorpe—"

"I hear you and Myra's nephew are old friends," he interrupted.

Liv let out a frustrated breath. "I don't see what that has to do with you."

"Just weeding out the competition," he said smoothly. He liked holding her close, waiting for the slight resistance of her body to melt.

"Competition?" Liv would have drawn away, but she was trapped in the jacket. "What are you talking about?"

"I'll have to learn about the other men you let hold you so I can dispose of them." Thorpe pulled her fractionally closer. The heat of his body seemed to skim along her skin. His eyes were direct on hers. "I'm going to marry you."

Liv's mouth dropped open. She hadn't thought it was possible for Thorpe to shock her again. He was a man she had learned to expect anything of. But not this. Here was a calm, matter-of-fact statement. He might have been saying he was going to be her partner for the next round of bridge. After a close, thorough study of his face, Liv could have sworn he was completely serious.

"Now I know you're crazy," she whispered. "Really, really mad."

His brow lifted in acknowledgment, but he continued in a reasonable tone. It was the tone more than anything else that left her baffled. "I'm willing to give you six months to come around. I'm a patient man. I can afford to be; I don't lose."

"Thorpe, you're in serious trouble. You should ask

for a leave of absence. Pressure does strange things to the mind."

"I think it'll be simpler if I'm straight with you." He was smiling now, amused by her reaction. Her eyes were no longer shocked, but wary. "Now you'll have time to get used to the idea."

"Thorpe," she said, "I'm not going to marry anyone. I'm certainly not going to marry you. Now, I think you should—"

She found herself cut off again as he took her mouth. Her small sound of protest was muffled, then silenced as his tongue slowly seduced hers. She was pressed against him, her arms still pinned straight down at her sides. But he felt the resistance melt, just as he had wanted. His own desire pounded. Her mouth wasn't submissive, but active on his. She sought more, even as he did.

Clouds covered her mind and there was only sensation. She could feel the somehow soft and strong texture of his lips, the slow, sure movement of his tongue. If they had been free, she would have wrapped her arms around him and clung. Only her mouth and the pressure of her body told him that she wanted him. Just as his told her.

She was suddenly and completely a creature of the flesh. She wanted nothing more than to be touched by him. Her skin burned for it; her body ached. She murmured something neither of them could understand. Thorpe could feel her response. He wanted her desperately. The thought ran through his mind that she had been right to call him mad. He wanted her to the point of madness. If they had been alone . . . If they had been alone . . .

Gradually, he brought himself back. There would be

other times, other places. Banking his desire, he lifted his mouth from hers. "What was it you were going to tell me to do?" he murmured.

Her breathing was unsteady. She struggled to remember who she was, who it was who held her, what he had just said to her. As he smiled at her, her brain began to clear. "See a doctor." She couldn't manage more than a whisper. Her body was tingling. "Quickly, before you really crack."

"Too late." Thorpe drew her back for a last, burning kiss. Stunned by her completely uninhibited response, Liv pulled out of his arms. She ran a hand through her hair.

"This is crazy." She kept the hand aloft, gesturing with it as if to make him see reason. "This is really crazy." Steadying, she took a quick breath. "Now, I'll admit I'm attracted to you, and that's bad enough; but that's the limit. I'm going to forget all of this." She slipped his jacket from her shoulders and dropped it into his hand. "I want you to do the same. I don't know how much you had to drink in there, but it must have been too much."

He was still smiling at her, a patient smile. "You wipe that grin off your face, Thorpe," she ordered. "And—and stay away from me." She stormed to the terrace doors, then turned her head to look at him a last time. "You're crazy," she added for good measure before she yanked the doors open and dashed through them.

Chapter 5

THERE WAS A WHITE ROSE ON LIV'S DESK IN THE MORNING. It stood in a slender porcelain vase, a bud only, with petals tightly closed. Of course, she knew who had sent it. Baffled, she dropped into the chair behind her desk and stared at it.

When she had returned to the card table the evening before, she had promised herself she wouldn't think of her conversation with Thorpe. A sane person didn't dwell on the words of a lunatic. Yet there had been a long, quiet stretch in the night when she had lain awake in bed. Every syllable of their conversation on the terrace had played back in her head. And now he was sending her flowers.

The smart thing to do would be to dump it, vase and all, into the trash and forget it.

Liv touched a fingertip to a white petal of the rose. She couldn't bring herself to do it.

It's just a flower, after all, she reminded herself. Harmless. I just won't think about where it came from. Briskly, she pulled a sheet of copy toward her. She had a news brief to give in fifteen minutes.

"Liv, thank God you're here!"

She glanced up as the assignment editor barreled down on her desk. "Chester?" He was an excitable, usually desperate man who lived on antacids and coffee. She was accustomed to this sort of greeting from him.

"Take crew two and get out to the Livingston Apartments in Southeast. A plane just crashed into the sixth floor."

She was up, grabbing her purse and jacket. "Any details?"

"You get them. We're going live as soon as you're set up. An engineer's going with you. Everybody's scattered around town or down with the flu." His tone hinted that the flu was no excuse for being unavailable for assignment. "Go, they're in the van." He popped a small, round mint into his mouth.

"I'm gone." Liv dashed for the door.

It was worse, much worse than she could ever have imagined. The tail section of the plane protruded from the face of the building like the shaft of an arrow. It might have been taken from a scene of a movie, carefully staged. Fires, started by the impact, belched out smoke. The air radiated with waves of heat and smelled pungently. The building was surrounded by fire engines and police cars, and they were still coming. Fire fighters were geared up, going in or coming out of the building, or spraying it with the powerful force of their hoses. The lower floors were being evacuated. She could hear the weeping and the shouts above the wail of sirens and crackle of the fire.

Behind the barricades, the press was already at work. There were cameras and booms, reporters, photographers and technicians. All were moving in their special organized chaos.

"We'll stay portable," she told Bob as he hefted the camera on his shoulder. "For now, get the building on tape, a full pan of these trucks and ambulances."

"I've never seen anything like this," he muttered, already focusing in on the visible section of the plane. "Can you imagine what it's like inside there?"

Liv shook her head. She didn't want to. There were people inside there. She forced back a swell of nausea. She had a story to report.

"There's Reeder." She glanced in the direction Bob indicated. "Assistant fire chief."

"Okay. Let's see what he can tell us." Liv worked her way through the crowd. She was jostled now and again, but she was used to that. She knew how to snake through masses of people to her objective. And she knew the crew would follow behind her. Coming to the edge of the barricade, she secured her position and took the mike from her soundman.

"Chief Reeder, Olivia Carmichael with WWBW." She managed to get the mike out to him by leaning over the barricade and planting her feet. "Can you tell us what happened, and the status of the fire?"

He looked impatiently at the mike, then at Liv. "Charter plane out of National." His voice was curt, gruff and as impatient as his eyes. "We don't know the cause of the crash yet. Four floors of the building are involved. Of the six floors, three have been evacuated."

"Can you tell me how many people are on the plane?"

"Fifty-two, including crew." He turned to bark an order into his two-way.

"Has there been any contact with them?" Liv persisted.

Reeder gave her a long, silent look. "My men are working down from the roof and up from the lower floors."

"How many people are still in the building?"

"Talk to the landlord, I'm busy."

As he walked away, Liv signaled to Bob to stop the taping. "I'm going to try to find out how many people are still inside." She turned to the sound technician. "Go back to the radio; find out if the desk knows the flight number yet, the plane's destination, any clue to the cause of the crash. We'll set up for a live bulletin." She checked her watch. "Five minutes, right here."

She turned to push through the crowd again. There was a woman sitting alone on the curb. She was dressed in a worn robe and clutched a photo album to her breast. Liv backtracked from her search for the building's landlord and went to her.

"Ma'am."

The woman looked up, dry eyed, pale. Liv crouched down beside her. She recognized the look of shock.

"You shouldn't be sitting out here in the cold," Liv said gently. "Is there somewhere you can go?"

"They wouldn't let me take anything else," she told Liv, pressing the album closer. "Just my pictures. Did you hear the noise? I thought it was the end of the world." Her voice was reed thin. The sound of it pulled at Liv. "I was fixing tea," she went on. "All my china's broken. My mother's china."

"I'm sorry." The words were pitifully inadequate.

Liv touched the woman's shoulder. "Why don't you come with me now. Over there. The paramedics will take care of you."

"I have friends up there." The woman's eyes shifted to the building. "Mrs. McGiver in 607, and the Dawsons in 610. They have two children. Did they get out yet?"

Liv heard another window explode from heat. "I don't know. I'll try to find out."

"The little boy had the flu and had to stay home from school." Shock was giving way to grief. Liv could see the change in the woman's eyes, hear it in her voice. "I have a picture of him in here." She began to weep—deep, tearing sobs that pulled at Liv's heart.

Sitting on the curb beside her, Liv gathered the woman into her arms. She was fragile, almost paper thin. Liv was very much afraid that the picture would be all that was left of the Dawson boy. Holding her close, Liv wept with her.

She felt a hand on her shoulder. Looking up, she saw Thorpe standing tall beside her.

"Thorpe," she managed as he stepped in front of them. Her eyes were eloquent. Thorpe lifted the old woman from the curb gently. She was still clutching the album. He slipped an arm around her, murmuring in her ear as he led her toward the paramedics. Liv let her forehead drop to her knees.

She had to pull herself back together if she was going to do her job. A reporter couldn't afford personal involvement. She could hear someone coughing violently as smoke clogged her lungs. The wind brought it still closer.

"Liv." Thorpe took her arm and drew her to her feet.

"I'm all right," she said immediately. She heard

another explosion. Someone screamed. "Oh, God." Her eyes flew back to the building. "How many people are still trapped in there?"

"They haven't been able to break through to the sixth floor yet. Anybody still on it, or in that plane, is gone."

She nodded. His voice was calm and unemotional—exactly what she needed. "Yes, I know." She took a deep, cleansing breath. "I need something to put on the air. I have a stand-up to do." She looked at him again. "What are you doing here?"

"I was on my way in to the station." There was a smear on her cheek from the smoke and ash. He rubbed it off with his thumb. He kept his voice light. "This isn't my beat, Liv. I'm not here for a story."

She looked past him to where paramedics were working frantically on a burn victim. "I wish to God I weren't," she murmured. From somewhere to the left, she heard a child screaming for her mother. "I hate this part of it—poking, prying into people's pain."

"It isn't an easy job, Liv." He didn't touch her. He wanted to, but knew that wasn't what she needed.

She looked over as her crew made their way toward her. Liv took the scribbled note from the sound technician with a nod.

"All right, we shoot from here with the building at the back." Drawing a breath, she faced the camera. "After I'm into it, I want you to pan the building." She took the mike again and waited for the cue that would patch her into the station. "Then focus in on the plane before you cut back to me. Keep in the background noise." In her earphone, she heard the countdown to cue.

"This is Olivia Carmichael, outside the Livingston Apartments, where at nine-thirty this morning charter flight number 527 hit the sixth floor of the building." Bob panned the building as she continued. "The cause of the crash has not yet been confirmed. Fire fighters are evacuating the building and working to gain access to the sixth floor and the plane. There were fifty-two people on board, including crew, en route to Miami." The camera came back to her. "There is no report as yet on the number of casualties. Burn and smoke-inhalation victims are being treated here by paramedics before being transported to the hospital."

Thorpe stood back and watched as Liv continued the report. Her face was composed, but for her eyes. The horror was there. Whether she knew it or not, it added to the impact of her facts and statistics. There were still traces of soot on her cheek, and her skin was dead white against it. A viewer looking beyond the words would see a woman, not just a reporter. She was good at her job, he reflected, perhaps because she constantly struggled to tamp down her emotions. The effort showed from time to time and made her more accessible.

"This is Olivia Carmichael," she concluded, "for WWBW." She waited until they were off the air, then whipped off the earphone. "All right, get some tape of the paramedics. I'll find out if they've gotten through to the sixth floor yet. Get a courier out here. They'll need whatever we've got for the noon news."

Liv felt the control slip back into place. She wasn't going to fall apart again.

"Very efficient," Thorpe commented.

Liv looked at him. He was all quiet intensity, all understated strength. It disturbed her that for just a brief moment she had needed him—simply needed to know he was there to lean on. It was a luxury she couldn't afford to allow herself.

"The trick is being good at it," Liv repeated. "Let's say we finally have a point of agreement."

He smiled and brushed a stray lock of hair from her forehead. "Want me to hang around?"

She stared at him, struck with conflicting emotions. Why was he so easily able to move her? "Don't be nice to me, Thorpe," she murmured. "Please don't be nice to me. It's simpler when you're a louse."

He bent and touched her lips with his. "I'll call you tonight."

"Don't," she returned, but he was already walking away. Swearing, Liv spun around. She couldn't worry about Thorpe. She still had information to gather and a story to finish.

Liv watched the tape on the eleven o'clock news. It was a different feeling than she had experienced during her own earlier broadcast. Sitting behind the desk, giving her report and watching herself on the monitor, she could separate her emotions from her job. Now, alone in her apartment, watching the tape as any other viewer, the tragedy washed over her again. Sixty-two people had died, and fifteen more had been hospitalized, including four fire fighters. The reports weren't official yet, but it looked as though a pilot error had been responsible.

Liv thought of the woman she had tried to comfort on the curb—the precious photo album she had clutched, the stunned grief, then the mourning. There had been no survivors from the sixth floor.

The time of day had been a blessing. Liv had said so herself in her report. Most of the apartments had been vacant. Children had been in school, adults at work. But the little Dawson boy in 610 had had the flu.

Rising, Liv snapped off the set. She couldn't think

about it, couldn't dwell on it. She pushed at her temples. It was time to take a couple of aspirin and go to bed. Nothing could change what had happened in the morning hours, and it was time to find her distance again.

It occurred to her, as she crawled into bed, that she had missed dinner. Hunger might be partially responsible for the severity of her headache, but she was too weary to take anything more than the aspirin. Shutting her eyes, she lay in the darkness.

This is what she had decided she wanted. Quiet, privacy. No one to depend on—no one to answer to. What she had now was hers; what mistakes she made were hers. That was the best way.

She opened her eyes to stare at the ceiling, wondering just when she had begun to doubt that.

The phone beside her shrilled, and Liv sat straight up. She fumbled for the bedside lamp, then picked up a pencil even as she lifted the receiver. Who but the desk would call her at midnight?

"Yes, hello."

"Hello, Liv."

"Thorpe?" Liv dropped the pencil and lay back. He was incredible.

"Did I wake you?"

"Yes," she lied. "What do you want?"

"I wanted to say good night."

She sighed, then was grateful he couldn't see her smile. She didn't want to give him any encouragement. "You woke me up to say good night?"

"I've been tied up. I just got home." Thorpe yanked off his tie. If there was one thing he hated about the job, it was ties. "Want to know where I've been?"

"No," Liv returned dauntingly, and heard him chuckle. Damn it, she thought, then propped her pillow behind her. She did want to know. "All right, where were you?"

"At a meeting with Levowitz."

"Levowitz?" Her attention was caught. "The bureau chief?"

"That's the one." Thorpe pried off his shoes.

"I didn't know he was in Washington." The wheels began to turn in her head. Levowitz wouldn't make a trip from New York to D.C. without good cause. "What did he want?"

"Harris McDowell's going to retire at the end of the year. He offered me the spot."

The news wasn't nearly as surprising as his casualness. Being offered McDowell's job was nothing to take lightly. Exposure, power, money. To be considered capable of stepping into McDowell's shoes was no idle compliment. It was an accolade.

Liv searched around for something to say, and settled on, "Congratulations."

"I didn't take it."

Now she waited a full beat. "What?"

"I didn't take it." Thorpe pulled off his socks and tossed them in the direction of the hamper. "You're off this weekend—" he began.

"Wait a minute." Liv sat up straighter. "You turned down the most prestigious position in CNC or any other news organization in the country?"

"You could put it that way if you want." He lit a cigarette from his second pack that day.

"Why?"

Thorpe blew out a stream of smoke. "I like working the field. I don't want to anchor, at least not in New York. About this weekend, Olivia."

"You're a strange man, Thorpe." She settled back against the pillows. She couldn't quite figure him out.

"A very strange man. Most reporters would kill for the job."

"I'm not most reporters."

"No," she said slowly, considering. "No, you're not. You'd make a good anchor."

"Well." He smiled as he unbuttoned his shirt. "That's quite a compliment from you. Want some company?"

"Thorpe, I'm in bed."

"If that's an invitation, I accept."

Unable to do otherwise, she laughed. "No, it's not. I haven't had a conversation like this since high school."

"We can go out and neck in the back seat of my car."

"No thanks, Thorpe." Relaxed, she snuggled down into the pillows. When was the last time, she wondered, that she had had a foolish conversation in the middle of the night? "If you only called to say good night . . ."

"Actually, I called about tomorrow afternoon."

"What about it?" Liv yawned and closed her eyes.

"I've got two tickets for opening game." He stripped off his shirt and tossed it to follow the socks.

"Opening game of what?"

"Good God, Liv, baseball. Orioles against the Red Socks."

He sounded so sincerely shocked by her ignorance, she smiled. "Dick Andrews handles sports."

"Broaden your outlook," he advised. "I'll pick you up at twelve-thirty."

"Thorpe," she began, "I'm not going out with you."

"It's not a seduction, Liv; that comes later. It's a ball game. Hot dogs and beer. It's an American tradition."

Liv turned off the light and pulled the covers up over her shoulders. "I don't think I'm making myself clear," she murmured.

"Try it again tomorrow. Palmer's pitching."

"That's very exciting, I'm sure, but—"

"Twelve-thirty," he repeated. "We want to get there early enough to find a parking place."

Sleepy, she yawned again and let herself drift. It was probably simpler to agree. What harm could it do? Besides, she'd never been to a ball game.

"You're not going to wear one of those hats, are you?"

He grinned. "No, I leave that to the players."

"Twelve-thirty. Good night, Thorpe."

"Good night, Carmichael."

She was smiling as she hung up. Just before she drifted into sleep, she realized her headache had disappeared.

Chapter 6

Memorial Stadium was packed when they arrived. Liv was to learn that Baltimore was very enthusiastic about their Orioles. There were not, as she had presupposed, only men wearing fielders' caps and clutching beers in the stands. She saw women, children, young girls, college students, white- and blue-collar workers. There must be something to it, she concluded, to draw out so many people.

"Third base dugout," Thorpe told her, gesturing down the concrete steps.

"What?"

"That's where we're sitting," he explained. "Behind the third base dugout. Come on." Taking her arm, he propelled her down. She frowned out at the field, trying to put together what she knew of the sport with the white lines, brown dirt and grass.

"Know anything about baseball?" Thorpe asked her.

Liv thought a moment, then smiled at him. "Three strikes and you're out."

He laughed and took his seat. "You'll get a crash course today. Want a beer?"

"Is it un-American to have a Coke instead?" While he signaled a roving concessionaire, Liv leaned against the railing in front of her and studied the field. "It seems simple enough," she commented. "If this is third base here, then that's first and second." She gestured out. "They throw the ball, the other guy smacks it and then runs around the bases before someone catches it."

"A simplistic analysis of the thinking man's sport." Thorpe handed her the Coke.

"What's there to think about?" she asked before she sipped.

"Strike zones, batting averages, force-outs, double play balls, switch hitters, wind velocity, ERAs, batting lineup, bull pen quality—"

"All right." She stopped him in midstream. "Maybe I do need that crash course."

"Have you ever seen a game?" Thorpe leaned back with his beer.

"Snatches on the monitor during a sportscast." She glanced around the stadium again.

The sun was bright and warm, the air cool. She could smell beer and roasted peanuts and hot dogs. From somewhere behind them, a man and woman were already arguing over the game that was yet to be played. There was a feeling of involvement she had completely missed in her occasional glimpses of a ball game on the television screen.

"This is a different perspective." She studied the scoreboard. Its initials and numbers told her little. "So, when does it start?" Liv turned to face Thorpe, to find him studying her. "What is it?" The unblinking stare made her uncomfortable. The distance she had planned on hadn't worked. Now she began to wonder if the casual friendliness she had decided upon would fare any better.

"I've told you. You have a fantastic face," he returned easily.

"You weren't looking at my face," Liv countered. "You were looking into my head."

He smiled and ran a finger down her fringe of bangs. "A man should understand the woman he's going to marry."

Her brows drew together. "Thorpe—"

Her intended lecture was cut off by the blast from the organ and the roar of the crowd.

"Opening ceremonies," Thorpe told her, and draped his arm behind her chair.

Liv subsided. *Just humor him,* she cautioned herself. The man is obviously unstable. She settled back to watch the hoopla of the season's start.

By the end of the first inning, Liv was lost, and completely fascinated. "No one got any points," she complained, and crunched a piece of ice between her teeth.

Thorpe lit a cigarette. "Best game I've ever seen was in L.A., Dodgers and Reds. Twelve innings, one to nothing, Dodgers."

"One point in twelve innings?" Liv lifted a brow as the next batter stepped into the box. "They must have been lousy teams."

Thorpe glanced at her a moment, saw she was perfectly serious, then burst out laughing. "I'll buy you a hot dog, Carmichael."

The batter dropped a short single into left field, and she grabbed Thorpe's arm. "Oh, look, he hit one!"

"That's the wrong team, Liv," Thorpe pointed out wryly. "We're rooting for the other guys."

She accepted the hot dog and peeled off a corner on the packet of mustard. "Why?"

"Why?" he repeated, watching as she squeezed the mustard on generously. "The Orioles are from Baltimore. The Red Sox are from Boston."

"I like Boston." Liv took a healthy bite of the hot dog as Palmer whipped a mean curve by the next batter. "Shouldn't he have swung at that one?"

"Don't like Boston too loudly in this section," Thorpe advised. The crowd roared as the batter grounded into a double play.

"Why didn't the man on first just stay where he was?" she demanded, gesturing with her hot dog.

Thorpe kissed her, surprising her with a full mouth. "I think it's time for that crash course."

By the bottom of the fifth, Liv was catching on to the basics. She'd taken to leaning over the rail as if to get a closer view. The score was tied at three to three, and she was too involved to be surprised her adrenaline was pumping. In her excitement, she had forgotten Thorpe was a lunatic. Her shield was slipping.

"So, if they catch the ball in foul territory before it hits the ground, it's still an out."

"You catch on fast."

"Don't be a smart aleck, Thorpe. Why are they changing pitchers?"

"Because he's given up two runs this inning and he's behind on this batter. He's lost his stuff."

She leaned her chin on the rail as the relief pitcher took the mound to warm up. "What stuff?"

"His speed, his rhythm." He liked the way she was absorbed in what was happening on the field. "He isn't getting his change-up over, and his slider isn't working."

She gave Thorpe a narrow look. "Are you trying to confuse me?"

"Absolutely not."

"How long have you been coming to games?"

"My mother took me to my first when I was five. Washington had the Senators then."

"Washington still has plenty of senators."

"They were a ball team, Liv."

"Oh." Again, she rested her chin on the rail. He grinned at her profile. "Your mother took you? I would have thought baseball a father-son sort of thing."

"My father wasn't around. He wasn't much on kids and responsibilities."

"I'm sorry." She turned her head to look at him. "I didn't mean to pry."

"It's no secret." He shrugged. "I wasn't traumatized. My mother was a terrific lady."

Liv looked out to the field again. Strange, she mused, she hadn't thought of Thorpe as ever being a child, with a family, growing up. She tried to picture it. Her vision of him had been limited to a tough, hard-line reporter with a gift for biting exposés. Thinking of him with a childhood, perhaps a difficult one, altered the view. There were entirely too many facets of him. She had to remind herself she didn't want to explore them.

But—what had he been like as a boy? How much had the early years influenced the way he was today?

There was sensitivity in him. The rose—the damn rose. Liv thought of it with a sigh. It made it difficult to remember that distance was necessary. And his sexuality. He knew how to arouse a woman, even a reluctant one. Arrogance, yes, but he was so blatantly at ease with it, the trait was somehow admirable. And his skill in his profession couldn't be faulted. She couldn't term him power or money hungry—not when he had casually refused a position most reporters would slit throats for.

I'd better be careful, she decided. I'm dangerously close to liking him.

Thorpe watched her profile, observing the play of emotions over her face. When she forgot her guards, he reflected, she was clear as glass. "What are you thinking?" he murmured, and cupped the back of her neck with his hand.

"No comment," Liv returned, but couldn't bring herself to discourage the familiarity. She couldn't find the will to push it away. "Look, they're ready to start again."

"The count's still three and one," Thorpe explained. "The runner on second's charged to the first pitcher. If he scores, it goes against him, not the relief."

"That seems fair," Liv commented as the batter knocked a foul tip straight at her. In automatic reflex, she reached up to protect her face and snagged the ball. As she looked down at it, stunned, the impact stung her palms.

"Nice catch," Thorpe congratulated, grinning at her astonished face.

"I caught it," she said in sudden realization, then gripped the ball tighter. "Do I have to give it back?"

"It's all yours, Carmichael."

She turned it over, rather pleased with herself. "How about that," she murmured, then suddenly giggled.

It was the first time he had heard the young, carefree sound from her. It made her seem seventeen. He had to check the urge to pull her against him and just hold her. She had never appealed to him more than she did at that moment, with the sun full on her face and a baseball clutched in her hands. Love for her was abruptly and unexpectedly painful.

He lost track of the game. It was Liv whose head shot up at the hard crack of ball on bat. Her eyes grew wide as she jumped from her seat with the rest of the stadium. She grabbed Thorpe's arm, dragging him with her.

"Oh, look! It's going all the way over the fence! That's a home run, isn't it? A home run, Thorpe!"

"Yeah." He watched the ball drop over the green barricade. "Home run. First one of the year."

"Oh, it was beautiful." She was caught in the loud blast of celebration music, the cheers of the crowd. Liv turned, giving Thorpe a quick, spontaneous kiss. It was over before she could be surprised by her own action, but he pulled her back for a deeper, lingering one. The shouts went on around her, lost in the fast, rocketing beat of her heart. She gave him pressure for pressure, taste for taste.

"Could be," Thorpe murmured as he drew his lips an inch from hers, "there'll be a whole volley of long balls."

Breathless, Liv eased out of his arms. In them, she lost everything but need. "I think one's enough," she managed. Because her legs weren't as steady as they might have been, she sat back down. She was closer to the edge than she had realized. It was time to take a few steps back. "Are you going to buy me another hot dog?" she demanded, and smiled at him. She ignored the tingling that still brushed along her skin. "I'm starving."

The rest of the game was a shrewd defensive battle. Liv had difficulty keeping her attention focused. She was too aware of Thorpe, too aware of the pulsing needs he had aroused, could arouse, so easily. She saw his hands and was reminded of the rough palms. She saw his arms and remembered there were muscles that could make her feel soft and safe. Liv didn't want to be soft. It made it too easy to be hurt. She didn't want to rely on anyone for safety again. It was too easy to be disappointed. She saw his mouth and knew how well it seduced. She told herself that to be seduced was to be weak and vulnerable. His eyes were intelligent, shrewd, saw too much. The more he saw, the greater the risk that he could gain an emotional hold on her.

She had allowed herself to be involved before. She still bore the scars. For years she had lived on the belief that the only way for her to keep her serenity was by withdrawal. She was coming to realize that Thorpe could change this. For the first time, she understood that she was afraid of him—of what he could come to mean to her.

Friendship, she reminded herself. That was all there was going to be. Just simple friendship. She spent the last two innings convincing herself it was possible.

"So we won." Liv checked out the final score on the board. "Five to three." She rubbed the foul ball between both palms.

"It's *we* now, huh?" Thorpe grinned and tugged on her hair. "I thought you liked Boston."

Liv leaned back in her seat and propped her feet on the rail as the crowd began to file out of the stands. "That was before I understood the intricacies of the game. You know, it's amazing how deceptive television can be. It's faster, more intense than I thought. Do you come often?"

He watched as she passed the ball from hand to hand and studied the field. "Are you fishing?"

"Just a casual question, Thorpe," she said coolly.

"Whenever I can," he answered, still smiling. "I'll take you to a night game next. It has a whole different feel."

"I didn't say—"

"T.C.!"

They both looked up as a man worked his way through the aisles toward them. He was short and stocky, with stone gray hair and a lived-in face. It was lined and pitted, with a square jaw and crooked nose. Thorpe rose to accept a bear hug.

"Boss, how are you?"

"Can't complain, no, can't complain." He drew back far enough to study Thorpe's face. "Good God, you look good, boy." With a meaty hand, he slapped Thorpe on the back. "Still watch you every night on the TV giving those politicians hell. You always were a sassy young pup."

Liv remained seated and watched the exchange in silence. She was fascinated to hear Thorpe referred to as a boy and a young pup. Thorpe was a good half foot taller than the man who grinned up at him.

"Someone has to keep them straight. Right, Boss?"

"You bet your—" Boss stopped himself and glanced down at Liv. He cleared his throat. "Gonna introduce me to your lady, or are you afraid I'll steal her away from you?"

"Liv, this old schemer is Boss Kawaoski, the best catcher ever to harass an umpire. Boss, Olivia Carmichael."

"Why sure!" Liv's hand was captured in the gnarled, broad one. "The lady on the news. You're even prettier face to face."

"Thank you." He was beaming at her out of eyes that seemed a trifle myopic.

"Careful, Liv." Thorpe slipped an arm around her shoulder. "Boss has a reputation as a lady-killer."

"Ah, sh—" He cleared his throat quickly again, and Liv struggled with a grin. "Shoot," he modified. "Wouldn't do to have my missus hear you talk that way. What'd you think of the game, T.C.?"

"Palmer's still dishing it out." He pulled out a cigarette and lit it. "It looks like the Birds have a tight team this year."

"Lots of new blood," Boss added, glancing wistfully out at the field. "The young left fielder has a mean bat."

"So did you, Boss." Thorpe looked back at Liv. "Boss carried a .324 average the year he retired."

Not completely certain of the meaning, Liv tried a safer angle. "Did you play for the Orioles, Mr. Kawaoski?"

"Just Boss, miss. I played for the Senators. That was twenty years ago." He shook his head at the passage of time. "This one used to hang around the clubhouse making a nuisance of himself." Jerking a thumb at Thorpe, he grinned. "Wanted to be a third baseman in those days."

"Did he?" Liv gave Thorpe a thoughtful look. Somehow, she had never considered him wanting to be anything but what he was.

"Wasn't so good with a bat," Boss reminisced. "But he had a great pair of hands."

"I still do," Thorpe said dryly, and gave Liv a broad smile which she ignored. "How are things going at the store, Boss?"

"Just fine. My wife's running it today. She didn't want me to miss opening game." He ran a hand along his squared chin. "Can't say I argued with her much.

She'll be sorry she missed you. Alice still lights a candle for you every Sunday."

"Give her my best." Thorpe crushed the cigarette under his heel. "This is Liv's first game."

"Well, no fooling." Boss's attention was switched as Thorpe had intended. Liv noted the move and filed it. Boss glanced at the baseball still clutched in her hand. "Caught yourself a foul too, first time out."

"Beginner's luck," she admitted, and held it out to him. "Would you sign it for me? I've never met a real ballplayer before."

Slowly, Boss turned the ball over in his hand. "Been a long time since I put my name on one of these." He took the pen Liv offered. "A long time," he repeated softly. He signed his name carefully around the curve of the ball.

"Thank you, Boss." Liv took the ball back from him.

"Thank *you.* Almost makes me feel like I could still pick a man off of second. I'll tell Alice I saw you." He gave Thorpe a final thump on the shoulder. "And the pretty news lady," he added. "Come by the store."

"First chance I get, Boss." Thorpe watched him move through the thinning crowd and up the steps. "That was a very nice thing you did," he murmured to Liv. "You're a perceptive woman."

Liv glanced down at the signature on the ball. "It must be hard to give up a career, a way of life, thirty years before most people have to. Was he very good?"

"Better than some." Thorpe shrugged. "That hardly matters. He loved the game, and the playing of it." Sweepers were already pushing their brooms through the narrow aisles, and Thorpe took her arm to lead her up the steps. "All the kids loved him. He never minded being hounded or catching a few pitches after a game."

"Why does his wife light a candle for you on Sundays?" She had told herself she wouldn't ask, that it was none of her business. The words were out before she could prevent them.

"She's Catholic."

Liv let that pass a moment as they walked toward the parking lot. "Don't you want to tell me?" she asked at length.

He jingled the keys impatiently in his pocket, then drew them out. "They run a small, independent sporting goods store in Northeast. A few years ago, they were having some trouble. Inflation, taxes, the building needed some repairs." He unlocked Liv's side of the door, but she didn't get in, only stood and watched him.

"And?"

"Twenty years ago ballplayers, average ballplayers like Boss, didn't make a lot of money. He didn't have much saved."

"I see." Liv slipped into the car as Thorpe rounded the hood. Leaning over, she unlocked the handle for him. "So, you lent him money."

"I made an investment," Thorpe corrected as he shut the door. "I didn't offer a loan."

Liv watched him as he started the ignition. She could see he didn't like her touching on this aspect of his life. She persisted. It was simply a reporter's habit, she told herself, to press for details. "Because you knew he wouldn't accept a loan. Or that if he did, it would put a dent in his pride."

Thorpe let the car idle and turned to her. "That's a lot of supposition on a very brief encounter."

"You just told me I was perceptive," she pointed out. "What's the matter, Thorpe?" A smile tugged at her mouth. "Don't you like people finding out you can be a nice guy?"

"Then you're expected to be nice," he told her. "I don't make a habit of it."

"Oh, yes." She was still amused, and the smile grew. "Your image. Tough, unsentimental, pragmatic."

He kissed her firmly, impatiently. Her surprise spun into longing. She felt his fingers tighten on her skin, and she opened for him. If it was a mistake, she had to make it. If it was madness, she'd find sanity later. In that moment, she only wanted to renew the pleasure he could give her.

His mouth was enough—enough to satisfy the slowly growing hunger. It wasn't the time to question why he was the one, the only one, who was able to crack the shield she had erected. She wanted only to experience again, to feel again.

His heart beat against hers, lightly, quickly, making her understand the hunger was mutual. She was wanted—desired. What would it be like to make love with him? What would it be like to feel his skin against hers? To have his hands touch her? But no—she couldn't let herself imagine. She couldn't stop herself from imagining.

He let his lips wander to the crest of her cheekbone, then on to her temple. "I'd like to continue this someplace more private. I want to touch you, Liv." His mouth came back to hers, hot, possessive. "All of you. I don't want an audience." He drew back until his eyes locked on hers. He saw desire, and his own clawed at him. "Come home with me."

Her heartbeat was echoing in her head, fast and furious. For the first time in years, it would have been so simple to say yes. She wanted him, shockingly. It overwhelmed her. How had it happened so quickly? If someone had suggested a month before that she would be tempted to make love with Thorpe, she would have laughed. Now, it didn't seem ludicrous at all. It seemed natural. It frightened her. Liv drew out of his arms and ran a hand through her hair. She needed some room, some time.

"No. No, I'm not ready for this." She told herself to take a deep breath, and did so carefully. "Thorpe, you make me nervous."

"Good." He fought back a powerful surge of need and leaned back. "I wouldn't want to bore you."

She managed a husky laugh. "You don't bore me. I don't know exactly what my feelings are toward you. I'm not even sure you're quite stable. This—this delusion you have about getting married . . ."

"I'm going to remind you of this conversation on our first anniversary." He put the car in first. If he was driving, he might keep himself from touching her again. Thorpe was discovering he wasn't as patient as he had thought.

"Thorpe, that's ridiculous."

"Think of what it's going to do for the ratings."

She wondered how he could be likable one minute, desirable the next, and then infuriating. Liv was torn between laughing and beating her head against the windshield in frustration.

"Okay, Thorpe," she began, opting for patience as he joined a stream of traffic. "I'm going to make this crystal clear in the simplest terms I can. I am not going to marry you. Ever."

"Wanna bet?" he countered smoothly. He shot her a grin. "I've got fifty says you will."

"Do you seriously expect me to bet on something like that?"

"No sporting blood." He shook his head. "I'm disappointed, Carmichael."

Liv narrowed her eyes. "Make it a hundred, Thorpe. I'll give you two-to-one odds."

He grinned again and cruised through a yellow light. "You're on."

Chapter 7

PRIME MINISTER SUMMERFIELD'S DEATH WAS UNEXPECTED. The fatal stroke which ended the British official's life left his country saddened. It sent the world press into a fever of preparation. There were special reports to air, recaps of Summerfield's forty-year career in British government to assemble, reactions to gather from the heads of other countries. How would the death of one man affect the balance of power in the world?

Two days after the prime minister's death was announced, the president was in *Air Force One,* crossing the Atlantic to attend the funeral. Thorpe was with him.

As press reporter, it would be his job to stick by the president, as close as a reporter was allowed, then share his information with the other news people who took the same journey on the press plane. He had a crew, pooled from the networks, ready to film any pertinent business on the flight. The cameraman, lighting and sound technicians were settled in the rear of the plane with their equipment close at hand. Their colleagues and backups were following on the press plane. In the forward portion of *Air Force One* were the president, first lady, and their entourages—secretaries, secret service, advisors. The mood was subdued.

Behind Thorpe, members of the pool crew played a quiet game of poker. Even the swearing was low key. On most trips, he would have joined them, whiled away the hours with a few hands, a few stories . . . but he had a lot on his mind.

The job itself would keep him occupied on the plane ride. He had research and information to put together and pick apart, a loose script to outline for the day of the funeral. Then, in London, it would be up to him to keep close to the president—watch for reactions, wait for a quote. The desire to be in the field and report his own stories had been the major element in his refusal of the anchor job in New York.

Thorpe would take what tidbits he could glean from the press secretary and use his own talents for observation and assimilation not only to give his own report, but to feed information to his colleagues.

Though the assignment was a plum, he almost wished it had been handed to Carlyle or Dickson, correspondents from the competing networks. He was on *Air Force One*. Liv was on the press plane.

She had kept her distance from him during the past few days, and Thorpe had given her room. He'd had little choice with the pressures of a top news story taking up his time. Yet the same story had brought them both, with frustrating consistency, to the same locations.

She'd been cool, he recalled, each time they had run into each other—at the White House gates, at the Capitol, at the British embassy. There had been no hint of the woman he had seen eating hot dogs and cheering over a home run. The ease with which she distanced him was more frustrating than he liked to admit. Even to himself. Impatience was dangerous, he knew. But his was growing.

She wasn't indifferent to him, he thought, as he scowled out of the window. A bit of turbulence made the plane tremble slightly as he pulled out a cigarette. No matter what she said, or how she acted, she couldn't erase the way she responded to him. There was hunger, and no matter how she struggled against it, the hunger won whenever he held her in his arms. Thorpe was willing to settle for that. For now.

"Three kings!" Thorpe heard the muttered expletive from the seat behind him. "Hey, T.C., let me deal you in before this guy cleans us all out."

As he started to agree, Thorpe saw the president slip inside his office with his secretary and speech writer.

"Later," he said absently, and rose.

When was the last time I went to England? Liv wondered. As she thought back, she remembered the summer she had been sixteen. She had traveled with her parents and her sister in first class. She had been allowed to nibble caviar and Melinda had been given champagne. The trip had been Melinda's eighteenth birthday present.

Liv remembered how her sister had chattered endlessly about the parties she would go to, the balls, the teas, the theaters. Clothes had been discussed unceasingly until her father had buried himself behind a copy of the *Wall Street Journal*. Too young for balls, ambivalent about dresses, Liv had been bored to distraction. The caviar, an unwise sampling of her sister's champagne and air turbulence had proven an unfortunate combination. She'd been ill—to her sister's disgust, her mother's surprise and her father's impatience. For the rest of the journey she had been looked after by a flight attendant.

Twelve years ago, Liv thought with a sigh. Things had certainly changed. No champagne and caviar on this trip. Unlike *Air Force One,* the press plane was both crowded and noisy. The card games here were less restrained. Reporters and crew from Washington stations roamed up and down the aisles, gambled, argued, slept—finding ways to ease the tedium of a long plane flight. Still there was an air of anticipation, of energy. The Big Story.

Liv busied herself with working on notes while two correspondents across the aisle speculated on the political ramifications of Summerfield's death. He'd been a reserved, almost bookish member of Britain's Conservative party. Yet underneath, Liv mused as she scribbled down her thoughts, there'd been a fine edge of steel. He hadn't been a man to be tampered with, or intimidated by tricky diplomatic maneuvers. She made notations on three potentially volatile situations he had handled during his term as prime minister, and other legislative triumphs, small and large, during his government career.

Liv had done quite a bit of research during the past two days, boning up on parliamentary procedure and Summerfield in particular. She had needed a firm handle on British politics in order to convince Carl to send her on the story. His argument that Washington politics were her forte had been only the first stumbling block. Thorpe, as usual, had been a larger one. Pressing down hard on her pencil with this thought, Liv snapped off the point.

Thorpe was going to England. Thorpe had been assigned as the president's press reporter. Thorpe would be traveling on *Air Force One* with the presidential entourage and the crew pooled from the various networks. WWBW could use Thorpe's feed without dipping into the budget for the funds to send a reporter and crew of their own.

It had taken Liv an hour of calm, lucid reasoning, and a further hour of determined arguing, to change Carl's mind. Afterward, she had been torn between cheering or screaming in frustration. *Thorpe.* Whatever she did, wherever she went, he was always there to make things twice as difficult for her.

And not just professionally.

She couldn't stop thinking about him. During the day, with the countless pressures of the job, he would crop up—either in person or by name. Then she would remember the dance at the embassy, the embrace on the terrace, the laughter at the ball game. At night, when she was alone, he would invade her mind, sneak into her thoughts. No matter what Liv did to prevent it, he would just suddenly *be* there. The way he laughed, the ironic lift of brow, the hard, rough hands. And worse, much worse, there were times she was certain she could taste his mouth on hers. That's when the needs would grow out of nowhere—unexpected, vibrant. She was never certain whether to be angry or terrified.

He had no right to bother her this way, she thought furiously as she groped in her briefcase for another pencil. He had no right to upset the order of her life. *And that bet.* Liv closed her eyes on a sigh of frustration. How had she ever allowed him to annoy her into making that ridiculous bet?

Marriage! Could he possibly be unbalanced enough to think she would seriously consider marriage? With him? What sort of man would waltz up to a woman he knows can barely tolerate his presence and announce his intention to marry her? A foolish one, Liv decided with a shrug, then caught her bottom lip between her teeth. Or a very shrewd one. Uncomfortably, Liv felt T.C. Thorpe fell into the latter category.

Of course, it didn't matter how shrewd he was; he couldn't *trick* her into marriage, and she would never be talked into it. So, she was perfectly safe.

Liv stared down at her notes and wondered why she didn't feel that way.

"Mike." Thorpe slipped into the seat beside Press Secretary Donaldson.

"T.C." Donaldson closed a file folder and gave Thorpe a careful smile. He was a man who looked like someone's kindly uncle: a little plump, beginning to go bald. His mind, however, was sharp and disciplined.

"What have you got to give me?" Thorpe asked him, and settled himself comfortably.

Donaldson raised both brows. "What's there to give?" he countered. "A state funeral, condolences, support, some pomp and ceremony. You'll have a lot of top officials, past and present, rubbing elbows. Royalty too. Good copy, T.C." He reached in his pocket for his pipe, then slowly began to pack it. "There'll be plenty to fill your time for the next couple of days. You've got the president's itinerary."

Thorpe watched Donaldson push tobacco into the bowl with his thumb. "He's going to be busy."

"He's not going to London to sight-see," Donaldson said dryly.

"None of us are, Mike," Thorpe reminded him. "All of us have our jobs. I wouldn't want to think you were making mine tougher by holding back on me."

"Holding back, T.C.?" Donaldson gave a quick laugh. "Even if I did, you usually manage to ferret out enough to get by."

"I notice there's a couple extra secret service aboard," Thorpe put in casually.

Donaldson went right on filling his pipe. "First lady's aboard, too."

"I counted her men, too." Thorpe waited a moment before going on. "The funeral of a man like Summerfield brings diplomats from all over the world." He paused, accepting coffee from the flight attendant while Donaldson eyed him over a lighted match. "Representatives from every country in the UN, and a few more. It promises to be quite a turnout."

"Depressing business, funerals," Donaldson commented.

"Mmm. Depressing," Thorpe agreed. "And dangerous?"

"All right, T.C., we've known each other too long. What are you fishing for?"

"Vibrations," Thorpe told him with a cool smile. "Any vibrations of trouble, Donaldson? Any reason the president or any of those other high political officials should be extra careful paying their last respects?"

"What makes you think so?" Donaldson countered.

"An itch," Thorpe said amiably.

"You'd better scratch it, T.C.," Donaldson advised. "I've got nothing for you."

As if considering the matter, Thorpe sipped his coffee. "Summerfield wasn't popular with the IRA."

Donaldson gave a dry chuckle. "Or the PLO, or a dozen other radical organizations. Is that a news bulletin, T.C.?"

"Just a comment. Can I get a statement from the president?"

"Pertaining to what?"

"His views on Summerfield's policy with the Irish Republican Army, and thoughts on the new prime minister."

"The president's views on the IRA are already documented." Donaldson chewed on the stem of his pipe. "Let's get Summerfield buried before we start on the new P.M." He shot Thorpe a straight look. "It might not be wise to talk about your hunch, T.C. No use giving people ideas, is there?"

"I only give people the facts," Thorpe said carefully, and rose. "I want to get some film."

Donaldson pondered a moment. "I'll arrange it, but no sound. We're going to a funeral. Let's keep this low key."

"My thoughts exactly. You'll let me know if there are any changes?" Without waiting for an answer, Thorpe wandered back to the card game.

"I want some film as soon as Donaldson clears it," he instructed the crew. Glancing down, he noted the cameraman held two pair. "Silent," he told the sound technician. "You can relax. Get a shot of the first lady working on her needlepoint." He grinned as the cameraman raised the bet.

"Looking for the homey touch, T.C.?"

"That's right." Leaning closer, he lowered his voice. "And see if you can get in a pan of the secret service."

The cameraman cocked his head to shoot Thorpe a look and met the cool stare. "Okay."

"Call." The lighting technician tossed in his chips. "What d'ya got you're so proud of?"

"Just a pair of eights," the cameraman said with a smirk. "And a pair of queens."

"Full house." The lighting technician spread his cards. Thorpe went back to his seat with mumbled curses following him.

He had always had an uncanny sense of intuition. The few moments with the press secretary had sharpened it. There was definitely more security on this trip than usual—enough to alert Thorpe.

Terrorism was a common word in the world today. It didn't take heavy thinking to conclude that when you brought heads of state from all over the globe together, political violence was more than a remote possibility.

A bomb threat? An assassination attempt? A kidnapping? Thorpe studied the quiet, three-piece-suited secret service agents. They'd be on the lookout, and so would he. It would be a long three days.

And the nights? he wondered. After the president's safely tucked away out of the reach of the press? He and Liv would stay at the same hotel. With luck—and a little strategy, he added thoughtfully—he could arrange to keep her close for most of the trip. At the moment, Thorpe considered proximity his biggest asset. Proximity, he amended, and determination.

Restless, Liv set aside her notes. She was unable to concentrate. She could not get Thorpe off her mind. It didn't help to be aware of how often they were going to be thrown together on this assignment. At least in Washington there were a number of stories to cover in the course of a day. This time, there would be only one. And Thorpe had the upper hand.

If she wanted a concise, thorough report, she would have to take whatever information he would give her. She would have to meet and talk with him on a scheduled basis. Of course, she reminded herself, regardless of everything else, he was a professional. That she couldn't fault him for. The information would be clear and incisive. If only it didn't have to come from him.

Kicking back her seat, Liv shut her eyes. Why was it her luck that Thorpe had been chosen as press reporter? If circumstances had been different, she would soon be three thousand miles away from him. Though she didn't like admitting it, she needed the distance. There had to be a way to stay clear of him. For the next couple of days, she would have to be on her toes just to keep up with the story and all the angles. He'd be busy too. That should solve a great deal of the problem.

When it came to free time, Liv decided she would make herself scarce. He was too thick skinned to respect her refusals or her coolness. If a no or a cold shoulder didn't work, unavailability was the next step. It was a pity they had to share the same hotel.

Nothing can be done about that, she reminded herself. But . . . she could see to it that she spent very little time in her room and very little time alone. It should be simple enough to lose herself in the crowd of press people that were about to descend on London.

With a small sound of disgust, she shifted in her chair. She didn't like playing hide-and-seek. But it's not a game, she told herself. It's more like war—a war she forgot to fight when he got too close. Yearnings, yes, she felt yearnings when he held her, when his mouth—

Shaking her head, she pushed the seat straight up. It wasn't Thorpe, she insisted silently. It was simply time she started feeling again. Five years was a long time to bury yourself. Clearly, too clearly, she saw his face in her mind's eye. And his smile—the charming, self-assured smile. She was definitely going to keep her distance.

The landing was smooth. Thorpe had had to stick to the president for another two hours before he could set off for his hotel. He had film, plenty of film to feed back to the States, along with his commentary. As he checked his watch and adjusted for the time difference, he noted CNC would have his report for the evening broadcast. With a revamp and update at eleven, he'd done his job for the day.

He watched London whiz by. It had been a good many years since he'd been there. Six? he mused. No, seven. But he thought he could still find the pub in Soho where he had interviewed a nervous attaché from the American embassy. Then there had been that little gallery in the West End where he had met a fledgling artist with a Rubenesque body and a voice like thick cream. Fleetingly, he recalled the two very exhilarating nights they had spent together.

Seven years ago, he thought, before he had settled in Washington. Before Liv. This London assignment was going to be different. He wasn't interested in two exhilarating nights with an unknown woman; he wanted a lifetime. And one woman. *Liv.*

Stepping out of the cab, Thorpe hefted his bag himself. He'd learned long ago to travel light. There was a damp chill in the air—the result of a drizzle which had stopped only moments before. People on the sidewalk were hunched inside jackets and moving quickly. As he stepped inside the hotel lobby, Thorpe saw the crowd of reporters checking in. His hopes to get to his room for a shower before the briefing were immediately aborted.

"Thorpe."

Shifting his bag, he smiled at Liv. She nodded politely.

"What have they got set up for us?" he asked, and was told there was a temporary press room on the second floor. "Okay, let's head up and I'll brief you." Before Liv could lose herself in the crowd, he had her arm. "How was your flight?"

"Uneventful." Knowing she could hardly snatch her arm from his without causing comment, Liv answered casually. "And yours?"

"Long." He grinned at her as they squeezed into the elevator. "I missed you."

"Stop it, Thorpe," she said crisply.

"Stop missing you? I'd be glad to if you'd stop avoiding me."

"I haven't been avoiding you. I've been busy." The crush in the elevator had her pressed tight to his side. After shifting his bag to his other hand, Thorpe slid an arm around her shoulders.

"Crowded in here," he said amiably when she shot him a narrow glance. Above the smells of tobacco, old cologne and light sweat, her scent lifted, sweet and clean. He had to control a desire to bury his face in her hair and lose himself in it.

"You'll make a scene, won't you?" she said softly, under the hum of conversation.

"If you'd like me to," he agreed. "I want to kiss you, Liv," he whispered, bending close to her ear. "Right here, right now."

"Don't!" There was no room to push away from him.

She could only look up and glare. It was her first mistake.

His mouth was inches from hers. His eyes, calmly amused, stared back into hers. There was a surge of need, a devastating sexual pull. Her mind went blank.

When the elevator doors opened, people began to file out around them. Liv stood still, trapped not by the arm around her shoulders but by the look of quiet, patient knowledge in his eyes.

"Come on, T.C., let's get this show on the road."

Thorpe didn't answer. He smiled at Liv and led her into the corridor. "We'll have to save it for later," he told her.

Freed of the trance, Liv stepped out of his reach. "There *is* no later," she snapped, then cursed herself as she took a place in the press room.

It took Thorpe less than thirty minutes to brief his colleagues and send them rushing off to complete their own reports. When he finally reached his own room, he had put in a twenty-hour day. Heading for the shower, he stripped on the way.

Liv walked into her room and let the bellboy bring in her bags. She waited while he fussed around the room opening drapes, checking the towel count. What she wanted was a pot of tea from room service, and her bed.

Jet lag, she thought wearily as she stuffed a pound note into the bellboy's hand. Why was it her sister never suffered from it no matter how many times she zipped here or there, country to country, party to party? If she had been Melinda, she would never have settled down with a cup of tea and a quiet room. She would have changed and rushed out to take in London's night life.

But she wasn't Melinda, Liv reminded herself as she

slipped out of her suit jacket. And she had already crammed a day and a half into a scant twenty-four hours. Tomorrow, Liv mused, stepping out of her shoes, there wouldn't be a moment's rest. Glancing in the mirror, she spotted the faint shadows of fatigue. It wouldn't do to have them show up on camera. A cup of tea, then a quick glance at her notes before sleep, she decided. She was heading for the phone to order when she heard the knock on the connecting door.

She frowned at it, then gave a sigh of annoyance. If one of the other reporters wanted to party or discuss the angles of the Summerfield story, she wasn't interested.

"Who is it?"

"Just another member of the working press, Carmichael."

"Thorpe!" The word came out in a rush of indignation. Without thinking, she flicked the lock and opened the door. He was leaning against the jamb, smiling, dressed only in a worn terry cloth robe. His hair was still damp from his shower, and the scent of soap and shaving lotion clung to him. "What are you doing here?" she demanded.

"Reporting the news," he said soberly. "It's my job."

"You know very well what I mean," she tossed back between her teeth. "What are you doing in the room next to mine?"

"The luck of the draw?" he ventured.

"How much did you give the desk clerk to arrange it?"

He grinned. "Liv, I don't have to respond to a leading question. You'll have to get that corroborated and ask me again." Still grinning, he let his eyes roam down to her stocking feet. "Going out?"

"No, I am not." Liv folded her arms and prepared to deliver a heated setdown.

"Good. I'd prefer a cozy evening at home." He took a step into her room. Liv's hand shot up to his chest. "Now look, Thorpe." Her palm had connected with his naked chest where the robe crossed over, and the sudden movement spread the material farther apart. Little more than dark, springy hair covered him to his waist. He continued to smile, unabashed, when she dropped her hand. "You're insufferable."

"I do my best." Lifting his hand, he twined a lock of her hair around his finger. "If you'd rather go out," he began.

"I am not going out," she repeated furiously. "And there's not going to be any cozy evening either. I want you to understand—"

"Haven't you ever heard that colleagues on foreign soil have to stick together?" His grin was suddenly boyish and impossible to resist. Liv struggled to keep her lips in a straight line.

"I'm making an exception in your case. Thorpe." She added on a note of exasperation, "Why won't you leave me alone?"

"Liv, it isn't traditional for a man to leave his fiancée alone."

His tone was so reasonable it took her a full ten seconds to react. *"Fiancée?* I am *not* your fiancée," she shouted at him. "I am *not* going to marry you."

"You want to add another hundred to the bet?"

"No!" She poked her finger into his chest. "Now you listen to me, Thorpe. Your delusions are your own business; leave me out of them. I'm not interested."

"You might be," he said pleasantly. "Some of my delusions are really fascinating."

"And I'm not going to sleep next door to a lunatic.

I'm getting another room." With that she whirled away.

"Afraid?" he asked, following her as she snatched up her bag.

"Afraid?" Liv tossed the bag back down and spun back. "The day I'm afraid of you—"

"I was thinking more of yourself." He tilted his head and studied her furious face. "Maybe you're not sure you could resist—ah, tapping on my door."

Speechless, Liv stared at him. "Tapping?" she managed in a sputter. "You think—you think I find you so irresistible, so—so . . ."

"Desirable?" he suggested helpfully.

Liv clenched her hands into fists. "I don't have any trouble resisting you, Thorpe."

"No?"

Before she could take a breath, she was in his arms. Before she could think to protest, his mouth was on hers. Pressed close—so close her body seemed to mold itself to his without her will. His mouth was firm, not impatient so much as insistent. This time, rather than tempting her surrender, he demanded it. The control, though it balanced on a fine edge, was his. With his fingers in her hair, he pulled her head back and plundered, deeper and still deeper.

"No trouble, Liv?" he murmured, lifting his mouth a whisper from hers.

Her breath was trembling. She shook her head before she attempted to speak. But he gave her no chance.

Again, his lips took hers, this time with the fire of possession. A moan of pleasure escaped her as she instinctively reached for him, tangling her fingers in his damp hair to pull him closer. Sharp, small needs began to race along her skin. He seemed to know, for his hands followed them with uncanny accuracy—a fingertip down her spine, a thumb at the sweep of her hip, his palm at the long length of her thigh.

Liv explored his face with her own hands, running her fingers over the angles and planes as if she would sculpt it. Her touch only heightened his demand, so that he crushed her to him, bending her back from the waist. Like putty, she moved to his command. Then he molded her. Under his hands, her breasts rose and fell with her quickened breathing. The nipples were taut, straining against the material of her blouse while he circled a fingertip over them.

There was no thought of resistance. She wanted the burn of his mouth, the scorch of his touch. When his lips moved to her throat, she tilted her head to give him absolute freedom. The moist heat of his tongue on her skin sent ripples of pleasure through her. She was lost in the dim, shadowed world of desires. His naked chest was pressed hard against her breasts. Caught tight, with arms that wrapped possessively around her, Liv yielded to him, to her own desire. His mouth lingered at the curve of her neck, just above the collar of her blouse; then, with deliberate leisure, he took his lips upward, lingering at the pulse in her throat, then the line of her jaw. When his mouth came back to hers, it was as though all the hunger and thirst she had ever known were concentrated in that one touch of lips.

Passion went from dark to bright. A harsh, blinding light seemed to explode in her brain. It left her limp. With a muffled cry that was half surrender, half terror, Liv leaned against him.

Unprepared for the sudden weakness, Thorpe drew her away to study her. In her eyes he could see traces of desire, hints of fear and confusion. The eyes alone were a more impenetrable defense than all her angry words or fierce denials.

Tenderness. He couldn't fight his own surge of tenderness. Taking her now would be simple, but having her physically was only part of what he wanted. When they finally made love—and he had no doubt that they would—she would come to him without fear. He would wait for it.

Smiling, he touched his lips briefly to hers. He wanted to see the flash of temper again. "In case you change your mind about resisting me, Carmichael, I'll leave my door unlocked. You don't even have to knock."

He sauntered away, shutting his connecting door with a gentle click. It took ten seconds before the heavy thud of her thrown shoe sounded against it. With a grin, Thorpe switched on the television to see what the British news had to offer.

Chapter 8

WITH A LOW, MONOTONOUS BUZZ, THE ALARM WOKE LIV at six A.M. She reached for the button automatically, then lay staring at the bland, impersonal room without the least idea where she was. London, she remembered, and rubbed her fingers over her eyes.

She hadn't slept well. Sitting up, Liv brought her knees to her chest and rested her forehead on them. Blast Thorpe! She'd spent half the night tossing and turning with doubts and desires that hadn't existed before he had touched her. Her purpose for being in London was professional. Even if she had the time, she didn't have the inclination for anything else. She simply didn't want to be involved with him. Why couldn't he see that?

Because, she thought wearily, saying something and acting on it are two different things. How could she convince him she didn't want to be involved when she responded totally every time he took her into his arms? Yes, she had wanted him. In that flash of a moment when she had been held close, mouth on mouth, she would have given herself to him. Her will had bent to his. That frightened her.

The problem, as she saw it, had to be resolved within herself first. The most important thing to do was to change the wording: not that she didn't want to be involved, but that she refused to be involved.

Rising, Liv prepared to shower and dress. There was too much to do that day to sit and brood about a personal dilemma. In any case, she thought it gave Thorpe too much importance to brood about him at all. How he would enjoy knowing she had done just that!

She had packed a very somber suit, charcoal gray and tailored. After doing up the final button, Liv gave herself a quick, professional study in the full-length mirror. She would do. A dab of extra makeup concealed the faint shadows under her eyes. *Thorpe again,* she thought resentfully.

The slim briefcase would carry her notes along with an extra pad and a supply of pencils. Tossing her coat over her arm, she prepared to leave. A slip of white on the floor by the connecting door caught her eye.

Liv stared at it for a moment. It looked suspiciously like a note. The best thing to do, she thought, would be to ignore it. She walked all the way to the front door before she gave up and went back. Stooping, she scooped the paper up.

"Good morning."

That was all it said. A laugh escaped her before she could stop it. He's mad, she decided again. Absolutely mad. On impulse, she ripped off a sheet of her own notepaper and scribbled a similar greeting. After slipping it under the connecting door, she left the room.

As arranged, she found her crew in a corner of the hotel's coffee shop. "Hey, Liv." Bob sent her a quick smile. "Want some breakfast?"

"Just coffee." She took the communal pot and poured. "I feel like I need a gallon of it."

"It's going to be a long day," he reminded her, and dug into his eggs.

"Starting immediately," she agreed. Absently, she shook her head at the waiter. "I want a stand-up in front of Westminster Abbey before the crowds get there, and another at 10 Downing Street. With luck, we might get some tape of Summerfield's widow. I imagine they'll start lining the streets a good hour before the funeral procession is scheduled." One of the crew tempted Liv with a piece of toast, but she smiled and shook her head. "We'll want some pans of the crowd on tape to use with a voice-over later."

"I've got to pick up some souvenirs for my wife and kids." Bob shot Liv a grin as she picked up her coffee. "Look, Liv, I got enough grief because I took off for London without them; if I don't bring back a few goodies, I'm going to be sleeping on the sofa."

"You should be able to squeeze out a few minutes for shopping between setups," she said. As she spoke, her eyes roamed the room, skimming over the faces of other reporters.

"Looking for somebody?" Bob asked, and cut into a sausage.

"What?" Distracted, she looked back at him.

"You've been scanning the room since you sat down. Are you meeting someone else?"

"No," she said, annoyed that she had unconsciously been looking for Thorpe. "You all better hurry," she told the crew in general. "The schedule's tight."

For the next ten minutes she drank her coffee with her back to the rest of the room.

The weak sunlight brought little warmth as Liv stood across from Westminster Abbey. She waited, going over her notes for the stand-up one last time as the crew set up their equipment. She estimated the spot would take forty-five seconds. Behind her the abbey's towers rose into a murky sky. London was gray under the clouds, the air heavy with threatening rain. At the moment, she gave no thought to the city around her, but was totally focused on the forty-five seconds of tape that was to come.

"Come in on me," she instructed the cameraman. "After the intro, I'm going to turn to the side and gesture back at the abbey. I want a slow pan; then come back on me at the finish."

"Gotcha." Bob waited until his lighting man had rechecked his meter. "Okay?"

Liv took the mike, then nodded. She ran through it once. Dissatisfied, she ran through it a second time. A faint breeze tugged at her hair as she spoke of the ceremony that was to come. Thoroughly, as though she had not worked the timing to the second, she talked of the abbey's history. When the camera came back to her, she looked into the lens with direct, serious eyes.

"This is Olivia Carmichael reporting from Westminster Abbey, London."

"Well?" Bob shifted his weight to his hip.

"It's a wrap." She checked her watch. "All right. We go to Downing Street. There're two hours before the ceremonies start. That should give us enough time for a quick stand-up and a few man-on-the-streets. We'll want another briefing with Thorpe before we feed what we have back to the station."

Thorpe had time for three cups of coffee while he waited for the president. His brief meeting with Donaldson had disclosed only that the president had spent a comfortable evening and had arisen early. But Thorpe was not satisfied.

Outside, the limo waited with secret service hovering discreetly in the background. Thorpe drew on a cigarette, standing coatless, heedless of the chill spring morning. His cameraman whistled tunelessly while the rest of the crew held a mumbled conversation. Thorpe didn't pay attention. He was watching the secret service. They were quite obviously on the alert.

The moment the president stepped outside, things came to life. Thorpe heard the whirl of the camera going on. He had the mike in his hand. Almost without thought, he filed what the first lady was wearing. There would be those who would demand an exact account.

"Mr. President."

The president stopped by the door to the limo and turned to Thorpe. A brief nod kept the guards at arm's length. "T.C.," he said solemnly. "A sad day for England, and for the world."

"Yes, Mr. President. Do you feel Prime Minister Summerfield's death will have an effect on your foreign policy?"

"Eric Summerfield's death will be felt keenly by all men of peace."

A roundabout way to say nothing, Thorpe thought without rancor. It was the name of the game. He also knew protocol. He wouldn't be allowed hard-line questions on the morning of the funeral. "Mr. President," he added, changing tactics, "have you any personal memories of the prime minister?"

If he was surprised by the altered tone, he continued smoothly. "He could walk for miles." The president smiled. "I discovered that at Camp David. Eric Summerfield liked to think on his feet."

With that, the president slipped into the limo beside his wife. Still vaguely dissatisfied, Thorpe waited for his press car.

His commentary, and the film of the funeral procession, would be broadcast via satellite. Thorpe set up less than a block away from Westminster Abbey, where the service would be conducted. His coverage promised to be a long, involved dissertation on what dignitaries had come to pay their respects, and in what order they arrived.

Thorpe announced the sighting of the royal family's limo, then others, sprinkling in tidbits of Summerfield's career and personal life. The streets were jammed with people, yet the background noise was minimal. When they spoke, onlookers spoke in hushed tones, as if they were inside the abbey.

He glimpsed Liv once, but there was no time for a personal encounter. As he talked into the mike, she was in the corner of his eye, the corner of his mind. His body tensed a split second before it happened.

A car broke through the police barricade and headed, at high speed, for the heart of the funeral procession. There was the sudden, shocking sound of gunfire. People who had lined the streets to watch scattered in a melee of fear and confusion. Cameramen raced for a better shot at the scene. Mike in hand, Liv dashed forward, reporting on the run. Thorpe was there ahead of her.

The procession was at a standstill. Bullets ripped holes in the tires of the speeding car, sending it skidding, careening out of control. The windshield cracked in a spider web of lines as the car swerved, held on course, then swerved again. It rammed into the curb and came to an abrupt halt.

Four men leaped out, rifles blazing. Bullets flew indiscriminately—toward the cavalcade, into the crowd. There were screams and a new rush of panic. People were knocked underfoot while others scrambled for safety.

Liv pushed her way through, dashing after her cameraman. She had to shove and duck as she fought against the flow of the crowd, which rushed pell-mell in the opposite direction. Shots rang out over the shouts of anger and terror. She took a sharp blow on the arm as someone clawed his way past her. Never faltering, she continued forward, speaking into her mike.

Thorpe caught Liv's wrist as she started to brush by him. Pulling her back, he kept his body firmly planted in front of hers. He'd seen a bullet smash into the pavement no more than three feet from where he stood.

"Don't be a damn fool," he snapped before he lifted his mike again. "Four men," he continued without taking his eyes off the scene, "masked and armed with high-powered rifles . . ."

Liv jerked her wrist out of his hold. Because her way was blocked, she was forced to give her report from where she stood. Over Thorpe's shoulder, she could see the wrecked car and the gunmen. There was no need to give Bob instructions. He was down on one knee at the front of the crowd, taping the shooting as coolly as he would have taped a garden party. From whatever cover they could find, members of the world press did their job. In a medley of languages, the word of the attack went out over the airwaves.

An explosive blast of gunfire erupted. Then there was sudden and ominous silence.

Thorpe continued to report after the four men lay sprawled in the street. His voice was objective, if hurried. He had to give the facts as he saw them. He had chosen television news for just this purpose. The immediacy. It would always be the newsman's greatest challenge—to report accurately what was happening as it happened, without a script, without preparation. His adrenaline was pumping. His instincts had been right on target.

For the next fifteen minutes, he talked nonstop until the crowd was calmed and the procession continued on to the abbey. The service would go on. Inside, the London correspondent for CNC would take over. It would give Thorpe time to dig up information on the attack. He signed off and signaled his cameraman.

"You had no right," Liv began immediately.

"Shut up, Olivia." He hadn't realized until that moment just how furious he was. As he turned his mike over to the sound technician, his hand shook slightly. She could have been killed, he thought grimly. Standing right beside him, she could have been killed.

Incensed, she drew herself up straight. "Who do you think you are—" The furious question was cut off when he grabbed her arm.

"Somebody had to stop you before you ran out into the crossfire. *You damn idiot!*" He stopped, took her shoulders and shook her. "Who'd give your precious report if you walked into a bullet?"

Liv jerked away from him. "I had no intention of walking into a bullet. I knew exactly what I was doing," she said coldly.

"You weren't thinking about anything but getting on top of the action." He was shouting now, drawing the curious attention of a few of their colleagues. "Did you think you could ask politely for them to stop shooting and give you an interview?"

Almost as bewildered as she was infuriated, Liv stared at him. "I don't know what you're talking about," she said. "I didn't do anything any other reporter wouldn't have done." With a quick move of her hand, she pushed back her tousled hair. "It was exactly what you did yourself. You had no business interfering with my work."

"Interfering with your work?" he repeated incredulously. "There were four crazy men with high-powered rifles out there."

"Damn it, I know that!" Exasperated, she gestured with her mike. "That's the story. What's the matter with you?"

Thorpe stared back at her. He was overreacting and knew it. But the fury wouldn't die. To keep from shaking her again, he jammed his hands into his pockets. He wasn't able to deal with knowing she could be in any sort of danger . . . and that he could do nothing about it.

"I've got a story to cover," he said tersely, and left her there.

Placing her fists on her hips, Liv glared after him. Glancing to the side, she caught Bob's questioning stare. After blowing out a frustrated breath, she went to him. "Come on, get the rest of the crew. We've got a story to cover."

Liv interviewed officials, bystanders, police. She spoke to a pale, shocked woman who had a flesh wound in her upper arm from a stray bullet. Liv had to lean heavily on crowd reaction and speculation as the facts were still very thin: four unidentified men on what could be considered nothing less than a suicide mission.

Twenty-four people had been injured, more from crowd panic than from bullet wounds. Only six had to be hospitalized, and only two of them had serious injuries. Liv dashed down names and occupations as she worked her way through the remaining crowd.

If the terrorists had counted on aborting the prime minister's funeral service, they hadn't reckoned with British sangfroid. The ceremony went on as scheduled inside the centuries-old abbey while the press and police functioned outside.

Ambulances came and went along with official vehicles. The wrecked car was towed away. Long before the service was over, there was no sign of any disturbance on the street.

From her vantage point, Liv watched the royal family exit the abbey. If the security had been tightened, it remained discreet. She waited until the last limo had driven off. Rubbing the bruise on her arm, she watched camera crews breaking down their equipment. She'd been standing for hours.

"What now?" Bob asked her as he loaded his camera in its case.

"Scotland Yard," she said wearily, and stretched, arching her back. "I have a feeling we're going to spend most of the afternoon waiting."

She couldn't have been more right. With a pack of other reporters, print and television, she waited. They were given a bare dribble of information in an official statement and sent on their way. By six o'clock that evening, there was nothing to add to her report but a recap of the morning's events and a statement that the terrorists were as yet unidentified. Liv shot a final stand-up in front of Scotland Yard, then headed back to the hotel.

Exhausted, she soaked for an hour in the tub and let the fatigue drain. Still, when she had toweled off and slipped into her robe, she was restless. The room was too quiet, too empty, and she was still too keyed up from the events of the day. She began to regret that she had turned down the crew's offer to join them for dinner.

It was still early, she noted. Too early. She didn't want to face another night alone in a hotel room. If she chose, there were any number of reporters she could seek out for company over a drink or a meal. But Liv found she didn't want to spend her evening rehashing and speculating over the day's events. She wanted to see London. Forgetting her weariness, she began to dress.

It was cool outside, with the dampness that had threatened all day still lingering. She had a light coat thrown over her slacks and sweater. Without thinking of direction, she began to wander. Traffic clogged the streets, so that the smell of exhaust tickled her nostrils. She heard Big Ben strike eight. If she was going to have dinner, she should find a restaurant. But she kept walking.

Again, she was reminded of the trip a dozen years before. She had traveled in a Rolls then, from monument to monument. There had been a garden party at Buckingham Palace. In a pale rose organdy dress and picture hat, Melinda had curtsied to the queen. Liv remembered how badly she had wanted to visit the Tower of London. Her mother had reminded her the National Gallery would be more instructive. She had studied the paintings dutifully and thought how badly she would have liked to have seen the inside of a pub.

Once, not so many years ago, Doug had spoken of taking a trip to London. That had been in their college days, when there had still been dreams. They had never had the money to spare for the plane fare. Then, there had been no love left to spare for dreams. Liv shook herself out of the mood. She was here now, free to see the Tower of London or a pub or to ride the subway. But there was no one to share the adventure with. No one to—

"Liv."

With a gasp, she turned and collided with Thorpe. He steadied her with a hand on her arm. For a moment she stared at him, completely disoriented.

"Alone?" he asked, but didn't smile.

"Yes. I . . ." She groped around for something to say. "Yes, I thought I'd do some sight-seeing."

"You looked a little lost." After releasing her arm, he stuck his hand in his pocket.

"I was just thinking." She began to walk again, and he fell into step beside her.

"Have you been to London before?"

"Once, a long time ago. Have you?"

"In my salad days." They walked for a time in silence. The restraint she sensed in him was something new, but she said nothing, letting him chose his own time. "There's nothing new on the terrorists," he told her after a moment.

"Yes, I know. I spent the afternoon at Scotland Yard. I suppose they could have been independent."

Thorpe shrugged. "They had very sophisticated, very expensive equipment, but they didn't seem to know how to use it. They were the only fatalities."

"It was stupid," Liv murmured, thinking of the four men who had held the limelight for one brief, fleeting moment. "A senseless thing to die for."

Again, they lasped into silence, walking in the chilly evening. The streetlamps were lit. They passed under the light, into the shadows and back into the light. Abruptly, he laid a hand on her shoulder. "Liv, there were a lot of bullets flying around out there today."

"Yes?"

"It was a miracle that none of the press or bystanders were killed."

"Yes."

She wasn't going to make it easy for him. Thorpe let out an impatient breath. "If I overreacted this morning, it was because I stopped thinking about you as a reporter. I only remembered you were a woman and I didn't want you hurt."

In silence she studied his face. "Is that an apology?" she asked him.

"No, it's an explanation."

Liv considered for a moment. "All right."

"All right what?"

"I consider it a reasonable explanation." She smiled then. "But the next time you get in my way on a story, you're going to get a very unladylike elbow in the ribs. Understood?"

He nodded, returning the smile. "Understood."

"Have you had dinner, Thorpe?" she asked, as they began to walk again.

"No, I've been getting the runaround from Donaldson."

"Hungry?"

He glanced down at her, one brow lifted. "Is that an invitation, Olivia?"

"No, it's a question. Answer yes or no."

"Yes."

"Someone told me that colleagues on foreign soil should stick together," she commented. "What are your views on that?"

"I would be inclined to agree."

Liv took his arm. "Come on, Thorpe, I'll buy you dinner."

Chapter 9

THEY FOUND A NOISY, CROWDED CHOPHOUSE AND squeezed into a corner table. Thorpe glanced around at the line of customers packed together at the counter. In the air was the scent of grilled meat and frying oil. Overhead were brilliant fluorescent lights.

"Very romantic," he commented. "I'm a sucker for atmosphere on a date."

"This isn't a date," Liv reminded him as she slipped out of her coat. "I'm testing a theory. You should be careful not to spoil it."

"Spoil it?" He gave her an innocent stare. "How?"

Her only answer was a narrowed look.

When they had ordered, Liv settled back in her chair to soak up the atmosphere. At the counter, two men argued heatedly over a horse race. Over the hiss and sizzle of cooking meat was a constant buzz of conversation. It was precisely the sort of place she had wanted to experience when she had been a teenager on her first trip to London.

In silence, Thorpe watched her, noting that her eyes went from person to person with no loss of fascination. Gone was the faint sadness he had seen on her face when he had first met her on the street. What had she been thinking about? he wondered. Or was it whom? There was still too much he didn't know. And, he thought, it would still be some time before she told him.

"What do you see?" he demanded.

"London." Liv smiled back at him. "A lot more of London than you can see by looking at monuments and museums."

"Apparently you like what you see."

"I only wish we weren't due to leave in the morning. I'd like another day."

"What would you do with it?"

Liv lifted her shoulders. "Oh, see everything, everyone. Ride a double-decker bus. Eat fish and chips in a newspaper."

"Go to Covent Garden?"

She shook her head. "I've been to Covent Garden. I'd rather go to the docks."

Thorpe laughed, lifting his beer. "Have you ever been to the London docks, Olivia?"

"No. Why?"

"I wouldn't advise it. At least not alone."

"You're forgetting I'm a reporter again," she reminded him.

"So would the dock workers," he said dryly.

"Well." She shrugged before leaning back in her chair. "In any case, we go back tomorrow."

"What are your plans then?"

"After I check in at the station I'm going to sleep for the rest of the weekend."

"When's the last time you saw Washington?" he asked, as grilled pork chops were set in front of them.

"What are you talking about? I see Washington every day."

"I mean for fun." He picked up his fork. "Have you ever played tourist in D.C.?"

Liv frowned as she cut into the meat. "Well, I suppose . . ."

"Ever been to the zoo?"

"Of course, I did a story on . . ." She paused and looked up. He was grinning at her. "All right, what's your point?"

"That you don't relax enough."

Liv lifted a brow. "I'm relaxing now, aren't I?" she asked.

"There isn't time for me to show you London properly," Thorpe put in. "Why don't you let me show you Washington?"

Warning signals sounded immediately. Liv toyed with her meal as she formulated a safe answer. "I don't think so," she said carefully.

Thorpe smiled and went on eating. "Why not?"

"I don't want you to get the wrong idea, Thorpe."

"What's the wrong idea?" His voice was bland and friendly. Glancing down at her hands, he remembered how her fingers had moved over his face when he kissed her.

"Look." Liv paused, wanting to choose her words carefully. "I'm not totally averse to your company, but—"

"Carmichael, you slay me with compliments."

"But," she continued, shooting him a look, "I'm not

going to become involved with you, and I don't want you to think otherwise." Because the words made her feel ungracious, she unbent a little. "We can be friends . . . of a kind, I suppose."

"Of what kind?"

"Thorpe," she said impatiently. "Stop it."

"Liv, as a reporter, I need concise information." He gave her an easy smile before he sipped at his beer.

"As a reporter," she countered, "you should be intuitive enough to understand my meaning."

Leaning closer, he grinned. "I'm crazy about you, Carmichael."

"You're crazy period," she corrected, and tried to ignore the sudden increase in her pulse rate. "But I'm trying to overlook that so that we can deal together amicably. Now if you'd just agree to keep things on a friendly basis," she continued.

"What's your definition of friendly?" he inquired.

"Thorpe, you're impossible!"

"Liv, I'm just trying to understand the issue. If I don't have the facts straight, how can I reach a viable conclusion? Now, as I see it"—he took her hand—"you're willing to admit you can tolerate my company. Is that right?"

Liv drew her hand from his. "So far," she said warily.

"And you're willing to take the second step and be friends."

"Casual friends." Though she knew he was leading her, she was as yet unable to see the trick.

"Casual friends," he agreed. Lifting his beer, he toasted her. "To the third step."

"What third step?" Liv demanded, but he only smiled at her over the rim of his glass. "Thorpe . . ."

"Your dinner's getting cold," he warned, then gave

her pork chops an interested glance. "Are you going to eat all that?"

Distracted from the point she had been going to make, Liv looked down at her plate. "Why?"

"I missed lunch."

Liv laughed and cut another slice. "So did I," she told him. She ate every bite.

When they stepped back outside, it was raining lightly. Liv lifted her face to it. She was glad Thorpe had found her—glad to have had his company over dinner. If it didn't make sense, it didn't matter. If it wasn't safe, she didn't care. She had needed an evening with someone who could make her laugh, make her think. Make her feel. If it was Thorpe, she wasn't going to question why tonight.

A few stolen hours was all she wanted. A few hours to forget all the promises she had once made herself. She didn't need the promises tonight. Tonight she was free of the past, free of the future.

"What are you thinking?" Thorpe turned her into his arms as she laughed.

"That I'm glad it's raining." Still laughing, she shook back her hair. Then his mouth was on hers. Liv threw her arms around his neck and gave herself totally to the moment.

He hadn't meant to kiss her. God, he hadn't meant to. He had only so much control to call upon. But at that instant, when she laughed and lifted her face to his, he couldn't resist. There was rain in her hair, on her cheeks. He could taste it on her lips.

He had never sensed this sort of abandonment in her before. It fanned his desire to a consuming fire. Couldn't she see how much he loved, how much he needed, and have pity on him if nothing else? Dear God, he thought, as he devoured her willing mouth, he was desperate enough to take pity if it was all she could give him. Crushing her to him, Thorpe buried his face against her throat.

Liv stepped back, drawing out of his arms to lean against a lamppost. Her heart was racing with a terrifying euphoria. The speed and force of her own passion left her shaken. And she had sensed something in him, a desperation that she didn't dare accept.

"Thorpe, I . . ." Swallowing, unable to admit what was happening to her, she shook her head. "I didn't mean for that—It just happened," she finished helplessly.

Still throbbing, Thorpe went to her. "Liv," he began, lifting a hand to her cheek.

"No, please." She closed her eyes. There was a tug-of-war inside her—pulling toward him, pulling away. Perhaps if she could forget everything, wipe the slate clean until that moment, then . . . But no, there was no pushing aside what had been. She wasn't yet ready to start again. "I can't," she whispered as she opened her eyes. "I just can't."

Instead of taking his hand from her cheek, he turned it over, letting his knuckles brush along her skin. It would have been impossible to have wanted her any more than he did at that moment. "Can't," he asked, "or won't?"

"I don't know," she murmured.

"What do you want, Liv?"

"Tonight . . ." She lifted her hand to his. "Just be my friend tonight, Thorpe."

There was a plea in her eyes that he couldn't ignore. "Tonight, Liv." He took her by the shoulders. "Friends tonight, but I won't make any promises about tomorrow."

"Fair enough." Some of the tension seeped out of

her. After a deep breath, she smiled at him. "Buy me a drink? I've waited twelve years to see the inside of a London pub."

His hold slackened slowly. She caught a glimmer of the effort it took for him to release her. "I know a little place in Soho if it's still there."

"Let's go see." Liv linked her arm through his.

It was there—a bit more dingy than it had been seven years before. When he entered, Thorpe wondered if it were the scent of the same stale beer and tobacco that hung in the air.

"It's perfect!" Liv told him as she gazed around through the curtain of smoke. "Let's get a table."

They found one in a corner. Liv sat with her back to the wall. Customers were shoulder to shoulder at the bar. From the familiarity, she concluded most of them were regulars. Off to the side, someone played a piano with more enthusiasm than skill. Several voices joined in song.

There was talk, a constant chatter. A voice would lift now and then, so that she caught snatches of conversation. The theme ranged from the attack on the funeral procession to someone's unsympathetic boss.

"What'll ya 'ave?" The barmaid who sauntered over gave them both a suspicious stare.

"White wine for the lady," Thorpe told her. "I'll have a beer."

"Ooh, Americans." That seemed to please her. "Doing the town?"

"That's right," Thorpe told her.

With a quick laugh, she walked back to the bar. "Got us a couple Americans, Jake," she told the bartender. "Let's 'ave some service."

Liv gave a low laugh. "How did you know about this place, Thorpe?"

"I was on assignment a few years back." He flicked his lighter at the end of a cigarette. "An American attached to our embassy here had delusions of being a master spy. He picked this place for the meet."

"Cloak and dagger." Liv leaned forward, resting her elbows on the wooden table. "And what came of it?"

"Zilch."

"Oh, come on, Thorpe." Disappointed, Liv shook her head. "At least make something up."

"How about I infiltrated an international spy ring single-handed and broke the story on the six o'clock news?"

"Much better," she approved.

"Here you go, ducks." The barmaid set the drinks in front of them. "Just whistle when you want another round."

"You know," Liv continued when they were alone again. "You just about fit the image."

"Image?"

"The tough, unflappable newsman." Liv sipped at her wine before she grinned at him. "You know, a trench coat with a few wrinkles, the world-weary face. You stand in front of a government building or a sordid pit and report the news in a drizzle. It has to be drizzling."

"I don't have a trench coat," he pointed out.

"Don't spoil it."

"Even for you," he said with a smile, "I'm not going to start doing stand-ups in a trench coat."

"I'm crushed."

"I'm fascinated."

"Are you? By what?"

"By your image of a field reporter."

"It was my image before I got into the game," she admitted. "I saw myself having meets with disreputable figures of the underworld in seamy bars and breaking world-shaking stories before breakfast. It was going to be one fast-paced story after another. Adventure, excitement, intrigue."

"No paperwork, stakeouts or time editors." Drinking his beer, he watched her. How could anyone remain so lovely after the day she had put in?

Her laugh was warm and appreciative. "That's it exactly. Reality came into focus in college, but I think I still had this image of high adventure and glamour. It stayed with me until I covered my first homicide." She gave herself a quick shake and returned to her wine. "That's the sort of thing that brings you back to earth quickly. Do you ever get used to dealing with that, Thorpe?"

"You don't get used to it," he countered. "But you deal with it."

She nodded, then pushed away the mood. The piano player had switched to a melancholy ballad. "Are you really writing a novel?"

"Did I say that?"

Over the rim of her glass, she smiled. "You did. What's it about?"

"Political corruption, naturally. What about yours?"

"I don't have one." With a spark of mischief in her eyes, she looked up at him. A dull, throbbing ache started in his stomach. "Actually," she began in lowered tones, then hesitated. "Can you be trusted, Thorpe?"

"No."

She gave a muffled laugh. "Of course not, but I'll tell you anyway. Off the record," she added.

"Off the record," he agreed.

"When I was in college and money was scarce, I did some writing on the side."

"Oh?" He wondered how money could have been scarce with her family background, but left the question unasked. "What kind of writing?"

"I did a few pieces for *My True Story.*"

After choking on his beer, he stared at her. "You're kidding! The confession magazine?"

"Don't get lofty. I needed the money. Besides," she added with a touch of pride, "they were pretty good little pieces."

"Really?" Thorpe gave her a lewd grin.

"Fictional," she stated.

"I'd like to read them . . . just for educational purposes."

"Not a chance." She glanced up as the crowd at the bar grew noisier. "What did you do in your misspent youth, Thorpe?"

"I had a paper route." He cast a casual glance over his shoulder at two men who were arguing over a game of darts.

"Ah, always the journalist."

"And chased girls."

"That goes without saying." Liv watched the dart players come nose to nose over their disagreements. Customers at the bar began cheerfully choosing sides. Thorpe reached for his wallet. "We're not leaving?" she asked as he pulled out bills.

"Things are going to get rowdy in a minute."

"I know." She grinned. "I want to watch. Do you want the guy in the hat or the one with the moustache?"

"Liv," he began patiently, "when's the last time you were in on a barroom brawl?"

"Don't be stuffy, Thorpe. I'm betting on the guy in the hat. He's smaller, but he's wiry." Even as she spoke, the man with the moustache threw the first punch. With a sigh of resignation, Thorpe leaned back. She'd be safer in the corner at this point.

Those at the bar turned to watch, holding their drinks as they shouted encouragement. Liv winced as her man took a jab in the stomach. Throughout the pub, customers began to pull out bills as they wagered on the outcome. The bartender continued to dry glasses. The two men came together in a furious hug, then toppled to the floor to wrestle.

Thorpe watched them roll around on the floor. A chair was knocked over, and a man with a glass of ale set it upright, sliding it out of range. He settled on it to root for the man of his choice. There were shouts of encouragement and advice.

It appeared Liv's prediction was a sound one, Thorpe decided. The man with the hat was slippery as an eel. He had his bigger adversary in a headlock, demanding that he give. With a face reddened with frustration and lack of air, he did.

"Want another drink?" Thorpe asked Liv as things quieted down again.

"Hmm?" She brought her attention back to him, then grinned at his dry expression. "Thorpe, don't you think this is the sort of thing that makes good copy?"

"If you're going to comment on a prizefight," he agreed, but smiled. "You surprise me, Olivia."

"Why, because I didn't scream and cover my eyes?" Laughing, she signaled the waitress herself. "Thorpe, they didn't do any more than give themselves a few bruises and something to talk about. The newsroom's more violent every day before deadline."

"You're a tough lady, Carmichael," he said, toasting her.

Pleased, she touched her glass to his. "Why, thank you, Thorpe."

It was late when they walked back outside. Liv heard the hour strike one. Stubbornly, the drizzle continued to fall. Lights reflected in shallow puddles and glimmered hazily through the misting rain. Though the air was chilled, the wine had warmed Liv, so that she felt glowing and wide awake.

"Do you know," she said as they walked slowly through Soho, "the first time I was in London I went to monuments and museums, teas and theaters. I feel as though I've seen more tonight than I did in that entire week." When he took her hand in his, she made no objection. There was something natural about walking with him in the early hours of the morning in a misting rain. "When I left the hotel tonight I was tired, depressed." She moved her shoulders. "Restless. I'm glad you found me."

"I wanted to be with you," he said simply.

Cautiously, Liv skirted around his statement. "I'm glad we're getting back in the middle of the weekend," she continued. "An assignment like this drains you, especially when you get a surprise like we had this morning."

"Not much of a surprise, really," he commented.

Liv looked up sharply. "Do you mean you were expecting something like that to happen?"

"Let's say I had a hunch."

"Well, you might have shared it with the rest of us," she said with a sound of exasperation. "After all, you were the press reporter."

"And as such, I'm required to share information and facts, not hunches." He grinned as she frowned up at him. "You should have been able to put two and two together for yourself, Carmichael. You have raindrops on your lashes."

"Don't change the subject."

"And every trace of your makeup's been washed away."

"Thorpe—"

"Your hair's wet."

With a sigh, Liv gave up.

"Tired?" he asked as they walked into the lobby of the hotel.

"No." She laughed. "Lord knows I should be."

"Want to go to the lounge for a nightcap?"

"Not if I want a clear head in the morning." She headed for the elevator instead. "I have to check in with Scotland Yard before we leave. Any connections there you want to share, Thorpe?"

Smiling, he pushed the button for their floor. "You'll have to dig up your own."

"I thought your turf was Washington."

"When I'm there," he agreed, and steered her into the corridor.

"You do have a connection," she said suspiciously.

"I didn't say that. In any case, the London correspondent will take the story from here."

Knowing she faced a dead end, Liv slipped her key into the lock. "That's unfortunately true. I hate not being able to follow up on it." She turned to smile at him. "Thanks for the company."

Without speaking, he lifted her hand to his lips. When the tremor shot down from her fingertips, she started to pull away, but he kept her hand firmly in his. He turned her palm up to plant another lingering kiss.

"Thorpe." Liv backed away, but her hand was still held fast in his. "We agreed to be friends."

His eyes were fixed on hers. The husky quality of her voice stroked along his skin. "It's tomorrow, Liv," he said quietly. "I didn't make any promises about tomorrow." Putting his hands on her shoulders, he turned her toward the door, and pushed her gently in. He let go of her only to close the door behind them.

She was in his arms again. Slowly, he ran his fingertips up the slim column of her neck. With his eyes on hers, he traced the shape of her ear, her cheekbones, then her lips. They trembled open at his touch as if she would speak. But no words came. With the same slow care, he took his mouth on the journey his fingers had completed. Light, butterfly kisses roamed over her neck and face, teased her mouth. He used neither pressure nor demand, but let her own needs hold her prisoner.

When he slipped his hands under her sweater, she made no attempt to stop him. Barely touching her, he ran the back of his fingers up her sides, then down again. He felt her quiver. Still, he deepened the kiss only slightly, a gentle exploration of the moist recesses of her mouth, a tender meeting of tongues.

Liv didn't resist him. It was as if she were too steeped in a conflict of her own making to reach for him or to push him away. Her breasts were firm and taut in his hands. The rough scrape of his palm against her sensitive skin brought a moan of pleasure from her.

Somehow instinct warned him she should be treated as an innocent—with care, with patience. Yet all the while his desire for her increased. Her trembling excited him, but he needed more. He needed her to touch him, to ask for him. The passion was there; he had tasted it before. He wanted it now. His mouth pressed down on hers, drawing it, coaxing it. She was fighting herself more than him. Her breathing was ragged, her body pliant, but there was still a thin wall he had not yet broken through.

Slowly, he unhooked her slacks, and with a groan, let his fingers reach for her. Soft—the incredible softness of her took him to the edge of control. For a moment she pressed against him convulsively. Life seemed to shoot into her entire body. Under his, her mouth was suddenly avid and demanding. Then she was pulling away, backing against the door. She shook her head frantically.

"No. No, don't do this."

"Liv." Pushed to the limit, Thorpe brought her back into his arms. "I won't hurt you. What are you afraid of?"

It was too close, much too close. Her voice sharpened in defense. "I'm not afraid of anything. I want you to go; I want you to leave me alone."

With his temper straining, his grip on her tightened. "The hell you do."

His mouth came down hard on hers as fury and frustration seeped through. Even as she tried to protest, her lips were answering his.

"Now look at me," he demanded roughly, drawing her back by the shoulders. "Look at me and tell me you don't want me."

She opened her mouth to tell him but the lie wouldn't come. She could only stand and stare at him. All of her courage deserted her. She was totally without defense.

"Damn you, Liv," Thorpe muttered abruptly. Pushing her aside, he slammed out of the door.

Chapter 10

When Liv walked into WWBW on Monday morning, her thoughts were calm. She had spent the remainder of her weekend assessing her relationship with Thorpe. *Relationship* was not quite the word she liked to use. It implied something personal. *Situation* was a better choice.

She had firmly decided against complications. It was true that she had found him more appealing, more enjoyable than she had thought she would. More fun. She had never considered Thorpe in the context of fun. He was an entertaining companion. And there was a quiet streak of kindness in him, which softened her.

Liv was a cautious woman; circumstances had made her so. But she was honest with herself. She knew the cool, controlled Olivia Carmichael who delivered the five-thirty news was only part of the whole woman. A great deal of herself had been in storage. She had put it there for her own survival. It was true that Thorpe had begun to pick the lock, but the years had given her strength. If she wanted to keep herself shut off, she would. It was that simple. Or so she had convinced herself.

Involvement didn't always follow a physical attraction. She had no intention of becoming involved with Thorpe. They would still work closely now and again, and perhaps she would even consider seeing him socially on occasion. Perhaps it was time to start picking up the pieces of her personal life. She couldn't mourn forever. But—she would not put herself into a position again where things could get out of hand with Thorpe. He wasn't a man to underestimate.

She had made a miscalculation when she had allowed her pride to push her into the ridiculous wager. A man like Thorpe, she mused, would only be all the more determined to have his way for the sheer devil of it. She should have simply ignored his fanciful statements about marriage.

The memory of his pleased, confident smile when she had accepted the bet still haunted her. He had looked too much like a cat who knew how to open the birdcage door.

But I'm not a canary, she reminded herself as she walked into the newsroom. And I'm not afraid of cats.

The newsroom was as it usually was. Noisy. Phones rang incessantly. Only the wall of television screens was silent. Interns bustled everywhere—college students learning the trade—running errands. The assistant director argued with a field reporter over the edited length of a segment. A crew headed out of the door with equipment and coffee cups.

"How many kittens?" she heard a reporter ask into a phone. "She had them *where?*"

"Liv." The assignment editor hailed her with an upraised hand. "The mayor's holding a press conference at two." He stuck out a piece of paper as he breezed by.

"Thanks." She wrinkled her nose at it. That might give her the time she needed to make the two million phone calls on her list.

"Who wants a kitten?" She heard the plea as she moved through the room. "My cat just had ten of them in the kitchen sink. My wife's going crazy."

"Hey, Liv." Brian caught her arm as she passed his desk. "I took two phone calls for you already this morning."

"Really?" She gave his jacket a critical glance. "New suit?"

"Yeah." He pulled a bit at the pearl-gray lapels. "What do you think?"

"Devastating," she said, knowing how Brian worried about his on-the-air image. He could agonize over the shade of his tie. "About the phone calls?"

"I was a little worried about the fit in the shoulders." He shifted them experimentally. "The first one was from Mrs. Ditmyer's secretary. Something about setting up a lunch date. The second was from a character named Dutch Siedel. Said he had a tip for you."

"Really?" Liv frowned thoughtfully. Dutch was the one dependable source she had on Capitol Hill. He was a page with visions of a hot political career.

"Who do you know named Dutch?"

Liv gave Brian a guileless smile. "He's my bookie," she said smoothly, and started to walk away.

"Full of surprises, aren't you?" Brian commented. "Who's the dude who keeps sending you flowers?"

That stopped her. "What?"

Brian smiled and examined his nails. "There's a fresh white rose on your desk, just like the one last week. The little intern with the frizzy hair said it came from upstairs." He shot her a teasing look. "There's been a lot of buzzing about Thorpe's visit to the studio last week. Collaborating on a big story?"

"We're not collaborating on anything." Liv spun on her heel and stalked to her desk.

There it was—white and innocent with its petals gently closed. She had a mad urge to crush it in her hand.

"Nobody ever sends me flowers."

Liv turned and glared at the woman typing at the desk behind her.

"You must have hooked a romantic." She sighed. "Lucky you."

"Lucky me," Liv muttered. What was the man trying to do to her? It occurred to Liv that the room had become suspiciously quiet. A quick sweep of her eyes caught several speculative glances and too many grins. Furious, she swooped up the rose, vase and all, and plunked it down on the other reporter's desk.

"Here," she said with a broad gesture. "You can have it." She stormed out of the room. It was time, she decided, as she heard the scattered laughter behind her, to lay down the ground rules.

Liv was out of the elevator in a flash when it stopped on Thorpe's floor. Still seething, she came to a halt at the receptionist's desk.

"Is he in?" she demanded.

"Who?"

"Thorpe."

"Well, yes, he is, but he has an appointment with the chief of staff in twenty minutes. Ms. Carmichael!" She stared in exasperation at Liv's retreating back. "Oh well," she murmured, and went back to her typewriter.

"Look," Liv began before the door had slammed shut behind her. "This has got to stop."

Thorpe lifted a brow and set down the pen he'd been writing with. "All right."

Her teeth clamped together at his amiable answer. "You know what I mean."

"No." He gestured to a chair. "But I'm sure you're going to tell me. Have a seat."

"This rose business," she continued, ignoring the chair and advancing to the desk. "It's embarrassing, Thorpe. You're doing it on purpose."

"Roses embarrass you?" He smiled at her, infuriatingly. "What about carnations?"

"Will you stop!" She leaned her palms on the desk much as she had done the first time she had stormed his office. "You might fool the brass with that crooked smile and choirboy look, but not me. You know just what you're doing. It's driving me crazy!" She paused a moment for breath, and he leaned back. "You know what a rumor factory this place is. Before noon, the entire newsroom is going to think I'm involved with you."

"So?"

"I'm *not* involved with you. I never have been and I never will be involved with you. I don't want my associates thinking otherwise."

Thorpe picked up the pen and tapped on the desk top. "Do you think being involved with me damages your credibility?"

"That has nothing to do with it." She snatched the pen out of his hand and tossed it across the room. "I'm *not* involved with you."

"The hell you aren't," he countered smoothly. "Wake up, Liv."

"Listen—"

"No, you listen." He rose and came around the desk. She straightened to face him. "You were kissing me two days ago."

"That has nothing—"

"Shut up," he said mildly. "I know what you felt, and you're a fool if you think you can pretend otherwise."

"I'm not pretending anything."

"No?" He lifted his shoulder a bit, as if he thought little of her statement. "In any case, sending you a rose is hardly comparable to groping in the editing room during a coffee break. If you want something tangible to be offended about, I can oblige you." He pulled her into his arms. For the first time, Liv noticed the glint of anger in his eyes. She refused to struggle. It would be humiliating because he was stronger. She tilted her chin and glared back at him.

"I don't imagine you have to put much effort into being offensive, Thorpe."

"Not a bit," he agreed. "I'm rather pressed for time right now, or I'd demonstrate. We can hash this out over dinner tonight."

"I'm not having dinner with you tonight."

"I'll pick you up at seven-thirty," he said as he released her and picked up his jacket.

"No."

"I can't make it before seven-fifteen." He kissed her quickly. "If we have things to say to each other, they should be said in private, don't you think?"

He had a point. And her mouth was still warm from his. "You'll listen to what I have to say?" she asked cautiously.

"Of course." He smiled and brushed her lips again, lightly.

She stepped back. "And you'll behave reasonably?"

"Naturally." He slipped on his jacket. She was wary of his easy agreement, but could hardly argue with it. "I've got to go. I'll walk you to the elevator."

"All right." As she walked with him, Liv wondered if she had won or lost the argument. A draw, she decided, was the best she could make of it.

Thorpe hesitated outside of Liv's apartment. He wasn't sure why he was doing this. He wasn't accustomed to rejection, particularly rejection from a woman. He had always had success both in his personal and professional life. The professional success he had worked for. Hard. Success in his private life had always come easily. He hadn't had to devote endless hours to research, endless miles to legwork to lure a woman into his arms, into his bed.

When he had been in his early twenties, pounding Washington pavements, making contacts, reporting on faulty sewage systems, he had had his share of desirable women. Some might have said more than his share. Later, when he had done an eighteen-month stint abroad, covering the delicate and explosive Middle East, there had still been women. And as his name had become more well known, his face more widely recognized, his choices had become varied.

He knew he had only to pick up his phone and dial to insure himself an evening's companionship. He knew scores of women—interesting women, beautiful women, famous women. He had come a long way from the boy who had hung around the old Senators' clubhouse.

Still, two things had remained the same. He was determined to be the best in his field, and when he wanted something, he went after it. Thorpe thrust his hands in his pockets a moment and frowned at Liv's door. Was that why he was here? he wondered.

But it wasn't as simple as that. Even standing there alone, he could conjure up her face, her voice, her scent. There had never been another woman in his life he could see so clearly when he was alone. There hadn't been another woman who could make him ache at the thought of waiting. She was a challenge, yes, and Thorpe thrived on a challenge. But that wasn't why he was there. He loved her. He wanted her. And, he was determined he was going to have her. He pressed the doorbell and waited.

Liv had her coat over her arm when she opened the door. She had no intention of letting him in. If she was going to be with him, she preferred a restaurant where there would be no danger of making the mistake she had already made too many times.

"I'm ready," she said in her most distant tone.

"So I see." He didn't move as she shut the door at her back. She was forced to push him out of her way or stand still. She stood still. He must have come straight from his broadcast, though Liv had no intention of admitting to him that she had watched it. He had removed his tie, however, and had loosened the first few buttons of his shirt. He looked as relaxed as she was tense.

"You're still mad." He smiled, knowing he was baiting her but unable to resist. He wasn't certain which expression he liked better: the grave sincerity in her eyes during a broadcast, or the controlled annoyance he so often saw when she looked at him.

Liv wasn't angry, but nervous—and furious with

herself for being susceptible to him. She could already feel herself unbending to that smile.

"I thought we were going to thrash this out over dinner, Thorpe, not in the hall of my apartment building."

"Hungry?"

She didn't want to smile, but her lips betrayed her. "Yes."

"Like Italian food?" he asked, taking her hand as they moved toward the elevator.

"As a matter of fact, I do." She gave a slight tug to release her hand, but he ignored it. "Good. I know a little place where the spaghetti is fantastic."

"Fine."

Twenty minutes later, they pulled up in front of the little place. Liv frowned at the high white building. "What are we doing here?"

"Having dinner." Thorpe parked the car, then leaned over to unlatch her door. She slid out and waited for him.

"They don't have an Italian restaurant in the Watergate."

"No." Thorpe took her hand again and led her toward the front doors.

Her suspicions began to peak. "You said we were going to an Italian restaurant."

"No, I said we were having spaghetti." After crossing the lobby, Thorpe punched an elevator button.

Liv gave him a narrow look. "Where?"

He guided her into the elevator. "In my apartment."

"Oh, no." She felt panic as the car began its climb. "I agreed to have dinner with you so we could talk, but I—"

"It's hard to talk seriously in a noisy restaurant, don't you think?" he said easily as the doors opened. "And I have a feeling you have a lot to say." Unlocking his door, he gestured her inside.

"Yes, I do, but . . ." The thick, aromatic scent of spiced sauce drifted to her. She crossed the threshold. "Who cooked the spaghetti?"

"I did." Thorpe slipped the jacket from her shoulders, then shrugged out of his own.

"You did not." She looked at him in frank disbelief. Did a man with rough palms, intelligent eyes and casual sophistication cook spaghetti?

"Chauvinist," he accused, and kissed her before she could prevent it.

"That's not what I meant." Liv was distracted by the kiss and the enticing smell coming from the kitchen. "I know lots of men who cook, but I—"

"Didn't think I could," Thorpe finished for her. He laughed, keeping his hands on her arms. Her skin was too smooth to resist. "I like to eat; I get tired of restaurants. Besides, I learned when I was a kid. My mother worked; I fixed the meals."

His hands were gliding gently up and down her arms until she felt her skin begin to pulse. It was an erotic sensation for him, as well as for her—work-roughened palms against satin smoothness.

"Don't," she whispered, afraid she would be unable to prevent herself from taking the small step forward into his arms.

"Don't what, Liv?" Watching the suppressed desire build in her eyes, he felt his own growing.

"Don't touch me like that."

For a moment, Thorpe did nothing; then casually, he removed his hands. "Are you any good in the kitchen?"

The ground solidified under her feet. "Not really."

"Can you toss a salad?"

Why was it so easy for him? she wondered. He could smile so effortlessly, while her knees were still trembling. "Probably, if I follow directions."

"I'll write some down for you." He took her arm in a friendly grip that still managed to shoot sparks down her spine. "Come on, give me a hand."

"Do you usually invite women to dinner, then put them to work?" It was important to match his mood and forget the moment of weakness.

"Always."

The kitchen was a surprise. Onions, garlic and potatoes hung in wire mesh baskets near the window, while copper-bottom pans dangled from hooks. There were utensils she had never seen before, all within easy reach of the stove or counter. Glass canisters stored colorful beans and different-shaped pasta. Her own kitchen was a barren desert compared to this. Here was a room of someone who not only knew how to cook, but enjoyed it.

"You really do cook," Liv marveled.

"It relaxes me—like rowing. Both take concentration and effort." Thorpe uncorked a bottle of Burgundy and set it aside to breathe. Liv was drawn to the simmering Crockpot.

"When did you have time to do this?"

He lifted the lid. "I put it on before I left for work this morning."

She narrowed her eyes at his easy smile. "You're terribly sure of yourself." It was astonishing how often he had made her angry in such a short period of time.

"Here," he said soothingly, and dipped a wooden spoon into the pot. "Taste."

Pride fell before hunger, and she opened her mouth

to obey. "Oh." Liv closed her eyes as the flavor seeped through her. "It's immoral."

"The best things tend to be." Thorpe dropped the lid on the pot again. "I'll do the bread and pasta; you do the salad." He was already filling a pan with water. Liv hesitated a moment. The sauce was still tangy on her tongue. Nothing, she decided, was going to stand between her and that spaghetti. "Everything's in the fridge," he added.

She located fresh vegetables, and after filling her arms with them, took them to the sink to wash. "I'll need a salad bowl."

"Second cabinet over your head." He added a dash of salt to the water after the flame was on under it.

She rummaged for the bowl as he began to slice bread. He watched her—as she stood on tiptoe to reach the bowl, her dress floating up then down with her movements; as she scrubbed a green pepper under a spray of water, her fingers gliding over the skin. She wore clear polish. Her nails were well shaped, carefully tended, but she never used color on them. It was something he had noticed. Her makeup was always subdued, understated, as were her clothes. Thorpe wondered if it was a purposeful contrast to her more flamboyant sister or if it was simply a matter of taste.

Liv carried the vegetables to the butcher block. She glanced up when Thorpe held a glass of wine out to her.

"Hard work deserves its rewards."

Before she could empty her hands and take the glass, he held it up to her lips. His eyes were steady on hers.

"Thanks." Her voice was as cloudy as her mind. She turned away quickly.

"Like it? You usually drink white." Thorpe lifted the glass and drank himself.

"It's good." Liv gave all her attention to choosing a knife.

Thorpe slipped one out of its slot and handed it to her. "It's sharp," he warned. "Be careful."

"I'm trying to be," she murmured, and set to work.

She could hear him moving around behind her, pouring pasta into boiling water, setting the bread under the broiler. His presence was invading her senses. By the time the salad was finished, her nerves were jangling. She took the wine he had left on the block and drank deeply. Settle down, she cautioned herself, or you'll forget what you came for.

"Ready?" His hands came down on her shoulders, and she just prevented herself from jolting.

"Yes, all done."

"Good. Let's get started."

A small smoked-glass table was set in front of a window. It was a cozy, intimate area, despite the open view of the city, raised from the living room by three steps and separated by an iron railing. There were candles of varying sizes and shapes burning through the room. The light was soft and flickering. The English bone china was another surprise. Liv tried to divorce herself from the atmosphere while Thorpe served the salad. She had come to talk. Perhaps it was best to ease into it gently.

"You have a beautiful apartment," she began. "Have you lived here long?"

"Three years."

"Did you choose it for its"—she paused and smiled—"colorful past?"

Thorpe grinned. "No. It suited my needs at the moment. I was in Israel when that went down. I've always regretted not being here to report the story."

He offered her oil and vinegar. "I know an assignment editor who tossed the story out when he got the feed. No time, and he thought no one would care about some minor break-in. I think he's selling used cars now in Idaho."

Liv laughed. "How long were you in the Mideast?"

"Too long." He caught Liv's questioning glance. "Hours of tedium and moments of terror. Not a healthy way to live. War opens your eyes, maybe too much, to what a human being's capable of."

"It must be very difficult," she murmured, trying to picture it. "Reporting a war, that kind of a war, in a foreign country."

"It was an experience," he said with a move of his shoulders. "The trouble is, when you're reporting, you tend to forget you're human too. For a while, up here"—he tapped his temple—"you're indestructible. The camera's a force field. It's a dangerous delusion—one that bullets and grenades don't respect."

She understood what he meant. She herself had once walked carelessly into a government building following a bomb detection team. Her mind had been on the story. It hadn't been until later that the full impact of her action had struck her.

"It's strange, isn't it?" she mused. "And it's not just reporters. Cameramen are probably worse. Why do you suppose that is?"

"Some like to claim it's a mission, a sacred duty to let the public know. I've always considered it simply a matter of being caught up in the moment. You do it because you're focused in on the story, and the story's your job."

"Tunnel vision," she said quietly, remembering he had used the phrase before. "That's not as romantic as a mission."

He smiled, watching the candlelight flicker over her skin. "Do you look for romance in your work, Liv?"

The question startled her, bringing her back. "No. No, I don't." Now was the time, she told herself. "Which is exactly why I agreed to have dinner with you tonight."

"To keep your romance separate from your work?"

Her brows drew together. Why did that sound so different when he said it? "Yes. . . . No," she amended.

"I'll get the spaghetti while you make up your mind."

Liv cursed herself and tore a piece of garlic bread in two. Why was it things never went as she planned when she was around him? And why did he always seem so on top of things? Straightening, she reached for her wine. She would simply start over.

"Here we go."

Thorpe placed a platter of thin pasta topped with the thick sauce on the table.

"Thorpe," Liv began. The aroma was irresistible, and she filled her plate as she spoke. "I really thought you understood what I said to you the other day."

"I understood perfectly, Olivia; you're very articulate." He helped himself when she had finished.

"Then you must see how difficult you're making things."

"By sending you a flower," he concluded, and offered her grated cheese.

"Well, yes." It sounded so silly when he said it. "It's very sweet, but . . ." Frowning, she rolled spaghetti onto her fork. "I don't want you or anyone else to think that it means anything."

"Of course not." He watched her sample the first bite. "How is it?"

"Fabulous. Absolutely fabulous." Liv let the pure

sensual pleasure of food spread through her slowly. "I've never tasted anything better." She rolled a second forkful and tried to remember what point she had been trying to make. "In any case, it's not the sort of thing associates do, you know." The second forkful proved as satisfying as the first.

"What isn't?" It gave him a great deal of satisfaction to watch her preoccupation with his cooking. Her tongue slid lightly over the fork.

"Send flowers," she stated. "To each other. Especially when there's rivalry as well. Local and national news are siblings. I know a bit about sibling rivalry."

"Your sister," he commented. The candlelight shot little flecks of gold into her eyes. He could almost count them.

"Mmm. With a sister like Melinda, I've had experience at being the underdog. I never minded; it makes you more inventive. The same goes for doing the local news."

"Is that how you look at it?" he asked curiously. He picked up one of her hands to examine the delicately painted nails. "As being the underdog?"

"You have the big budget," she pointed out. "The large exposure, publicity. But that doesn't mean we can't have the same quality on a smaller scale." There was a callus on his thumb. She could feel its light scrape across her knuckles. An unexpected chill shot straight down her spine. Carefully, Liv removed her hand and reached for her wine. "But that's not the point."

"What is?" Thorpe smiled at her—the slow, personal smile that scattered her wits. Liv hastily pulled herself together.

"You know how stories fly around a newsroom.

Internal stories," she specified as she returned to her dinner. "It's a difficult place to have any privacy. Privacy's important to me."

"Yes, it must be. There hasn't been any mention of you in the papers or glossies since you were a teenager. The Carmichaels always make good copy."

"I didn't fit the mold." She hadn't meant to say that, and was astonished it had slipped out. "What I'm trying to say," she continued, as Thorpe kept his silence, "is that once someone in your newsroom or mine gets hold of an idea, the next minute it'll be fact. Then the sky's the limit. You know how a simple coffee date can become a torrid lunchtime affair after the third telling."

"Does it matter so much?"

Liv gave a weary sigh. "Probably not from your standpoint, but from mine, yes. I have to deal with being the new kid on the block, and a woman. It's still hard, Thorpe. Whatever progress I make is always examined more closely than anyone else's right now. Is Carmichael seeing Thorpe because she wants to jump on the national news team?"

He studied her a moment. "You don't have enough confidence in yourself."

"I'm a good reporter," she countered immediately.

"I was speaking about you as a woman." He saw the shield come up and could have sworn in frustration.

"That's none of your concern."

"Isn't that what we're talking about?" he countered. "I sent a *woman* a rose, not a reporter."

"I am a reporter."

"That's your profession, not your sex." He lifted his wine and forced back annoyance. He knew anger was no way to get through to her. "It doesn't do to have thin skin in this business, Liv. If newsroom gossip bothers you, you're going to get a lot of bruises. Look in the mirror. People talk about a woman with a face like yours. It's human nature."

"It isn't only that." Liv subsided a bit. She had wanted to talk to him. It wouldn't help if she became angry. "I don't want any personal involvement—not with you, not with anyone."

Thorpe studied her in silence over the rim of his glass. "Were you hurt that badly?"

She hadn't expected the question, or the trace of sympathy in it. It cost her a great deal to keep her eyes level and composed. "Yes."

He left it at that. That she had made the admission instead of freezing was enough. He would wait for the rest. "Why did you come to Washington?"

Liv looked at him a moment. She had been prepared for further interrogation, but not for a casual change of subject. Warily, she allowed herself to relax again. "I'd always been interested in politics. That was my beat in Austin, though most of the time I did little but read the news on the air. When WWBW made the offer, I grabbed it." She began to give her attention to the meal again. "It's an exciting city, especially from a reporter's viewpoint. I wanted the excitement. I suppose I wanted the pressure."

"Have you thought of doing national news?"

She made a vague gesture with her shoulders. "Of course; but for now, I'm happy where I am. Carl's the best news director I've ever worked with."

Thorpe grinned. "He does have a tendency to become emotional."

Liv lifted a brow as she toyed with the last of her spaghetti. "Particularly when some hotshot from upstairs steals a story. I had to step on the toes of one of your associates after the mayor's press conference this afternoon."

"Is that so? Which one?"

"Thompson. The one with the big ears and flashy ties."

"A flattering description."

"Accurate," Liv countered, but a smile tugged at her lips. "In any case, I'd gone to a lot of trouble to set up a quick interview after the conference. He tried to cash in on it."

"You set him straight, I'm sure."

Liv let the smile form. It rather pleased her to recall how she had dispatched the enterprising Thompson. "As a matter of fact, I did. I told him to do his own legwork or they'd find him hung by his tie in the basement of the Rayburn Building." She paused consideringly. "I think he believed me."

Thorpe looked into the cool blue eyes. "I think I do too. Why didn't you just sic your cameraman on him?"

Liv grinned and scooped up the last of her spaghetti. "I didn't want a vulgar scene in front of the mayor."

"Want some more?" He gestured toward her empty plate.

Liv sat back with a sigh. "You've got to be kidding."

"Dessert?"

Her eyes widened. "You didn't really make dessert?"

Leaning forward, Thorpe tipped more Burgundy into her glass. "Drink your wine," he suggested. "I'll be right back."

He took the plates away with him. Liv gave a moment's thought to giving him a hand, then sat back. She was too content to move. It was foolish to deny she enjoyed his company. Liked talking to him. Arguing with him. She had nearly forgotten how stimulating an argument could be. He made her feel alive, vital. She didn't quite feel safe with him, and even that was exciting.

Liv glanced up as she heard him come back. At the sight of the dish of strawberries and cream he carried, she gave a low sound of pleasure.

"They look marvelous! How did you get your hands on strawberries that size this early in the season?"

"A reporter never reveals his sources."

She sighed as he set the dish on the table. "They look wonderful, Thorpe, but I don't think I can manage it."

"Try one," he insisted, dipping a berry into the fresh whipped cream.

"Just one," she agreed, and obligingly opened her mouth as he started to feed it to her. He smeared the cream along her cheek. "Thorpe!" Liv said on a laugh, and reached for her napkin.

"Sorry." He laid his hand on top of hers, preventing her from lifting the napkin. "I'll get it." Cupping her neck with his other hand, he slowly, lightly began to nibble the cream from her cheek.

Liv's laughter stilled. She didn't move, couldn't protest. Her mind and body were locked in the shock of sensation. Her skin seemed alive only where his tongue glided over it.

"Good?" he murmured, passing his lips over hers.

Liv said nothing. Her eyes were locked on his. Thorpe watched her steadily as he read the stunned passion in her eyes.

Slowly, he dipped a second berry and offered it. "Another?"

Liv shook her head, swallowing as she watched his teeth slice through the berry. Rising, she stepped down into the living room. She had to be on her feet to think, she told herself. In a moment, she would feel perfectly normal again. The trembling would stop—the heat would cool. A startled gasp escaped her when Thorpe turned her into his arms.

"I thought you'd like to dance," he murmured.

"Dance." She melted into his arms. "There isn't any music." But she was moving with him, and her head was already resting on his shoulder.

"Can't you hear it?" Her scent was teasing his senses. Her breasts yielded softly as he drew her closer.

She sighed and closed her eyes. The candlelight flickered against her lids. Her limbs felt heavy, much too comfortably so. She leaned on Thorpe. She tried to tell herself she had had too much to drink. That was what she was feeling. But she knew it was a lie. When his lips passed over her ear, she sighed again and shuddered.

I should go, she told herself. I should leave now, right now. Her fingers wandered into his hair. It's madness to stay. A slow, kindling longing was building as his body moved against hers. His hand slid up her spine and down again to settle at her waist. When she felt his lips on her neck, she gave a low sound, drugged in pleasure.

"I can't stay," she murmured, but made no effort to move from his arms.

"No," he agreed, as his mouth made a leisurely journey to hers.

"I should go." Her lips sought his.

"Yes." He slipped his tongue between her parted lips to touch hers. Liv felt her bones dissolve and her head spin.

"I have to leave."

"Mmm-hmm." Gently, he lowered the zipper at the back of her dress. She made a muffled sound as his hands ran over the thin chemise.

"I'm not going to get involved with you, Thorpe." Her mouth was moist and heated as he explored it.

"I know; you've told me."

Her dress slid to the floor.

She pressed closer and let his mouth find hers again. She was drowning, but the water was so warm, so soft. The need for him was sleepy, growing as he moved his hands over her. She was a prisoner of his touch—a touch that was gentle. She made no protest when he lifted her into his arms.

Moonlight filtered into the bedroom, shadowed light, softly white. Liv nearly broke through the surface.

"Thorpe—"

Then he kissed her again. Lost, longing, she clung to him as he lowered her to the bed. He undressed her slowly, with soft kisses and caresses. The words he murmured were quiet, stroking her nerves, arousing her body.

When his back was bare, Liv ran her hand over it. There was hard strength. She wanted him to be strong. Needed for him to be. He lowered the chemise to her waist, following the trail of his hands with his mouth.

Desire changed from dreamy to desperate in a flash. Liv moaned and pressed him closer until his mouth was hungry at her breast. Her movements under him were no longer languid, her hands no longer timid. She arched to help him strip the thin garment from her. He ran his hands up the inside of her thighs, and she felt a rush of heat engulf her. She crested on a moan, but he slid his fingers over and inside her, driving her up again.

She dug her nails into his shoulders. Nothing, no one, had ever made her feel like this—mindless, aching, glowing. Liv wanted him to take her, but he had other pleasures to give.

His tongue glided down her torso, flicking over the curve of her waist until she knew she would go mad. Wandering, he moved lower still, until on a strangled gasp, she peaked again.

Her responsiveness overwhelmed him, taking him beyond his own desire. He wanted her to experience every drop of pleasure he could give. She was sensitive to every touch, every thought. Though the moonlight gave her skin a marble hue, it felt like liquid fire under his hands. Need for her vibrated through him. Each time she moaned his name or reached for him, the shock of it rocketed straight through him. Desire pulsated from her—for him. That alone took him to the edge of reason.

His mouth crushed down on hers, and Liv answered the demand ravenously. All restraint had fled; all barriers were broken. She knew only a desperate need for fulfillment and the one man who could give it to her. She opened for him, then guided him inside of her.

Her gasp was muffled against his shoulder. She felt the muscles tense and ripple against her mouth as he took her beyond what she remembered, past what she had dreamed of. She gave herself up completely and went with him.

Thorpe lay wrapped round her, holding on to the warmth. For him, the world had whittled down to the bed—to the woman. Even in the dark he could see her, each curve of her body, each plane of her face. In all of his memory, he had never felt so involved, so totally united. Her skin was smooth against his, her nipples still taut as her breasts pressed against his chest. Her breathing was leveling slowly. He had known there was passion under her strict control, but he hadn't guessed the depth of it or what its effect on him would be. He was vulnerable, almost defenseless for the first time in his life.

Liv felt the intensity of passion drain into contentment. She had never experienced that sort of abandonment. Had that been missing all of her life? She was almost afraid to find the answer and what it would mean. One basic truth was that he had made her feel like a woman again, complete. The taste of him still lingered on her lips and tongue. She didn't want to lose it, or the warm security she now held nestled in her arms.

But who was Thorpe? she wondered. Who was he who had drawn from her what she had been unable, or unwilling, to give any man for more than five years.

"I promised myself this wouldn't happen," she murmured, and buried her face against his neck.

Her words forced Thorpe out of his dreamy state. "Regrets?" he asked carefully, and waited what seemed a lifetime for the answer.

"No." Liv gave a long sigh. "No regrets." She tilted her face back. "I never expected to be here with you, like this. But I don't regret it."

He relaxed again and held her closer. The soft, serious words stirred him. "Olivia, you're such a complicated woman."

"Am I?" She smiled a little and closed her eyes. "I've never thought so. Too simple perhaps, and single-minded, but not complicated."

"I've been working on sorting you out for a year and a half," he returned. "It isn't an easy job."

"Don't try." She let her hand roam over his shoulder again. She liked the feel of muscle, knowing he could control it into gentleness. "Thorpe, have you had many lovers?"

He gave a muffled laugh. "That's a delicate question to ask at the moment, Carmichael."

"I wasn't going to ask for names and numbers," she countered, sighing as his hand moved down her back. "It's just that I haven't really. I'm not very good at it."

"Good at what?" he asked absently. His casual explorations were teasing his own need for her.

She felt awkward suddenly, and searched for a phrase. "At—ah—pleasing a partner."

The movement of his hand stopped, and he drew back to study her face in the darkness. "Are you joking?"

"Well, no." She was embarrassed now. If she hadn't been so relaxed, she would never have put herself into such a position. She fumbled on. "I know I'm not very—exciting in bed, but—"

"Who the hell put that into your head?"

The sharp annoyance surprised her. *My husband* trembled on the edge of her mind. "It's just something I've known—"

He swore ripely and stopped her. "Do you think I was pretending just now?"

"No." She was confused suddenly, and unsure of herself. "Were you?"

He was angry, almost unreasonably so. Rolling, he pinned her beneath him. "I wanted you, from the first moment I saw your face. Did you know that?"

She shook her head, unable to speak. A fresh surge of passion raced through her at the press of his body, the grip of his hands.

"You're so cool, so aloof, and I could see all those

whispers of heat. I wanted you like this, naked in my bed."

His mouth crushed down on hers, bruisingly, furiously. Her lips were eager for his, accepting the anger, the demand, matching the hunger.

"I wanted to strip away the layers," he muttered. He moved his hands over her until she was writhing mindlessly. "I was going to have you—melt all that ice." His hand slipped between her thighs and she arched, yearning for him. "But there wasn't any ice, any need for games when I held you. If you didn't please another man, it was his fault. His loss. Remember it."

She was on fire. Her hands touched, searched, stroked on their own power while her mouth roamed his neck. She could feel his pulse go wild under her tongue. She pulled at him, dragging his mouth back to hers. The taste—his taste. She was desperate for it. He trembled with her.

Then the kiss was savage, staggering her with the knowledge that she had taken him beyond the civilized. This was no pretense. He was totally lost in her—in what they made together. She felt it, marveled at it, then swirled into a mist where no thoughts could penetrate.

She was limp, utterly spent, her breath and body shuddering. His weight was on her fully, and his back was damp under her hands. There was no measuring the time they lay there, replete in each other.

"I suppose you're right." His voice was dark and husky. "That wasn't very exciting."

Liv didn't think she had the energy to laugh, but it bubbled inside her, warm and comfortable. She didn't know how he knew exactly the right thing to say, but she accepted it. It was a novel and wonderful sensation, to laugh in bed. He lifted his head and grinned at her.

"Idiot," he said softly, and kissed her. Shifting, he gathered her to his side. She was asleep in moments and lay still. He held her.

Chapter 11

THE ALARM CLOCK WENT OFF WITH A SHRILL. AUTOMATI-cally, Liv reached over to shut off the blast and rolled into Thorpe. Her eyes shot open. Disoriented, groggy, she stared into his eyes while the bell continued to peal. Part of her mind registered the shadow of beard on his chin, the sleepy heaviness of his eyes as they looked into hers.

I slept with him, she remembered. Made love with him and slept the night in his bed. The knowledge registered slowly. She could feel a trace of astonishment in the full light of day, but though she searched and wondered, there were still no regrets. She had been given passion, gentleness, caring. How could there be regrets?

Thorpe reached behind him and snapped off the alarm. Silence was abrupt and complete. Saying nothing, he gathered Liv against him. He had seen the dazed surprise in her face, then the gradual understanding and acceptance. He found it amusing, and strangely endearing. This wasn't a woman who made it a habit of waking up in a man's bed.

The quiet morning cuddle was a new sensation, and Liv drifted with it. Undemanding intimacy. Tangled with him, she explored it sleepily. She wasn't certain what she was feeling. What emotion was this? Contentment? Happiness? Simple pleasure at being close enough to touch and be touched?

Something had changed. Doors had opened. She wasn't sure whether she or Thorpe had turned the lock, but it had been done. His breath was warm on her cheek, his arms lightly possessive around her. She was no longer alone. Did she want to be? She felt the pressure of his body against her. Yesterday she had been certain that solitude was the answer for her. But now . . .

She had made love with him. Shared herself. Taken from him. Liv wasn't a casual person. Intimacy was no small gesture for her. Intimacy meant commitment. To her, the two had always, would always, walk hand in hand. And yet, she had promised herself there would be no more commitments in her life, no more one-to-one relationships. There was too much in her past to remind her of the risks. He was becoming too important. She was becoming too vulnerable. It was much too easy to stay where she was, wrapped tight, held close. If she stayed too long, she might forget how quickly disillusionment came.

She shifted, wanting to break the bond before it became too strong. "I have to get up. I have to be in by nine-thirty."

Still silent, Thorpe brought her back to him. His mouth closed gently over hers. She was so soft, so warm. And her scent still lingered. He'd waited long, too long, to wake beside her. Now he wanted to enjoy the moment. He wanted to see how she looked in the morning, fresh from sleep, her eyes still heavy. He had slept beside her, awakened beside her. He didn't intend to be without her again.

Liv responded to the gentleness and the lazy arousal. For a moment she could pretend there was no outside world that demanded their involvement and no past to inhibit her. There was only the two of them. If she closed her eyes, she could imagine it was still night and they had hours left to hold each other. But time was passing. The sun was a pale yellow light through the windows.

"We have to get up," she murmured, almost wishing he would contradict her.

"Mmm." He shifted his head slightly to see the clock. "Apparently," he agreed, and settled for a last nuzzle of her throat. "I don't suppose your conscience would allow you to come down with a sudden case of laryngitis or a convenient fever?"

"Would yours?" she countered.

He laughed and kissed her. "At the moment, I have no conscience."

"I wish I could say the same." Easing away from him, she sat up, automatically pressing the sheet to her breast. "I'm going to need a robe."

"Pity." With a groan he rolled away from her and rose. "I'll supply you with a robe. And breakfast," he added as he padded to the closet. "If you handle the coffee."

She was a little stunned to see him stand naked in front of the closet. Straightening her shoulders, she told herself not to be a fool. She had just spent the night with him. His body was no secret to her now. But to see him, Liv thought, as he pulled out the first robe for himself. He was magnificently built—hard, lean, with broad sinewy shoulders and a long torso. She had indeed often thought he seemed streamlined in his clothes. Without them, he appeared more the athlete.

"Okay?" He pulled out a short, kimono-style robe in blue terry and turned to her.

She had lost what he had been saying. Her eyes lifted to the amusement in his. "What? I'm sorry."

"Can you make coffee, Liv?" He grinned as he held out the robe.

"Have you got a jar and a spoon?"

He looked pained. "Are you joking?"

"I was afraid you wouldn't. I'll manage, I suppose," she told him doubtfully, and slipped her arms into the robe.

"The percolator's on the counter; coffee's on the second shelf over the stove," he instructed as he swung into the bath. "See what you can do."

She wrinkled her nose as he shut the door, then rose from the bed.

In the kitchen, she found things precisely where he had told her. She ran water and measured coffee. Just barely, she could hear the sound of the shower running.

She found it an odd sensation to be poking around in his kitchen, naked under his robe. *I'm having an affair,* she thought. She held the top of the percolator aloft a moment, staring into space. She had made love with Thorpe, had spent the night in his bed, and was now preparing coffee in his kitchen. In his robe, she reminded herself, running a hand down the lapel.

With a quick shake of her head, she fit the lid on top of the pot. For goodness' sake, I'm twenty-eight years old. I've been married and divorced. I'm a professional woman who's been on her own for years. Why shouldn't I have an affair? People do every day. It's a part of life. It's very simple—even casual. To make anything else out of it is foolish. We're two adults who just spent the night together. That's all there is to it.

Even as she ran the last of these cool, sensible words in her head, Thorpe came into the room. Liv turned to say something mildly sarcastic about the coffee and found herself folded into his arms.

His mouth touched hers softly at first, twice. The third time, they lingered and grew hungry. She lifted her arms to bring him closer. Everything she had just told herself was forgotten. His hair was still damp as her fingers combed through it. The scent of soap and shaving lotion brushed at her senses. Everything seemed new and fresh, like a first romance.

His hands rested at the sides of her breasts, then lowered to her hips. It wasn't a desperate kiss, but a strong one. It brought echoes of the night back to her. Thorpe drew back a little to look at her.

"I like you this way," he murmured. "Barefoot, in a robe several sizes too big for you, with your hair a little mussed." He lifted a hand to it and disordered it further. "I'll be able to picture you this way when I watch the cool Ms. Carmichael deliver the news."

"Fortunately for the ratings, the viewers won't."

"Their loss."

"Not everyone appreciates the rumpled, just-out-of-bed look, Thorpe." The coffee was perking frantically, and she drew out of his arms. There were mugs suspended from hooks under the cabinets. Liv slipped two off and poured.

"But then I appreciate the calm, sleekly groomed look too," he pointed out, offering her a small carton of cream for her coffee. "Actually, I haven't found anything about you that doesn't appeal to me."

Liv laughed and glanced up at him. "Are you always so agreeable before your coffee, Thorpe?" She handed him a mug. "I'd better shower while you drink this. It might sour your mood." He started to lift it to his lips, and she placed a hand on his arm to stop him. "Remember, before you drink it, you did promise to fix me breakfast."

She left him, taking her own mug with her.

Thorpe glanced back down at his coffee, then sipped doubtfully. It wasn't quite as bad as she had prophesied. Obviously, he thought, as he drank again, the kitchen wasn't her area. It was his, he concluded philosphically, and went to the refrigerator. He could hear the shower running. He liked knowing she was close—only a few rooms away. He took out a slab of bacon and heated a pan.

Thorpe wasn't a man to delude himself. They had made love—they would make love again—but Liv's feelings were not as defined as his. It was uncomfortable to find himself in the position of caring deeply for someone who didn't return the same depth of emotion. She could, he told himself as the bacon sizzled. She was fighting it. He was too confident a man to consider he might lose in the end.

Even in the bright sunlight of the kitchen he could remember her open giving of the night before—her initial hesitation, the gradual change to aggression and passion. Whatever she said, she was a complex woman, full of hidden corners and contradictions. He wouldn't have it any other way. Since he had fallen in love, he preferred it to be with a woman who had a few eddies and currents. Fate might have bound him to a tamer type.

Olivia Carmichael was the woman for him, and he was the man for her. He might have to be patient until he convinced her, but convince her he would. Thorpe smiled as he cracked an egg into a bowl.

As it had the night before, the scent coming from the kitchen drew Liv irresistibly. Standing in the doorway, she stared at the platter Thorpe was piling with bacon, golden eggs and lightly browned toast.

"Thorpe," she said, inhaling deeply, "you're amazing."

"You just noticed?" he countered. "Grab a couple plates," he ordered, jerking his head toward the proper cabinet. "Let's eat before it gets cold."

Liv did as he bade, plucking up the flatware as well before she followed. "I have to admit," she said as she took her chair at the table, "that I'm in deep awe of anyone who can fix a meal and consistently have everything ready at the same time."

"What do you eat at home?"

"As little as possible." She began to help herself from the platter. "Mostly I use all those little boxes that say "Complete Meal Inside." Sometimes there really is."

"Liv, do you have any idea what sort of things they put inside those little boxes?"

"Please, Thorpe." She shoveled a forkful of eggs into her mouth. "Not while I'm eating."

He laughed and shook his head. "Didn't you ever learn to cook?"

Liv lifted a shoulder. She remembered the meals she had fixed during her marriage. They had usually been hurried—dinners put together before she had dashed on to the evening shift at the station, a quick something after classes. She had cooked adequately, even well on sporadic occasions. But there had been so little time and so many obligations. She skipped back over that to give him the answer.

"When I was growing up, my mother didn't consider it important. In fact," she added after finishing off a slice of bacon, "she didn't care to hear about the few times I poked into the kitchen to see what was going on. That wasn't our territory."

Thorpe buttered a slice of toast and considered how remarkable diverse their backgrounds had been. He and his mother had been close, both from necessity and out of love. Liv and hers had been distant, perhaps from a simple lack of understanding.

"Do you go back to Connecticut often?"

"No."

There was a signal in the one word. *Don't press too close.* Thorpe recognized it and detoured.

"How's your schedule today?"

"Packed. The first lady's dedicating that children's center at eleven. Dell's due into National at one, though I doubt we'll be able to get near him, and I have another stakeout at the school board this afternoon." She finished off the rest of her eggs. "I'm scheduled to tape another promo. The general manager's nervous about the ratings."

"Aren't they all." He glanced at her empty plate. "Well, at least you're fortified."

"If that's your subtle way of saying I stuffed myself, I'll overlook it." Rising, Liv began to gather the plates. "Since you cooked it, I'll wash up while you dress."

"Very democratic."

She kept her eyes on the plates and platters. "I'll need to go back to my apartment to change before I go in. I'll take a cab."

"Don't be ridiculous."

Unsure of her moves, Liv lifted the stack of plates. "It's silly for you to drive halfway across town, out of your way. It would be simpler—"

He stopped her by taking the stack of plates out of her hands and setting them back on the table. Placing his hands on her shoulders, he studied her face. It was in his eyes again—the searching, the depth of intensity that was inescapable.

"Liv, last night meant something to me. Being with you means something to me." He could see the quick flicker of emotions as she digested his words. "No cabs."

"No cabs," she agreed, then slipped her arms around him to hold him tightly. The gesture surprised him, moved him. Liv closed her eyes and held on. She had been afraid he would agree without a second thought. The sensible part of herself had told her it would be best—keep it light, keep it sophisticated. Take a cab and see you later. But her heart wanted more. And her heart was beginning to outweigh everything else.

"Will you wait for me tonight?" he murmured into her hair. "Until after my broadcast?"

She tilted her face to his. "Yes." As his mouth touched hers, she thought fleetingly that the ground she was treading on might be dangerous; but she hadn't felt so alive in years.

It was five thirty-two when Thorpe stood in the control room and watched Liv through the window. He paid scant attention to her report on a robbery at a local chain store, or to the technical aspects of television that went on around him. She had, quite simply, been on his mind all day. He'd wanted to see her again before it was his turn in front of the camera.

"Punch up camera one," Carl ordered from his seat

in front of the wall of monitors. She was there too, reproduced eight times in the black-and-white preview monitors and the live color ones. Her voice came through in stereo from the speakers. At his left, an engineer worked at the sound board.

"Camera two."

Brian's image replaced Liv's on the live monitor. At Carl's next order, the graphics were punched up to flash behind him.

"Thirty seconds to commercial."

Brian continued smoothly to the cut.

Carl drew hard on a cigarette and shot a glance over his shoulder at Thorpe. "See you around here more now than when you worked here," he commented.

"I've more incentive," he answered easily.

Carl studied Liv's image in the monitor and gave a grunt of agreement. He'd always liked Thorpe as a man, respected him as a reporter. He wished that he had been able to keep him on staff. Carl gave a sigh and crushed out the cigarette. He doubted he'd keep Carmichael more than a couple of years. He'd been around too long to expect anything different.

"Thirty seconds."

Thorpe looked back through the window. Liv was talking to Brian. She laughed at something and shook her head. Was it his imagination or did she seem more relaxed, more free? It would be well over an hour before he could touch her again.

Camera one was focused on her, and on cue she began the next segment of the broadcast. Thorpe left the control room with her voice still echoing in his mind.

With the show over, Liv went back to the newsroom. She had weighed the pros and cons of going upstairs to meet Thorpe, and had decided that to wait for him in her own territory would generate less speculation—and less gossip. She was not ready to put her personal life on display.

She missed him. The fact had surprised her, but there was no denying it. Her day had been hectic, at moments frantic, but somehow he had hovered on the edges of her thoughts throughout it.

Keeping to her desk, she began to go over her next day's schedule. Her eyes drifted again and again to the clock. Why, when the day had flown by, did one hour seem to be an eternity?

"This lady looks like she wants a cup of coffee."

Glancing up, Liv smiled at Bob and held out a hand. "I always knew you had great perception."

"I'd rather be irresistibly sexy," he commented, and sat on the corner of her desk.

"Of course you are." Her eyes laughed at him over the rim of the plastic cup. "I constantly have to restrain myself!"

"Yeah?" He grinned at her. "Can I tell my wife?"

"I'll leave that up to your own discretion."

"I worked with Prye today." Bob sighed into his coffee cup. "You know the little thirty-second stand-up he did in front of the Kennedy Center."

"Mmm-hmm." Liv knew what was coming, and settled back in her chair.

"Fourteen takes. You wouldn't believe how many times that guy can blow a line. He got irked when I asked him if he wanted us to make up some idiot cards for him. We should have more respect for the talent." He snorted, and gulped down more coffee. "He wouldn't know talent if it walked up and chewed on his ankle."

Liv opted to play the diplomat. She was well aware

that Prye had a running battle with the crews. "The stand-up came across very well."

"Lucky for him he doesn't have to go live. If I had my choice," he said, and winked at her, "I wouldn't work with anyone who didn't have great legs. You know"—he cocked his head to study her—"you look different."

She lifted a brow. Could it be that a night of love and freedom had left some noticeable change? "If you're trying to save yourself from Prye tomorrow," she said lightly, "I've already talked to the desk about having you work with me."

He grinned again. "Thanks, but I'd rather have a wild weekend in Acapulco."

"Acapulco," she repeated, pretending to consider it.

"We could use your expense account."

"Liv's already occupied this weekend," Thorpe said mildly. Both Bob and Liv turned to look at him. He glanced down at her, then back at the cameraman. "She's going to be rowing."

"No kidding?" The information seemed to give Bob more reason to grin. "I guess I'll have to settle for Sunday dinner at my in-laws." He rose and, giving Liv a brief salute, left them.

"Thorpe." He had her arm and was already propelling her through the room. "I haven't made any plans for the weekend."

"I have," he returned amiably. "And you're included."

"I have this small idiosyncrasy," she told him when they stepped outside. "About having a voice in my own plans."

"I'm flexible." He opened the car door for her,

leaned on it and smiled. "If you'd rather go to Acapulco, I can arrange it."

It was difficult to feel annoyed when he was smiling at her. She let out a small huff of a sigh. "I might consider rowing," she said, and gave in to the urge to touch his mouth with hers. "If you man the oars."

Chapter 12

So much could change in a week. Liv could almost forget what it was like to be alone—truly alone. The nights no longer held absolute silence. She could almost forget what it was like to have no one but herself to depend upon. There was someone in her life again. She no longer attempted to reason out how he had gotten there.

She was growing to rely on Thorpe's companionship. She was growing to enjoy the pleasures of intimacy. Simply, she was growing to need Thorpe.

As the days passed, she found she looked forward not only to their conversations, but even to their arguments. He stimulated her, forced her to think fast if she wanted to hold her own. Intellectually, they complemented each other. There were times, she knew, he sharpened his wit on her, just as she did on him.

His strength was important to her. There was something rock solid about him. She had once looked for the solidity in someone else and had been disappointed. She wasn't looking for protection. She had been through too much to doubt her own ability to deal with whatever life tossed at her. When you had gone through the worst and survived, nothing could ever hurt you in quite the same way again. But if she chose a partner, a companion, a lover, he had to have strength.

She was still cautious. There were still guards over her emotions. But they were growing weaker.

As he had promised, Thorpe took her to a night ball game.

"I'm telling you, he should look for another profession," she stated as she stuck the key in the lock of her door. She brooded over the faults of the plate umpire as she shrugged out of her jacket. "Don't they have to go to school or something before they become umpires?"

"Or something," Thorpe agreed, not even trying to hide a grin. Liv had been indignant over the umpire's calls during the entire drive home.

"Well," she concluded, "he must have gotten dreadful marks. I wouldn't be surprised if he's a nasty person who kicks his dog."

"A sentiment probably shared by a number of ballplayers." Thorpe slipped out of his jacket and tossed it to join hers. "Maybe it's time you took over the sportscast, Liv."

She gave him an arch look. "I might do very well," she returned. "After a few more games, I could probably report a play by play as well as I do a filibuster. Would you like a brandy?"

"Fine." He smiled at her back as she fixed the drinks.

"Leaving the play by play aside for the moment and concentrating on filibusters, what do you think of Donahue's chances?"

"Slim," Liv responded, and turned back with two snifters.

"I talked to him today." Taking the brandy from her, Thorpe drew Liv down on the couch beside him. "Right before he went onto the floor. He's brown-bagging it. He must have had five ham sandwiches and a half a dozen doughnuts."

Liv laughed. "Well, at least he won't go hungry. That should give him the stamina to keep his filibuster going—if his voice holds out."

"He's determined," Thorpe commented. "He told me he's going to outlast and outtalk every one of his opponents. If force of will and ham on rye can do it, Donahue's got it made." Liv settled back against his shoulder, and his arm automatically encircled her. "The gallery was packed for most of the day."

"We did some man-on-the-streets," Liv murmured, sleepy now with contentment. "Most people were there from pure curiosity rather than any interest in the issue. But a full gallery and a filibuster make good press. That might keep Donahue going a few days longer."

"He made it through day five."

"I'd like to see him win." She sighed. How had she ever been comfortable without his arm around her? "I know it's unrealistic, and the bill will pass eventually, but still . . ."

He listened to her slow, quiet voice. There was a parallel between Donahue and himself, he thought. Thorpe had launched his own filibuster with Liv. He was just as determined as the senator to win a full victory. It wasn't enough just to be able to hold her. He wanted, needed, a lifetime. How much longer was it going to take? There were times when the need for caution frustrated him to the point of anger.

He set down his drink, and then hers. Liv lifted her face for the kiss, but it was not as she had expected. His mouth was fierce. She was pressed back against the cushions of the sofa with his body fitted to hers. He tugged at her clothes impatiently. This was something new. Always, there had been a thread of control in his lovemaking, as if he compensated for the difference in their physical strengths with gentleness. Now, she felt the urgency as he pushed open her blouse to find her.

His mouth was locked on hers, so that she couldn't speak, or even moan, as he stripped off her jeans. She fumbled with his sweater, wanting to be flesh to flesh, but the press of their bodies together hampered her. With a low, savage oath, Thorpe stripped it off himself, pulling it over his head, then letting it fall to the floor.

His mouth was suddenly everywhere—tasting, ravishing. She was pliant, fluid under his touch. She flowed wherever he took her, rising and falling to his whim. There was a wildness in him she had only glimpsed before.

He took her on the couch as if it had been years since their last joining. The desperation went on and on until she knew there could be no more either of them could want or give. Then he was pulling her to the floor with him, heating her again while her body was still humming.

She moaned his name once, half in protest, half in disbelief, as her passion mounted again.

"More," was all he said before his mouth took hers.

His hands were as avid as they had been at the first touch, and her body as receptive. There was in her now an overwhelming need to possess, to be possessed. No longer was she only guided. Her hands sought him, found him, while her mouth clung hot and fast to his.

She was shuddering without being aware of it. She heard only his labored breath in her ear when she wrapped around him. Need and fulfillment seemed to burst within her at once. Then she was once more pliant, once more limp. This time, Thorpe lay beside her and let his body rest.

Yet he couldn't prevent himself from touching her still. Her skin drew him, and the curve where waist flared to hip. His hands were gentle now. He kissed the slope of her shoulder, the delicate line of her jaw. He heard her sigh as she moved closer to him.

As fiercely as passion had whipped through him before, now love ached inside him.

"I love you." He felt her immediate stillness and realized he had spoken aloud. Cupping her chin in his hand, he lifted her face to his. "I love you," he said again. He hadn't meant to tell her in exactly this way, but now that it had been done, he kept his eyes on hers. He wanted her to understand he meant what he said.

She heard the words, saw them repeated in his eyes. Something moved inside of her like a tug-of-war, toward him and away. "No." She shook her head and the word was weak. "No, don't. I don't want you to."

"You don't have any choice." The statement was calmer than his mood. Her answer, and the anxiety in her eyes, cut at him. "And, it seems, neither do I."

"No." Pushing away, she sat up to cradle her head in her hands. Old doubts, old fears, old resolutions crowded at her. Pressure was squeezing her in a tight fist. "I can't. . . . You can't."

Love—that dangerous, dangerous word that left you naked and senseless. Accepting it was a risk, giving it a disaster. How could she let herself be caught in the web again?

Thorpe took her shoulders and turned her to face him. Her response left him hurt and angry. The pale, miserable look on her face only added to it. "But I do love you," he said curtly. "Not wanting me to doesn't change it. I love you, have loved you for quite some time. If you'd bothered to look, you'd have seen that."

"Thorpe, please . . ." She could only shake her head. How could she explain to him? What did she want to explain? She wanted him to hold her until she could think clearly again. Love. How did it feel to know she was loved? If she could have a few moments. If her heart would stop pounding.

"I'm not interested in only having your body, Olivia." She could hear the temper and frustration in his voice. She stiffened against it. No, she would not be pressured. She would not be maneuvered. She was still in charge of her own life. He could feel the change. His fingers tightened on her skin in impotent fury.

"What do you want?"

"A great deal more," he said deliberately, "than you're willing to give me. Trust, I suppose, would be a good start."

"I can't give you any more than I have." She wanted to tremble, to weep, to cling to him. She kept her eyes level. "I don't love you. I don't want you to love me."

Neither knew the extent of pain their words caused the other. She saw only a flare in his eyes that made her realize how strictly he controlled his own violence. If he had had less of a grip on himself, she felt certain he would have struck her for the cold dispassion of her words. She almost wished he would. At the moment, she would have gladly exchanged physical pain for the emotional one.

Slowly, he released her. He hadn't known he could be hurt like this. In silence, he dressed. He knew he had to leave quickly, before he did something he would detest himself for. She wouldn't drive him to that. Not by rejection, or her damn coolness or anything else. He'd leave her to herself, since that's what she wanted. The sooner she was out of his sight, the sooner he could work on forgetting her. He cursed himself for being a fool even as he shut the door behind him.

The sound of it closing brought Liv's head around. For a full minute, she stared at the panel. The silence welled up around her. Curling into a ball, she lay on the rug and wept for both of them.

The normal routine of a day was like an obstacle course. Getting up, dressing, driving through rush hour traffic. To Liv, it all seemed larger, more complicated than it ever had before. In a morning crammed with appointments, she went through the hours with a combination of nervous energy and dull fatigue. Her thoughts could never be completely centered on her objective when Thorpe was always just around the edges. She had begun to taste happiness again, and now . . .

Everything had happened so fast. Liv hadn't expected him to love her. She knew enough of him, understood enough of him to be certain he wasn't a man to love lightly. His energy and power would be bound up in it. When a man like Thorpe loved a woman, she was loved completely. Perhaps that was what frightened her most.

Yet, what she felt now as she finished up an interview wasn't fear; it was emptiness. Before Thorpe had become a part of her life, she had accepted the emptiness. The void had been filled, as nearly as possible, with her work and her ambition. It was no longer enough. During the morning, a dozen things happened that she found herself wanting to share with him. Years had passed without her feeling the need to share with anyone, and now it was inescapable. But she had pushed him away.

What should she do now? How could she make him understand that while part of her wanted to love him, to be loved by him, another part was like a rabbit under a gun. Frozen. Terrified.

How could she expect him to understand? she asked herself as she mechanically negotiated through afternoon traffic. She was no longer sure she understood herself. Put it on hold for a while, she advised herself. Have lunch with Mrs. Ditmyer, relax, and then try to think fresh again.

Hoping she could take her own advice, Liv pulled into the parking lot beside the restaurant. It was the perfect way to take her mind off things, she decided. Part business, part social. A glimpse at her watch told her she was barely five minutes late. Nothing major. It wouldn't do to keep Myra Ditmyer waiting long.

I like her, Liv thought as she entered the restaurant. She's so . . . alive. Greg was lucky to have her for an aunt, for all her matchmaking tendencies. Liv could only wish the cards had dealt her a similar relative. A woman like that would be sturdy as a boulder when the world crumbled under your feet.

Liv shook away the thought. There was also the matter of her position in Washington political and social circles. Since Myra had taken it into her head to notice her, Liv might as well take advantage of the side benefits.

"Mrs. Ditmyer's table," she told the maître d'.

"Ms. Carmichael?" He smiled when she inclined her

head. "This way please." Liv followed him, amused. As a Carmichael she recognized deferential treatment. As a presswoman, she had learned not to expect it.

"Olivia!" Myra greeted her as though they were the fastest of friends. "How charming you look. And how lovely it is to have men staring again. Even if they're only speculating whether I'm your mother or your maiden aunt from Albuquerque."

Liv was laughing even as the maître d' assisted her into her chair.

"Mrs. Ditmyer, I knew having lunch with you would be the high point of my day."

"What a sweet thing to say." She beamed, pleased with herself. "Paul, do see about some sherry for Ms. Carmichael."

"Of course, Mrs. Ditmyer." The maître d' bowed away from the table.

"Now then." Myra folded her hands on the table expectantly. "You must tell what wonderfully exciting things you've been doing. I'm sure running around reporting on political corruption and world-shaking events must keep you forever in a spin."

Liv laughed. It was impossible not to be relaxed and exhilarated simultaneously in the woman's company. "It seems a crime to disappoint you, Mrs. Ditmyer, but most of the time I spend waiting at airports or outside the gate at the White House. Or," she added with an apologetic grin, "on the telephone finding out where I'm going to wait next."

"Oh, my dear, you mustn't burst my bubble." Myra sipped her own glass of sherry. "I'm perfectly content if you make something up, just so it's exciting. And call me Myra; I've decided we're going to get along famously."

"Do you know, I believe we will." Liv shook her

head. "I'm sorry to say we can't all be Woodwards and Bernsteins. But I suppose all reporters run into a fat story now and again. Right now, the heat is on Senator Donahue's filibuster."

"Ah, Michael." Myra smiled, then nodded with approval as Liv's sherry was set in front of her. "Feisty old devil. I've always been fond of him. Nobody rhumbas like Michael Donahue."

Liv nearly choked on her sherry. "Is that so?"

"I shall have to introduce you next month when I give my Spring Ball. You do rhumba, don't you, dear?"

"I'll learn."

Myra smiled in her dazzling way, then crocked a finger at the waiter. "I, unfortunately, will have to make do with the fruit salad. My dressmaker's sighing horribly these days." She gave Liv a wistful glance that wasn't envious so much as reminiscent. "The scampi's exquisite here."

"Fruit salad will do nicely," Liv returned. "Being able to sit down for lunch is treat enough. I still have to thank you for asking me," Liv went on, as the waiter moved away. "It really isn't often I have the opportunity to have an hour like this in the middle of the day."

"But of course you can justify the luxury by terming it as partly business." Myra laughed at Liv's expression. "Oh, no, my dear, you mustn't think it offends me. Why not in the least. It's actually part of my intention. Now . . ." She leaned forward a bit like a general preparing to outline a plan of attack. "You must tell me what special project you have in mind. I know you must have one; it's simply in your character."

Liv sat back. Though she held the glass of sherry, she didn't drink. She was too enthralled with the woman across from her. "Myra, I believe you would have made a fabulous reporter."

A pleased pink flush spread on her cheeks. "Do you really? How marvelous. I do so love to nose around, you know."

"Yes," Liv answered faintly.

"So." Myra spread her hands, palms up. "Tell me what you have in mind."

Liv shook her head and smiled. "All right. I've been toying with trying a news special, probably slotted for late night. A personal view of women in politics. Not only women politicians, but women married to politicians. How they deal with the stress business—family, public exposure, traveling. I'd like to think I could deal with both sides of the coin that way. Women who are immersed in government for varying reasons."

"Yes . . ." Myra pouted in thought. "That might prove quite interesting. It can be the very devil on a marriage, you know. The campaigning, the staff dinners, the state dinners, the protocol. Lengthy separations, high pressure. It's a horse race, my dear. One long, never ending horse race. And the women . . ." She smiled again and swirled her sherry. "Yes, indeed, it might be interesting."

"I've been knocking it around with Carl for a couple of months. He's the news director," Liv explained. "I think he'd go for it, if and when I can give him an outline and some firm names. I suppose seeing Amelia Thaxter at the embassy started the wheels turning again."

"A remarkable woman," Myra commented. She smiled, somewhat dismally, as the fruit salad was placed in front of her. She wasn't the sort of woman who liked moderation, even gastronomically. "As dedicated as they come, and quite devoted to her constituents. Quite sincerely devoted. She made a choice between marriage and a career long ago. Some women can't mix the two." She smiled at Liv then and plunged her fork into a chunk of pineapple. "Oh, I'm not talking out of school. She'd tell you herself if asked. I believe she'll be quite interested in your project. Yes, and Margerite Lewellyn—nothing she likes better than to talk about herself. Then there's Barbara Carp . . ."

Liv listened, not touching her own lunch as Myra rattled off names of women political figures and the wives of some of Washington's top brass. This was a great deal more than she had expected. And as she spoke, Myra became more animated with the idea.

"What fun," she concluded. "I believe you'll do a marvelous job of it. I think I'll make a few phone calls when I get back."

"I appreciate it," Liv began, hardly knowing what to say. "Really I—"

"Oh, fiddle." Myra waved away the thanks with her fork. "It sounds a great deal more fun than planning another dinner party. Besides"—she gave Liv another of those blinding smiles—"I fully expect to be interviewed myself."

"That is an opportunity I wouldn't miss for the world," Liv said sincerely. "Myra," Liv said, and applied herself to her own salad, "you are amazing."

"I do try to be. Now, that's all the business nicely settled." She gave a self-satisfied sigh. She liked this girl. Oh, yes, she liked this girl very much. And when Myra Ditmyer made up her mind about someone, it was as firm as one of her husband's court decisions. "I must tell you, I had no idea when I made that little arrangement about the bridge party that you and Greg knew each other. I love being surprised."

"He was a very good friend." Liv poked at her salad. "Seeing him again was good for me."

Myra watched her carefully. "I said I was surprised. But then . . ." She saw Liv's eyes rise to hers. "It didn't take me long to put the pieces together. When he was in college, Greg had written me often about Livvy. I remember hoping he was enjoying a nice, sweet romance. He was certainly captivated by her."

"Myra, I—"

"No, no, now, let me finish. Greg was always a faithful correspondent. So refreshing in a young man. He wrote me that his Livvy was involved with his roommate."

"It was all so long ago."

"My dear." Myra placed a hand on hers. "I apologize. But Greg was very intimate in his letters. I suppose he needed a sounding board for his feelings. They were quite real to him at the time. He was desperately in love with you, and as close to Doug as a man can be to another. Being in the middle was difficult for him, and perhaps because I was removed, he talked to me through his letters. He told me everything."

The look, the press of the hand, told Liv that Myra was being literal. There must be nothing about those years that she didn't know. Liv stared at her helplessly.

"Now, dear, have some more wine. I don't mean to upset you. We all learn to cope, don't we," she went on in an easy voice as Liv obeyed her. "To live with loss and pain and disappointment. One can't have lived to my age and not have run the gamut. It must have been dreadful for you. You probably thought you'd never live through it."

"No," Liv murmured. "No, I was sure I wouldn't."

"But you have." Myra patted her hand again, leaned back and waited.

Perhaps it was Myra's skill in dealing with people,

perhaps her genuine interest in them that caused Liv to respond to Myra's silence more than she would have to a dozen well-meaning questions.

"I thought for a while it would be better to die than to have to live with the pain. There didn't seem to be anybody. . . . My family," she said on a long breath. "I suppose they tried; in their way they were sympathetic, but . . ." She stopped and let out a quiet sigh that tugged at Myra's heart. "I wanted to scream; I wanted to tear something apart. Anything. They simply never understood that kind of need. A person's grief, a person's private torment should be just that. Private. It should be handled with dignity."

"Poppycock," Myra said rudely. "When you're hurt, you cry, and the hell with anyone who doesn't like to see tears."

Liv laughed. "I believe I could have used you then. I might not have made such a botch of things."

"It's entirely your own opinion that you did," Myra said sternly. "It might be time for you to give yourself a bit more credit. But, as I've said, you've lived through it, and this is today. Tell me about you and T.C."

"Oh." Liv looked down at her salad again in fresh bewilderment. What was there to say? She'd botched things again.

"I can hardly hold any hope that you and Greg will make a match of it." She saw Liv smile at that and continued. "But as T.C.'s one of my favorite people, I've decided to be content with that."

"I'm not ever going to marry again."

"Oh, what boring nonsense," Myra said good-naturedly. "T.C. and you have been seeing each other fairly regularly now, haven't you?"

"Yes, but . . ." Liv frowned a bit. Myra really had missed her calling.

"He's entirely too intelligent a man to let you slip through his fingers. I'd bet Herbert's prize golf clubs that he's already asked you to marry him."

"Well, no. That is, he told me I was going to, but—"

"Much more in character," Myra said, pleased. "Oh, yes, that's just like him. And, of course, that got your back up."

"He was so unbearably arrogant," Liv stated, remembering.

"And he loves you so dreadfully."

That stopped her. She could only stare.

"Olivia, a blind man could have seen it that night at my little bridge game. And my eyesight's very keen. What are you doing about it?"

"I've . . ." Liv felt herself deflate like a pricked balloon. "I've ruined it. Last night."

Myra studied her in silence a moment. Really, she thought, the child was so confused. Again she reached out to pat her hand. It was such a shame to see people waste time because they thought too much and acted too little.

"You know, unlike the maxim, life isn't short, Olivia; it's really terribly long." She smiled at the serious eyes on her face. "But not nearly long enough. I've been married to Herbert for thirty-five years. If I had listened to my parents, bless them, and my own better sense, I would never have married a man who seemed too stuffy, who was too old for me and entirely too work oriented. Think of all I would have missed. Life," she said positively, "is worth a few risks. To prove it," she added and sat back, "I'm going to have some of that lemon mousse. . . ."

Even hours later, preparing for broadcast, Liv couldn't get Myra's words out of her mind. It was time to do something, she decided in the middle of the sportscaster's report. Time to stop mulling things over point by point. If she wanted to be with Thorpe, she was going to have to tell him so.

The moment her broadcast was over, Liv went upstairs. Seeing her approach, the receptionist gave a fatalistic sigh.

"He's not here," she said, as she prepared to pack up her work for the day. "He's doing his report on location."

"I'll wait in his office." Liv breezed by before the other woman could comment.

What am I going to say to him? Liv asked herself the moment she shut the door behind her. *What can I say?* Pacing the room, she tried to find words.

It seemed odd to be there without him. The room was so much his. Scattered on one wall were pictures of him with various world leaders and government officials. He looked invariably relaxed—never stiff, never overawed. He was simply Thorpe, Liv mused. And that was enough. There were scrawled notes littering his desk, and a hefty pile of papers held down by a paperweight. She went to look out at his view of the city.

She could see the dome of the Capitol. With the sun beginning to set, it had a rosy hue, almost fairylike. Traffic was thick, but the heavy glass insulated her from the sound of it. She gazed out at the lines and circles of the streets, the old, stately buildings, the cherry blossoms just coming to bloom. It didn't have the movement or urgency of New York, she decided, but was beautiful in its way. Engrossed in her study, she never heard Thorpe come in.

Seeing her surprised him. He was uncustomarily thrown off-balance. He hesitated for a moment with his hand still on the knob. Very carefully, he shut the door at his back.

"Liv?"

She whirled, and he saw her expression range from surprise to pleasure to controlled anxiety. More than he had ever wanted anything, Thorpe wanted to take her into his arms and pretend the night had never happened.

"Thorpe." At the sight of him, all her planned speeches flew out of her head. She stood rooted to the spot. "I hope you don't mind that I just came in."

He lifted a brow and she saw it—the light mockery, the easy amusement. "Of course not. Want some coffee?"

He was so casual as he strolled over to the pot, she began to wonder if she had imagined that less than twenty-four hours before he had told her he loved her. "No, I . . . I came by to see if you'd come to dinner," she said impulsively. She could sense refusal and hurried on while his back was still to her. "Of course, I can't promise a meal like you could fix, but I won't poison you."

Thorpe abandoned the making of coffee, and turned to face her. "Liv, I don't think it's a good idea," he said quietly.

"Thorpe . . ." She turned away for a moment to gather strength. What she wanted to do was weep, and to use his shoulder to weep on. That wouldn't help either of them. She turned to face him again. "There are so many things you don't know, don't understand. But I want you to know, and to understand that I care. I care very much. Maybe more than I'm able to deal with." He could hear the nerves rushing through her voice as she took a step toward him. "I know it's a tremendous thing to ask, but if you could just give me some time."

It was costing her, he noted, to ask. Knowing her, he understood it had cost her to come to him this way. Hadn't he told himself to be patient? "I have some things to clear up here first," he said. "Would it be all right if I came by in an hour or so?"

He heard her small expulsion of breath. "Good."

An hour later, Liv was wound up tight. She tried to bank her nerves and concentrate on getting together a meal, but her eyes were forever fixing themselves on the clock.

Maybe I should change, she thought, and glanced down at her no-nonsense suit of charcoal gray. Even as she headed from the kitchen, the doorbell rang. Liv jolted. Oh, stop being ridiculous, she chided herself, but when she answered the door, her heart was thumping.

"Hi." She gave him a bright smile that was a little strained around the edges. "Your timing's good; I'll put the steaks on in a minute." She shut the door behind her and was already wondering what to do with her hands. "Steak's about the safest; I can't do too much to ruin it. Would you like a drink?"

I'm rambling, she thought. Good God. And he was looking at her again in that calm, steady way. She went to the bar without waiting for his answer. She could use one, even if he couldn't.

"Do you want scotch?" she asked, pouring first from the vermouth decanter for herself. She felt his hands on her shoulders.

She didn't resist when he turned her, didn't lower her eyes when his looked into hers. Without speaking, he simply gathered her close and held her. With a shuddering sigh, she clung to him and felt the tension flow from her.

"Oh, Thorpe, I nearly went crazy without you. I need you." That in itself was an awesome admission. They both held on to it. Liv lifted her face to his. "Don't go," she murmured. "Don't go tonight."

She pressed her mouth to his. The world focused for her again. "Make love to me," she whispered. "Now, Thorpe. Right now."

His mouth still on hers, he lowered her to the couch. He touched her gently, feeling the shape of her through her clothes. Her body was pliant, willing to be explored. Her breath trembled on his tongue. With unbearable softness, he kissed her again and again until Liv felt the total capitulation of mind, body, spirit. She felt no aching drive, no desperation, only a warm, liquifying surrender.

He undressed her slowly, layer by layer, piece by piece, letting his fingertips linger on the point of her breast, on the curve of her hip. Liv sighed and relinquished everything. He was in command, to take her wherever he wished.

His touch was light, almost reverent as he stroked her. Even when he wandered to the heated skin of her inner thighs, he moved without hurry. She began to shudder, to arch under him, but he lingered only briefly at her moist center before roaming on.

He teased the tip of her breast with his tongue, then stopped to savor. Liv felt the passion shoot from the sensitive skin he tasted to the pit of her stomach. It pulled at her until her movements were less languid. But he wouldn't be rushed. His mouth took the same slow, aching journey his fingertips had—over and over her while her skin hummed then quivered, then flashed with heat.

She heard herself calling him in a voice that was rough with needs. Her body was no longer passive, but crying out for him. Only him. He took her, but slowly, while she clung to him mindlessly, a breath away from heaven. Then his mouth was on hers and they rocketed through space together.

Chapter 13

"HEY." THORPE NUZZLED LIV'S NECK TO WAKE HER. "Going to sleep all day?"

She snuggled closer. "Um-hum." She kept her eyes shut. The feel of his body against her was all that she wanted at the moment. It could be night or morning or afternoon. She didn't care.

"It's after nine." He ran his hand down her back and heard her quiet sigh of pleasure. "We're going to spend the day in a boat, remember?"

Liv let her eyes open to slits. It was morning, she discovered. Saturday morning. And he was with her. With a sleepy smile, she tilted her face back to his. "Let's spend it in bed instead."

"The woman's lazy," he decided. And beautiful, he thought as he brushed the hair from her cheek. So achingly beautiful.

"Lazy?" Liv's left brow arched. "I've masses of

untapped energy." Her voice was slow and heavy as she shut her eyes again. "Masses," she repeated, and yawned.

"Oh yes, I can see that. Should we go to the Mall and jog first?"

She opened her eyes again. "Oh, I've a much better idea."

He hadn't expected the kiss to be so ardent, or her move to be so quick. She was suddenly lying across his chest with her mouth on his. His sound of pleasure was muffled. Then she touched him. His pulse jumped from an easy rhythm to a racing pace in the space of seconds. His blood, cool from the night's rest, flamed headily. Her hands were urgent, unexpectedly aggressive, her mouth hungry on his skin. He was caught up in her quickly, before he could fully register that she was leading him.

His instant response seemed to fill her with power. Her mouth was greedy on his, demanding and drawing, then roaming on to his neck, his throat, his shoulders. Her tongue darted out, tracing over his chest, lingering over his nipples, and then on.

When did she become so strong? he wondered, dazed. Or was he suddenly weak? He needed to have her now. Now. He could feel the blood pounding, in his head, in his loins, in his fingertips. Pleasure was a pain clawing at his stomach.

But when he tried to roll her over, she shifted, straddling him and crushing his mouth with her own. He was suffocating, but he pulled her closer. She was in his lungs, in his pores. Her movements on top of him were driving him mad.

Then he was inside her. Sanity shattered. The world exploded. He could hear the thunder of it roaring inside his head until he thought he would never hear anything else. Then it was Liv's breathing—short, shallow. She seemed to melt onto him as the strength seeped from her. He shuddered once, then cradled the back of her head in his hand.

My woman, he thought almost fiercely as she rested against him, still trembling. He let himself lie still until the intensity passed. There was still a need to be cautious. "I suppose you want an apology."

"Hmm?" He could hear the bafflement in the sigh.

"For calling you lazy."

Liv laughed and clung to him, then shifted to his side. "It does seem to be in order," she agreed, and prepared to snuggle again. "You can give it to me when I wake up."

"Oh, no." Rising, Thorpe grabbed her and hauled her unceremoniously, unsympathetically from the bed. "Rowing," he said as she tried to scowl at him.

"You're an obsessed man."

"Absolutely." He smiled before he kissed her nose. "I'll let you have the shower first."

"Thanks."

Her gratitude seemed a trifle mordant, but he grinned at her as she shut the bathroom door behind her.

Thorpe slipped on his slacks and gave an idle thought to fixing coffee. Instead, he reached for the pack of cigarettes that lay on the table beside the bed. From there, he could hear Liv humming as she started up the water for her shower.

Picking up his lighter, Thorpe flicked it and got spark but no flame. Mildly annoyed, he glanced around for matches, then opened the narrow drawer in the table, thinking he might find some there.

The photograph caught his eye immediately. It drew his attention first because Liv's apartment was so conspicuously bare of photos or personal mementos, and second because the child smiling back at him was strikingly beautiful. Lifting it out, he studied it.

It was a small snapshot framed in silver. The boy was hardly more than a year old, full in the cheeks and grinning broadly. His thatch of black hair was thick and left to fall around his face in a style that suited the freewheeling smile. The eyes were dark, dark blue, nearly cobalt, and filled with a mixture of mischief and delight. Here was a child a stranger on the street would stop to smile at—a child aunts and uncles would have to spoil. You could almost hear the laughter that was ready to burst through the grin.

With the photo still in his hand, Thorpe sat on the bed.

"I hope I used all the hot water," Liv said from behind the door. "It would serve you right for dragging me out of bed at the crack of dawn on a Saturday." She opened the door and stood for a minute looking down as she belted her robe. "I don't smell any coffee. The least you can do when . . ."

Her voice trailed off as she looked up and saw what Thorpe held in his hand. He watched the laughter and color flow from her face.

"Liv." He started to explain the hunt for the matches, then stopped. The words would hardly matter, even if they penetrated. "Who is he?"

Thorpe could count a full ten seconds before her eyes lifted to his. He watched her swallow, saw her bottom lip tremble; but when she spoke, her voice was clear and strong. "My son."

He had known it the moment he had seen the photo. The resemblance was unmistakable. Yet he felt a thud of shock at her answer. Keeping his eyes level, he too spoke calmly. "Where is he?"

Her face was dead white now. He had never seen eyes so dark, so full of thoughts and secrets and pain. A ripple of emotion shook her. "He's dead."

Quickly, Liv turned to the closet and began pulling out clothes. She saw nothing more than a blur of colors. She chose at random with hands that were too numb to shake. Even when she felt him take her shoulders, she continued, pushing at hangers and pulling out a blouse.

"Liv." It took a firm hand to turn her.

"I have to get dressed if we're going." She shook her head, already warding off questions as she tried to break his grip.

"Stop it." The command was curt, and the shake he gave her was strong enough to draw a quick breath from her. "No, don't do that. Not now, not ever again. Not with me." Then, before she could speak, he pulled her against him and held her.

She might have withstood the command. But he was offering comfort, strength. She leaned into him, and her defenses crumbled.

"Come, sit down," he said, "and tell me about it."

With his arm still around her, Liv sat on the bed. The snapshot lay beside her. She picked it up and set it in her lap. He didn't press her further, sensing she needed a moment before she could begin.

"I was nineteen when I met Doug." Her viewers wouldn't have recognized her voice now. It was small and hesitant and threaded with emotion. "He was studying law. He had a scholarship. He was a brilliant man, very free spirited, yet intense about what he was going to do. He was going to be the best defense attorney in the country. Change the system from within the system, challenge windmills, fight dragons. That was Doug."

When he said nothing, Liv drew a deep breath and

continued. Her voice grew stronger. "We were attracted to each other right away. Maybe partly because our backgrounds were so totally different and our ideals were so shiny. We sparked something in each other. And we were so young." She sighed, gathered strength and went on. "We married quickly, less than three months after we'd met. My family . . ." With a little laugh, she shook her head. "Well, leave it that they were surprised. Sometimes I'm afraid that might have been one of the reasons I married him. I don't like to think it was."

She stared off into middle distance, into her own memories. For a moment, Thorpe felt cut off from her. He shook the feeling off and continued to listen.

"It wasn't the sturdiest marriage—we were young and there were a lot of pressures. College. Doug was cramming for exams; I was interning at a local station and studying every spare minute. Money didn't matter much to either of us, luckily, because there wasn't a great deal of it. We had some good times, but Doug was . . ." She let out a long breath, as if searching for the proper words.

"He had a weakness for women. He loved me, I really believe he did in his own way, but he had a difficult time with fidelity. None of his—slips ever meant anything to him, and I wasn't very sexually experienced."

Thorpe found himself forced to choke words back. He didn't want to interrupt her now that she was talking, really talking, but the urge to curse the man she had married was almost too powerful to resist. He could remember very clearly her telling him, the first time they had made love, that she wasn't very good at pleasing a partner. Now, at least, he understood how the notion had been planted. He kept quiet and listened.

"We had Joshua within the year—hardly a year after we had first met. My family thought we were mad, starting a family so quickly and with an income far below what any of them could conceive trying to live on. But we both wanted a baby. We both wanted Josh. It seemed, for a time, he'd center our lives. He was so special." Her eyes fell to the photo in her lap. "I know all mothers think that about their babies, but he was so beautiful, so good-natured. He hardly ever cried."

She saw the tear fall onto the glass of the frame and squeezed her eyes shut. "We both adored him. It was impossible not to. For almost a year, we were happy. Really, really happy. Doug was a tremendous father. No job was too small or too demeaning. I remember once he woke me up, absolutely beside himself with pride when he had discovered Josh had cut a tooth."

Liv said nothing for nearly a full minute. Thorpe didn't want to prompt her. He understood her need to continue at her own pace. Keeping his arm around her, he waited.

"After I had graduated, we moved to New Jersey. Doug had a position with a small law firm, and I had landed a job with WTRL. I had the night desk at first. It wasn't easy on either of us. We were both just starting out, taking career crumbs, working obscene hours, raising the baby between us. I don't think Josh suffered. It certainly didn't seem so, he was such a happy baby. I was with him all day; Doug took over in the evening and put him to bed. Then, there was an incident with a law clerk Doug was attracted to. A small slip; he hadn't had one in a year. I overlooked it." She shrugged. "Tried to overlook it," she corrected herself. He blamed himself enough for it in any case. We tried to put things back together. We had the baby to think of. Nothing was more important to either one of us than Josh.

"Finally, I got off the night shift and onto days. I started reading the weather and doing a few minor reports. We spent a lot of time finding a sitter who satisfied both of us. Even then, we disagreed. Doug wanted me to stop working and stay home with Josh. I wouldn't do it." She pressed her fingers to her eyes a moment, then laid them back in her lap. "He was so well adjusted, so content. I loved him more than anything else in the world, but it didn't seem necessary, or even wise, for me to stop work, give up my career to be with him every minute. There were financial considerations, and my own needs. And I didn't want to smother him."

Her voice lost its strength and started to waver. "It was so tempting to just stay with him, spoil him. Doug used to say if I had my way I would have kept him a baby forever. I always thought he was trying to make Josh grow up too quickly. It was really sweet the way he'd buy him a football and talk about two-wheelers when Josh was only eighteen months old. But then he bought this huge swing set on Josh's second birthday. It terrified me, all those high bars. We argued about it a bit—not seriously. He laughed and called me overprotective. Then I laughed because Doug had been the one to research car seats for three weeks before he'd bought one. If I'd . . . If I'd stuck to my instincts, everything might have been different."

Liv stared down at the picture a moment; then, she pressed it to her breast. "The sitter called me at work to tell me Josh had taken a tumble from the swing. Just a bump on the head, she said, but I dropped everything, called Doug and rushed home. He'd gotten there even before I had. Josh seemed fine, but both of us were panicked. We took him straight to the emergency room at the hospital. I remember sitting there while he was being X-rayed. This big room, with all these black plastic chairs, metal ashtrays, and overhead lights. The floor tile was black with white speckles in it. I counted them and Doug paced.

"When the doctor came out, he took us both into this little room. He had a gentle voice. It terrified me. I could see it in his eyes before he said anything, but I wouldn't believe it. It wasn't possible." She pressed her hand to her mouth to try to keep the sobs from breaking through. Every detail was flooding back over her, and with them, all the pain. "I didn't believe it when he told us Josh had thrown an embolism. He was gone. Just like that."

Liv rocked back and forth, the photo pressed close as the sobs began to tear at her throat. "I don't even know what happened then. I got hysterical; they sedated me. The next thing I remember clearly was being at home. Doug was devastated. We couldn't seem to do each other any good. Instead, we lashed out. We said terrible things. He blamed me for not staying home watching our child. Caring for him. If I had been there, then maybe . . . And I clawed back. He'd bought the swing set. The damned swing set that had killed my baby."

"Liv." He wanted to wipe it all out—the pain, the grief, even the memories. She had the photo pressed against her breast as if she would try to bring it to life with her own heartbeat. What comfort could he offer? Not words; there weren't any. He could only hold her.

She dashed at the tears in her eyes as Thorpe drew her closer. Now that it was coming out, it was far from finished. She was functioning only on emotion now, and it had to run its course. "Greg came. He was Josh's godfather, our closest friend. God knows we needed somebody; our world had just fallen apart. He kept us from hurting each other more, but the damage was done. Josh was dead."

She gave a long sigh that rippled through her and had her shoulders trembling under his arm. "He was dead, and nothing could change it. There wasn't any blame. An accident. Just an accident."

She was silent for a long time. He could sense she was gathering her strength to continue. He wanted the pain to stop, wanted to help her close it off in the past where it had to stay. But even before he could speak, she continued.

"Greg took care of the arrangements—the funeral. I wasn't coping with it well. They were giving me something; I don't even know what it was. That first week, Doug and I were like zombies. My family came, but they didn't know me. They hadn't known Josh as I had. Every day I expected to walk by his room and hear him playing. I went back to work because I couldn't bear staying in the house waiting for him to wake up."

The tears were flowing as she spoke. Her voice was raw with grief. Whatever Thorpe had expected to find beneath the guards, it hadn't been this. She was blind with it now. He didn't think she was aware of him any longer, or of the arm that kept her close.

"The marriage was over. We both knew it, but we couldn't seem to bring ourselves to say the words. It was as if we were both thinking that if we hung on, he'd come back. We were polite to each other, tiptoeing around. I wanted someone to hold on to, someone to tell me . . . I don't know what words I needed to hear, but he didn't have them. I don't suppose I had them for him. We shared the same bed and never touched each other. We lived like that for over a month. Once I—once I asked him to come into Josh's room with me to help me—help me sort through his things. I knew I couldn't do it alone, and that it had to be done. He left the house, and didn't come back all night. He couldn't face it, and I couldn't face it alone. I had to call Greg, and we . . ." She pressed the heel of her hand to her forehead and tried not to choke over the words. "Doug and I never spoke of it again.

"Then Melinda came, my sister. She'd been fond of Josh. She used to send him useless, expensive little toys. Her being there seemed to help for a while. She was a distraction. She made us get out of the house, forced us to entertain her and keep our minds off . . . everything. I think it helped me, because I began to realize that Doug and I were only hurting each other by keeping up the pretense of being married. We had to stop. I decided to ask for a divorce before one of us did something unforgivable. It wasn't easy. I thought about it for days.

"I came home early one afternoon because I wanted to have a little time to sort out what I would say. I'd made up my mind to talk to Doug that night. When I got there, Doug's car was in the drive. I thought he might have been ill and come home. When I went upstairs, I found him in bed with my sister."

Very gently, she laid the photo back in her lap. "It was the final blow. My sister, my home, my bed. I left before either of them could say anything. I didn't want to hear. I didn't want to say the horrible things that I knew I'd say if I waited. I went to a motel. That's when I made up my mind that my parents had been right all along. If you live calmly, without disturbing your life with emotional attachments, you can't be hurt. That's how I was going to live. From that moment. No one, nothing, was ever going to take me to that point again. I'd had enough pain. I filed for divorce right away. Doug asked Greg to handle it for me. I never even spoke to him again, except through Greg. After a while I began to realize that Doug had just taken the step before I had. He'd used Melinda to end something that was killing both of us. That made it easier to forgive him. And because we'd had, and lost, something extraordinary together."

On the last word, she began to weep passionately, uncontrollably. As she turned into Thorpe, his arms cradled her to hold her until the grief passed.

Chapter 14

THERE WAS THE FAINTEST OF BREEZES OVER THE WATER. IT rippled over the reflections in the Potomac and just stirred Liv's hair. Now that they were there, stretched out under the sky, Thorpe was glad he had persuaded Liv to come. The sun and the activity would be good for her. Another woman, he thought, would have wanted to sleep off the strain of that much weeping. Not Liv.

She was still pale. Her eyes showed traces of the tears they had spent. But there was an unmistakable aura of strength about her. Thorpe admired her for it even as he loved her for it. Now, he felt he could understand why she had iced herself over. He had seen the face of the boy in the photograph—a face full of life and undiluted joy. He ached for her, for her loss. It was difficult for him to imagine Liv married, having a son, building a life with another man. A small house in the suburbs, a fenced yard, toys under the sofa—all of that seemed a world apart from the woman who sat across from him now. And yet, that had been her life not so many years before. It could be her life again, this time with him. Thorpe wanted it for her, and for himself.

More than ever, he knew there would be a need to move slowly with her. She was strong, yes, but she had been terribly hurt.

Doug, he thought, and experienced one moment of blazing anger. He didn't forgive as easily as Liv. The man, as he saw it, had done more than lose Liv through his own weaknesses. He had scarred her. Now it was up to Thorpe to show her, convince her that he meant to stand beside her. Always.

From where Liv sat, she could watch Thorpe row. His muscles rippled. There seemed to be no effort in the skill and strength he used to guide the boat over the river. He wasn't a man who had to flex his biceps to prove he was strong or masculine. He knew himself, and his confidence came from that knowledge.

So she had told him. Years had gone by since she had opened herself like that to anyone. There was nothing he didn't know about her now. Why had she told him? Perhaps, she mused, because she had known—or hoped—he would still be there when she had finished. And he had been: no questions, no advice, only support. He had known what she needed. When had she discovered what an unusual man he was? And why had it taken her so long? She felt relaxed and safe, and more at ease with herself than she could remember. The tears and the telling had purged the pain. For a moment, she closed her eyes and let her body enjoy the cleansing of her mind.

"I haven't thanked you," she said into the quiet.

"For what?" He brought the oars up and back in a long, steady stroke.

"For being there, and for not saying all those tidy little words people say when someone falls apart."

"You were hurting." His eyes were on hers again, looking deep. "Nothing I could say can erase what happened or make it easier. But I'm here now."

"I know." Liv sighed and leaned back. "I know."

They rowed for a time in silence. There were other boats here and there, dotting the river, but they didn't come close enough to exchange waves or greetings. It might have been their own private stream in their own private world.

"It's still early enough in the spring," Thorpe said, "that the river isn't crowded. I like to come at dawn in the summer, when the light's just breaking. It's amazing how quiet all those buildings look at sunrise. You can forget there'll be throngs of tourists tramping up the monument or packing into the Smithsonian. At dawn, it's hard to think about what's going on in the Pentagon or the Capitol. They're just buildings, rather unique, sometimes beautiful. On a Saturday or Sunday, when I haven't got a story weighing me down, I can just row, and forget all the times I've climbed the stairs, ridden the elevators and opened the doors in all those buildings."

"Funny," Liv mused. "A month or two ago, I would have been surprised to hear you say that. I pictured you as a man with one driving ambition, totally focused on his job, and his job alone. I never would have imagined you needing to get away from it, to separate yourself from the pace."

He smiled and continued to stroke steadily through the water. "And now?"

"And now I know you." She sat up and let the wind catch her hair. "When did you discover that rowing was your alternative to ulcer pills?"

He laughed, both amused and pleased. "You do know me. When I got back from the Middle East. It was hard over there. It was hard coming back. I imagine most soldiers feel the same way. Adjusting to normality isn't always easy. I started working out my frustrations this way, and found it became a habit."

"It suits you," Liv decided. "The understated physicality." She grinned as he arched a brow. "I don't imagine it's as simple as you make it look."

"Want to give it a try?"

She smiled and settled back. "Oh, that's all right. I'm better at spectator sports."

"It doesn't take much coordination," he added. Her eyes, which had begun to close, opened again. "Any kid with a week at summer camp can manage it." He was baiting her purposefully. He wanted to see that gleam of competition back in her eyes.

"I'm sure I could manage it just fine."

"Come on then," he invited, and locked the oars. "Give it a try."

She wasn't at all certain she wanted to, but the challenge was difficult to avoid. "Do you really think we should switch around? I wouldn't like to capsize in the middle of the Potomac."

"The boat's well balanced," he said easily. "If you are."

She stood up at that, though warily. "All right, Thorpe, move aside."

They changed positions with a minimum of fuss. Thorpe settled down on the small cushioned seat and watched Liv grip the oars. "Don't put a lot of power into it," he advised as she struggled for a moment to unlock them. "Just keep it as smooth as you can."

"I went to summer camp," she said sweetly, then scowled as her arms refused to coordinate with each other. "But then, usually we used canoes. I'm great with a paddle. There." She managed one shaky but reasonable stroke. "Now I'll get my rhythm. Take that smirk off your face, Thorpe," she added, and put all her concentration into her task.

Liv could feel twinges from muscles she hadn't put to use in years. It was a good, cleansing feeling. She could count to eight with each stroke and feel her shoulders strain then give with the movement. The oars scraped against her palms.

Oh yes, she thought, I can see why he does it. They were moving—not as cleanly as before, but moving nonetheless through the water under her power. There was no engine, no sail, no dependence on anything but her own effort. Her body, her will and the oars. Yes, she understood exactly what he meant. She believed she could have rowed for miles.

"Okay, Carmichael, time's up."

"Are you kidding? I just got started." She sent him a grim look and kept rowing.

"Ten minutes is enough the first time out. Besides"—he scooted across to her when she paused—"I don't want you to ruin your hands. I like them the way they are."

"I like yours." Taking his palm, she pressed it to her cheek.

"Liv." It was impossible to believe he could love her more at that moment than he had the moment before. Yet he did. Locking the oars, he drew her close to his side.

It was late afternoon before they walked back into Liv's apartment building. Each carried a paper sack filled with groceries.

"I know how to roast a chicken," Liv insisted,

pushing the button for her floor. "You put it in the oven and turn it on for a couple of hours. Nothing to it."

"Please." He gave her a pained look. "It might hear you." He cradled the sack that held the chicken more protectively. "There's an art to these things Liv. Seasoning, timing, preparation. If a chicken's going to give up its life for your consumption, the least you can do is have a little respect."

"I don't think I like the tone of this conversation." She glanced dubiously at his grocery bag. "Why don't we just send out for pizza?"

"I'm going to show you what a master can do with a two-pound roaster." Thorpe waited until they had stepped out of the elevator. "And then I'm going to make love to you until Sunday morning."

"Oh." Liv gave this a moment's thought and struggled with a pleased smile. "Only till then?"

"Until very late Sunday morning," he added, stopping to kiss her before she could locate her keys. "Maybe," he murmured against her mouth, "until very early Sunday afternoon."

"I'm beginning to appreciate the idea of this cooking lesson a bit more."

He let his lips wander to her ear. "I'm beginning to appreciate the idea of sending out for pizza. Later." His mouth came back to hers. "Much, much later."

"Let's go inside and take a vote."

"Mmm, I like your thinking."

"It's the Washington influence," she told him as she slipped her key into the lock. "There's no issue that can't be resolved with a vote."

"Tell that to the senators who are waiting for Donahue and his filibuster to run out of steam."

She laughed and turned the knob. "I'll tell you something, Thorpe," she said as she closed the door behind them. "I don't want to think about senators or filibusters." She shifted the bag in her arm so that she could bring her body close to his. "I don't even want to think about that two-pound roaster you're so crazy about."

"No?" His free arm came around her. "Why don't you tell me what you do want to think about?"

With a smile, she began to undo the buttons of his shirt. "Why don't I show you instead? A good video reporter knows that action's worth a thousand words."

He felt her cool, long fingers roam down his chest. He set down his bag, then took hers and let it lean against the closed door. "I've always said, Carmichael, you're a hell of a reporter." Her laugh was smothered against his mouth.

It was late Sunday evening. Liv sat close to Thorpe on the sofa. The entire weekend, she thought, had been like a dream. She had shared with him more than she had ever intended to share with anyone. But then, he had come to mean more to her than she had intended to allow anyone to mean to her again.

Last night, they'd laughed through the cooking and eating of dinner. It was so easy to laugh with him. So easy, when she was with him, to forget all the vows she had once made. He loved her. The knowledge still staggered her. This tough, relentless man loved her. He'd shown her gentleness and understanding—traits she had needed but had never thought to find in him. How different her life would have been if she had found him all those years ago!

But no . . . Liv closed her eyes. That would be like wishing Joshua out of existence. She wouldn't give up the memory of those brief years for anything. He'd been the focus of her world. Her child.

Perhaps because her time with him had been concentrated into two short years, she could remember almost every detail of it. Loving like that was the greatest wonder a woman could know. And the greatest danger. She'd promised herself never to experience it again.

Now there was Thorpe. What sort of life would she have with him? What sort would she have without him? Both of the questions, and their answers, frightened her.

Already, she thought as her head stayed nestled on his shoulder, he's gotten close enough to frighten me. I'm not certain I can turn back now. . . . I'm not certain I can go ahead. If things could go on just as they are . . . But the time was fast approaching when she would have to make a move, one way or the other.

He knows what he wants, she mused. There isn't a doubt in his mind. I wish I could see things as clearly.

"You're quiet," he murmured.

"I know."

"Yesterday morning's catching up with you." He wanted to draw her closer, to make her forget, but forgetting wasn't the answer for either of them. "It couldn't have been easy for you, talking it all through, feeling it all again."

"No, it wasn't easy." She tilted her head to look up at him. Her face was in shadows, but her eyes were clear on his. "But I'm glad it happened. I'm glad you know. Thorpe . . ." She let out a little breath. It was becoming more and more important that he know everything. "There was a time, right after Josh died, that I wanted to die too. I didn't want to live without him; I couldn't conceive of living without him. There wasn't enough strength in me to do anything solid about it, but if I could have died, just closed my eyes and died, I would have."

"Liv." He lifted a hand to her cheek. "I can't pretend to know what it's like to lose a child. That kind of grief can't be understood by anyone who hasn't experienced it."

"I didn't die," she continued, swallowing. "I ate, I slept, I functioned. But I buried part of myself with Josh. What was left, I smothered when I divorced Doug. It seemed the only way to survive. I've lived this way a long time, without considering any changes."

"But you didn't die, Liv." His hand slipped down to cup her chin. His eyes were direct on hers. "And changes are a part of living."

"Have you ever loved someone completely?"

"Just you," he said simply.

"Oh, Thorpe." Liv pressed her face against his shoulder. Emotion squeezed her heart. The words came so easily to him, and the feelings. She wasn't certain she was strong enough yet to accept them. "I need you. It scares me to death." She lifted her face again and her eyes were eloquent. "I know what it is to lose. I'm not sure I can survive a second time."

He was so close, so close to having her. He could feel it. If he took her in his arms, if he kissed her now, he might urge the words he needed from her lips. They were in her eyes. It took every ounce of his control not to push. Not today, he told himself. She's given you enough this weekend.

"Needing someone," he said carefully, "doesn't mean you have to lose them."

"I'm trying to believe that." She took a deep breath. "For the first time in five years, I want to believe that. It matters, when I thought it never would again."

After a moment, he lifted her hand and pressed the palm to his lips. "How much time do you want?"

The tears came instantly, silently. She hadn't had to

ask. He had known. He was giving her what she needed with no questions, no demands. "I don't deserve you." She shook her head. "I really don't."

"That's my risk, isn't it?" He smiled. "In my opinion, I deserve you completely, so that balances things."

"I need to do some thinking." She kissed him, then held on. "I have to be alone, because you make it hard for me to think."

"Do I?" He kissed her again. "All right," he agreed, pulling her with him as he rose. "But think fast."

"Tomorrow." She held him close for another moment. "Just until tomorrow." The arms around her had such strength. The man had so much to give. "Oh, God, am I a fool, Thorpe?"

"Yeah." He drew her back to frame her face in his hands. "I'm a hell of a catch, Carmichael; just remember that."

"I will," she murmured as he walked to the door. He paused, and turned back with his hand on the knob.

"Tomorrow."

"Tomorrow," she repeated when she was alone.

Chapter 15

THINGS WERE NOT AS CLEAR AS LIV WOULD HAVE LIKED them to be. Once before she had thought herself in love, and she had been wrong. What she had felt for Doug had been the impulses and dreams of youth. She was older now, and more cautious. Perhaps too cautious, she mused as she settled behind her desk. Yet, when she told Thorpe she loved him, she wanted to say the words without any cloud of doubt. He deserved that from her.

She didn't want to lose him. That above all was crystal clear. He had become the focal point of her life in a very short time. Dependence. No, she couldn't deny that she was dependent on him. But was that love?

Was it love when a man kept drifting into your mind? When you began to associate the tiny details of your day with thoughts of him? When you stored up the little pieces to share with him?

Liv could remember what it was like to lie beside him in the morning—the quiet, the warmth, the easy unity. She could remember how a look in his eyes could make her tremble with need even in a crowded room.

Was she in love with him? Why was she searching for another name for what she felt? The truth had been locked inside her for days. Now it was time to accept it. If she was going to ask Thorpe to take a risk, she had to be willing to take one herself. Love equaled vulnerability. He could hurt her, undoubtedly would from time to time. The shield was gone now. She would never be able to hide behind it again. Abruptly, she realized she didn't want to. What she wanted could be said in one word: Thorpe.

"Liv!"

She turned to the frantic assignment editor with a brilliant smile. "Yes, Chester." It was going to be a beautiful day.

"Take a crew. On the double. New Senate Office Building. Some guy, unidentified, is holding three hostages, including Senator Wyatt, in the senator's office."

"Good God." She was up, grabbing a pad and her purse. "Anybody hurt?"

"Not yet. As far as we know," he added, streaking toward Carl's office. "There's been some gunfire. Be careful. We want a bulletin fast."

"Twenty minutes." She was already out the door.

The Capitol Police had the building surrounded when Liv arrived. She glanced around for telltale signs of Secret Service men and FBI. When you knew what to look for, they stood out clearly. On the rooftops of neighboring buildings, she caught glimpses of sharpshooters taking position. Men armed with ugly-looking guns were going over strategy and positions on two-ways. The press area was already partitioned off and jammed with reporters and technicians. Everyone was talking at once, demanding answers, trying to sneak their way through the barricade to secure a closer position.

Liv pushed her way through and managed to get a mike out to a nearby uniformed officer. "Olivia Carmichael, WWBW. Can you give us a rundown on what's happened? Do you have an identification on the man who's holding Senator Wyatt? What are his demands?"

"He's a former aide; that's all I can tell you." That's all you *will* tell me, Liv corrected, noting the flicker in his eye. "He hasn't made any demands yet."

"How many weapons does he have? How did he get inside the building?"

"We don't know. We're only sure about the handgun. He isn't even answering the phone yet."

Liv was left with little more than nothing in the midst of a pack of hungry reporters. She had to find someone else—with a looser tongue. She could manage a quick bulletin, but she was going to have to do a lot of digging to put anything solid on the air.

Senator Wyatt. Liv remembered him very well from the embassy party. Jovial, pink-cheeked Senator Wyatt who had joked with her and told her to dance with Thorpe. She glanced across the street and studied the dozens of windows. It didn't seem possible he was in one of those rooms with a gun held to his head.

On the edge of the crowd, Liv spotted a familiar face. It was the receptionist who had kept her cooling her heels for two hours in an office two floors below Senator Wyatt's only a few days before.

"Ms. Bingham." Liv blessed the two hours and the

innumerable cups of coffee she had consumed in the woman's office. "Olivia Carmichael. WWBW."

"Oh, Ms. Carmichael, isn't it dreadful!" She stared up at the windows with her eyes wide and stunned. "They've cleared the whole building. I just can't believe it! Poor Senator Wyatt."

"Do you know who's holding him?"

"It's Ed. Ed Morrow. Who would have thought it? Why, I've ridden in the elevator with him just dozens of times." She lifted her hand to her throat at the memory. "I heard the senator had to let him go last week, but . . ."

"Why?" Liv had the mike under her arm and was scribbling quickly on her pad. The woman never seemed to notice. "I'm not sure. Rumor is Ed got himself tangled up in gambling—something illegal. He's always so polite. Who would have thought it?"

"The senator fired him?"

"Just last week." She nodded quickly three times, and her eyes were still wide. "He was supposed to clear out his desk today. He must have gone crazy. Sally said he shot twice in the hallway."

"Sally?"

"The senator's secretary. She was just down the hall when it happened. If she had been in the office . . ." She swallowed and fixed her eyes back on the building. "He's fired twice through the window since I've been out here. Do you think the senator's going to be all right?"

"I'm sure he's going to be fine." Even as Liv said the words, the sharp report of gunfire split the air.

"Oh God!" The receptionist gripped Liv's arm. "Is he killing them? He must be killing them!"

"No, no." Liv felt the cool lick of fear. "He's just shooting out of the window. It's going to be all right."

She had to corroborate the woman's identification of the gunman before she put it on the air. That was the job—one step at a time. She couldn't think about what was happening to the people inside. Not yet. "Is the senator's secretary still here?"

"She had to go with the police. She's back there somewhere."

"All right, thank you." Quickly, Liv began to work her way through the crowd again. Spying Dutch, she headed straight for him. If anyone could give her the details, he could.

It was closer to half an hour than the twenty minutes she had promised, but Liv delivered a straightforward, detailed stand-up with pans of the police and the crowd. The building across the street was quiet—too quiet for her liking. She would almost have preferred another volley of gunfire to the silence. Terror, she realized abruptly, was always silent.

"When the hell is he going to do something?" Bob muttered beside her. The tension was seeping into them all—police, bystanders, press. Everyone was waiting for the next move. "Major league coming up," he added. "There's T.C."

"I'll be right back," Liv told him. "Make sure the engineer's ready to patch us into the station if anything goes down." She made for Thorpe like a homing pigeon heading for roost. "Thorpe."

"Liv." He touched her cheek briefly. "I figured you'd be here."

"Is there anything new?" she asked, knowing there was more than a story involved this time. They both knew the man inside.

"They've established communications with Morrow. Wyatt's not hurt; neither are the aides. Yet. He doesn't seem to be quite rational. One minute he wants a half million in cash and a plane, the next gold and an armored car. He changes his mind every time they talk to him."

"How the hell did he get in there with a gun?" she demanded.

Thorpe gave a quick, mirthless laugh. His eyes never left the building across the street. "It isn't difficult for someone security's used to seeing to pass through. He had it in his jacket, I imagine, or it was already in his desk." He shifted impatiently. Liv could tell he wanted to move, wanted to do something. "I'd feel better if he were a professional. In the state he's in, it's too easy for him to make a mistake and take the hostages down with him." He swore with a quiet urgency she rarely heard from him. "He wanted to make certain he was getting full media coverage."

"You don't really think he's doing it for the publicity, do you?" The thought appalled her.

Thorpe shook his head. "I've dealt with him several times when I've set up meetings." He took out a cigarette. "He's a taut, hungry little man. A good mind, but the nerves show."

"Gambling, I'm told."

"So the stories go." Thorpe drew on the cigarette and let out a quick stream of smoke. "Too quiet," he muttered. "Too damn quiet."

Tension was palpable. It increased, almost visibly, as the minutes dragged by. How long, she wondered, could the taut, hungry little man Thorpe had described stand up under the strain? He'd taken an irrevocable step. How much further would he go? She waited, like the others, to find out.

"Thorpe." Liv recognized the man from the Secret Service, and frowned when he singled Thorpe out. "Chief Daniels wants you."

"Sure." Thorpe crushed another cigarette under his heel. "Her too," he added with a jerked thumb at Liv. "We're a team."

Liv bit back a smile. That was quite a change. Without a word, she followed behind them.

The communications van was set up well away from the press area. She glanced briefly at the equipment, the tape recorders, two-ways, phones, the men working in shirt sleeves. What could they want with Thorpe? she wondered. This had nothing to do with the press.

Chief Daniels pushed his glasses back onto his weary face. "T.C., Morrow's demanding to speak to you directly. You game?"

"Sure."

"The tape'll be running. Be careful what you say. If he makes any demands, don't promise, don't negotiate. Leave that to us." He spoke quickly and without inflection, but Liv caught the undercurrents. He didn't like this new twist. "You're not in a position to give him anything he wants. He's smart enough to know that. Whatever he asks for, you just tell him that you'll check and get back to him. Understood?"

"Understood."

He glanced at Liv and focused in on her press badge.

"She's with me," Thorpe told him easily.

"None of this goes on the air until I give the word." His eyes were hard, and close to hostile. "We're not going to give him a media free-for-all."

"Understood," Liv said calmly, then watched as Thorpe was handed a receiver.

"We'll ring." Daniels signaled one of his men. "Keep him talking as long as you can. If things start to get out of hand, we'll take over."

Thorpe nodded and heard Morrow pick up the phone on the first ring.

"T.C.?"

"Yeah. How you doing, Ed?"

Morrow laughed shakily. "Terrific. You going to do a report on me?"

"That's right. You want to tell me why you're up there and what it'll take to get you down?"

"You remember that day we sat in my office and talked about the Birds when Wyatt was held up in a meeting?"

"Sure." Thorpe caught a glimpse of Daniels's grim face as he held a headset to his ear. "End of last summer. The Orioles were fighting for first place." He drew out another cigarette and flicked on his lighter. "Seen any games this year?"

Liv could hear the echo of the frantic laugh come through the receiver. "I've already dropped twenty-five big ones on games this year."

"That's rough. You need money?" Thorpe's eyes were locked on Daniels's now. "Is that what you want for Wyatt's release?"

"I'll tell you all about it T.C., but just you. You come in and do one of your interviews right here. I've got an exclusive for you."

Liv could hear snatches, and what she heard was enough to have her grabbing Thorpe's arm in panic. Ignoring her, Thorpe kept his eye on Daniels.

"Too many hostages," Daniels said in an undertone.

"That'll give you one more hostage, Ed," Thorpe replied easily. "Doesn't seem like a very good deal."

"No, no, I see your point." Morrow's voice shook with nerves. "Maybe I'll send out the two aides for you. If you tell me you're coming up. You're as good as your word, aren't you, T.C.?"

"Two for one," Thorpe mused, watching Daniels

steadily while Liv gripped his arm tighter and shook her head. "But then, the aides don't mean much, do they?"

There was a long pause. Liv could feel the sweat beginning to trickle down her back.

"You come up, alone, no back-up, and I'll send out Wyatt. How's that for a deal? A one-time offer, T.C. You're not going to turn down a scoop like this, are you?"

"I'll have to check back with the big shots at CNC, Ed. Give me ten minutes. I'll get back to you."

"Ten minutes," Morrow agreed, and cut the connection.

Liv grabbed Thorpe's jacket and turned him to face her. "No." She shook her head frantically while her eyes mirrored her fear. "You can't. You can't think of doing such a thing. Thorpe, you can't."

"Hold on a minute." His voice was calm and practical as he set her aside. "Well?" he said simply to Daniels.

"Number one, we can't ask you to cooperate."

"So you're not asking," Thorpe countered. "What then?"

"People I have to talk to before we consider making an exchange like this." Daniels rubbed a hand over his mouth. He didn't like the taste of it. But there was a senator involved. Touchy, he thought. Very touchy.

"Then start talking to them," Thorpe suggested.

Daniels sent him a long look. "You'd better do some thinking while I do. It's not going to be a cozy interview."

"Thorpe." Liv's voice quavered with panic. She knew that look in his eyes. "No."

Thorpe took her gently by the shoulders. "Liv," he began.

"No, no, listen to me." She gripped the front of his jacket. "It's insane. You can't just walk in there; you're not trained for this sort of thing. And who's to say he'll let Wyatt go when you do? He'll—he'll have more bargaining power then. You must see that."

"He wants to talk," Thorpe pointed out, and started to lead her away. "Wyatt can't get him national coverage; I can."

"Oh God, Thorpe, he's not stable." She was weeping now and unaware of it. "He'll kill you, and the senator too. You don't have to go. They can't make you."

"No one's making me." He signaled a member of his crew and spoke in undertones. "Call the desk. Tell them I'm going to do an interview with Morrow in exchange for the hostages. Get a camera on the building in about ten minutes; some of them should be coming out. I'll need a tape recorder."

"No!" Liv's voice rose now, in direct contrast to his. She clutched at him as if she could hold him from what he intended to do. "You can't. Please, listen to me."

"Liv." He brushed the hair back from her face. "You'd do the same thing. It's part of the job."

"Your life isn't worth a Pulitzer."

He lifted a brow. "Some might disagree with that."

"Damn it, Thorpe." She had to think fast; she had to be rational or he'd never listen. "It's probably just a trick. He can let the two aides go, and with you and Wyatt, he'll have two important people. He must realize that the network would negotiate for your release. It's just the sort of thing he's looking for."

"Maybe. Maybe not." He kissed her then to quiet her, and then because he needed to.

"Oh, please, don't go." She clung to him, knowing she had already lost and unable to accept it. "I love you." Slowly, he reached up to take her shoulders and draw her back far enough to see her face. It was tear-streaked and desperate. "I love you," she repeated. "It's tomorrow, Thorpe. Stay with me."

"God." He rested his forehead on hers and let the feeling seep through him. He pulled her close again, bruisingly close. "Your timing, Carmichael, is incredible." When he kissed her again, he felt her lips tremble under his. "We're going to talk about this later. We're going to talk about it for a long time." He drew her away and smiled at her. "You'd better give your station the latest developments or you're going to find yourself scooped."

"Why won't you listen to me?" She was angry now as well as desperate. Even her love hadn't swayed him. "You can't go in there. I need you." She didn't care if the words were unfair, as long as they prevented him from crossing the street.

"I need you too, Liv. That doesn't have anything to do with me doing my job, or with you doing yours."

She didn't want logic; she only wanted him. She clutched at him fiercely. "I'm going to marry you."

He smiled again and kissed her nose. "I've known that for months. You're just a bit slow." Glancing up, he noted the camera pointing in their direction. "And now several hundred thousand people know it too."

"I don't care." Her penchant for privacy seemed suddenly absurd. "Thorpe, you can't ask me to face losing you." She grabbed the lapels of his jacket in hands that were damp with fear. "Damn you, I can't face it! I can't face it all again. I won't."

His grip was firmer now, and his eyes intense. "You listen to me. I love you, more than anything. Don't you forget it. We live with risk every day; if we don't, we're already dead. It hurts to be alive, Liv."

Pale and calm, she faced him. "I'll never forgive you

if you do this. I never wanted to love you. Now that I do, you're asking me to stand by and wait to lose you. I won't forgive you for that."

He watched her steadily. He saw the pain and the panic. He didn't want to hurt her. He would have done anything in his power to keep that look from her eyes, but he couldn't alter who he was or what he was. "Maybe you should think about who you fell in love with, Olivia. I haven't changed. I'm exactly as I was, and exactly as I'll be tomorrow. Now I've got a job to do. So do you."

"Thorpe—"

"Come on." He cut her off and began to lead her back. "Daniels should have finished talking to his people by now."

Liv stood back and watched, helpless, as Thorpe, Daniels and Morrow made the final negotiations for the exchange. There was nothing she could say, nothing she could do to stop him. He had told her she would do the same thing. She understood it, but it didn't matter. He was her love, her life. Everything that was important to her was bound up in him.

It's not fair! she thought on a fresh surge of desperation. She'd been given her second chance. Now she had to stand back and watch while it was put on the line. Myra's words played back in her head: life's not short, but it's never long enough. *Thorpe!* Her whole being cried out to him while she dug her teeth into her lip to keep silent. *Don't go! I have so much to say to you. So much time to make up for.* She wanted to tell him what he meant to her, how he had opened up everything she had closed.

Thorpe was checking the tape recorder as he listened to Daniels's instructions. Liv watched them, her eyes blinded by tears. Oh, Thorpe, she thought, I can't face the emptiness again. Not now that I know what it is to have you. I need to know you're there when I reach out. I want to love again, to hold your child in my arms. Oh, please, don't shut me off when I've just started to feel.

With a deep shuddering breath, she pressed her fingers to her eyes. She watched him again—the sharp athletic profile, the deep, intense eyes. *Is he frightened?* What's going on in his mind? Is he remembering that none of us is indestructible? But you have to be, Thorpe. For me. For us.

What does he need from me? *Not this,* she realized abruptly. He needs support, not a hysterical woman pulling at him, begging him to think of her. He needs his wits about him now. . . . If only I could go with him. But I can't. I can't *go* with him, but I can *send* something with him.

As she watched, the two aides were hustled out of the building and out of range. So Morrow had kept the first part of the bargain. There was only Wyatt now. Thorpe for Wyatt.

Drawing on all her strength, Liv stepped up to him. "Thorpe."

He turned to her. There were still tears on her cheeks, but he recognized the control.

"You always did go out of your way to scoop me on a story," she managed in a reasonably steady voice. "I hope this one's worth it. You better do a hell of a job in there. I need the copy for my broadcast."

He grinned as he kissed her. "Just don't step too close to my turf, Carmichael."

Liv clung for one last moment. "Catch my report at five-thirty."

"I've always been fond of you, T.C.," Daniels commented. "And it seems this lady is too." He gave Thorpe a long look. "You've still got time to back out."

"Thorpe walk away from an exclusive?" Liv pulled back and ordered herself not to shake. "You don't know him very well."

"You." He pulled Liv back a last time. "Think about where you want to spend your honeymoon. I lean toward Paris."

"You warned me you were a romantic." Then he was turning, preparing to cross the street. "Thorpe!" Liv couldn't prevent herself from calling out. When he turned she held back the plea and smiled at him. "If you get yourself killed, the deal's off."

He grinned. "Tonight we send out for pizza. I'll be back."

He was gone quickly, swallowed up by the building. The waiting began.

Thorpe had a pretty good idea of what he should do. The questions were already forming in his head as he rode the elevator with an armed guard. The trick would be to keep Morrow pacified, at ease. Talking. Keep him talking. He fully intended to come out in one piece. Lebanon had taught him a few things.

He'd ridden this elevator before, countless times. It was part of the routine. Hadn't Alex Haley interviewed Rockwell while the American Nazi leader had played with a gun? And that had been a hell of an interview. Reporters couldn't always choose the sane and the reasonable.

The elevator opened and he started down the hall. The tickle at the back of his neck told him there were more guns. He ignored them and knocked on Wyatt's outer office.

"T.C.?"

He heard Morrow's voice, strung out with nerves.

"Yeah. I'm alone."

"Come in slow. I've got a good view of the door."

Thorpe did as he was instructed. Morrow stood in the archway to Wyatt's inner office with his gun held to the senator's head.

"T.C." Wyatt's normally florid face was gray. "You've got to be crazy."

"How are you, Senator?"

"He's fine," Morrow snapped, his eyes darting behind Thorpe. "Shut the door and step away from it."

When Thorpe obeyed, he signaled him with a jerk of his head to come forward. He eyed the tape recorder. "Set it down and take off your jacket."

"No weapons, Ed," Thorpe said easily as he carefully stripped off his jacket. "Just the tape recorder. We made a deal." He gave Wyatt an apologetic smile. "You'll have to excuse us, Senator. Ed and I have a private interview."

"Yeah." Morrow stared at Thorpe a moment, then loosened his hold on Wyatt. "Yeah. You can go."

"T.C.—"

"I said you can go." Morrow's voice lifted. So did the gun. "He's here for me this time."

"Sorry, Senator." Thorpe's voice was calm and unruffled. His fingertips were prickling as he watched the gun hand tremble. "Ed and I have a lot to discuss. We'll set something up later."

With a nod, Wyatt started to turn.

"No." Morrow stopped him with the word. He licked his lips, then ran the back of his hand over them. "You back up, all the way out."

Thorpe waited as Wyatt followed Morrow's instructions. There was fear in the room; he could all but taste it. It didn't lessen even after the door closed behind Wyatt. Morrow stood a moment, staring at the door.

Thorpe didn't want him to start thinking too carefully. "All right," he said, and took a seat. "Let's get started." He turned on the tape recorder.

Outside, Liv watched the building steadily. Everything but her mind was numb. She couldn't feel her hands, her feet. She knew there was activity all around her—in the communications van, in the press area. Things were starting to hum. Her mind was focused on one thing. Thorpe.

Thorpe kept his questions brief. He wanted as little emotion as possible. "Ed, it might be more comfortable for both of us if you . . ." He made a gesture with his hand, palm lowered to indicate the gun. Morrow glanced at it, then shifted the revolver until it was no longer aimed at Thorpe's chest. "Thanks. Obviously, you chose Wyatt's office because you worked here," he went on. "Did you feel the senator was unjust in letting you go?"

"He's clean as a whistle, you know," Morrow answered. "Couldn't blackmail him. God I needed the money. In deep, T.C.—too damn deep. I thought about juggling some funds, but I didn't have enough time. He found out about the gambling, about the people I've been dealing with. Not the senator's kind of people." He laughed in a quick nervous giggle and shifted the gun again. It was pointed back at Thorpe, but Morrow didn't notice. "I thought I'd get something for taking him hostage, but they'd never let me get away with it, would they?" The look he gave Thorpe was lost and fatalistic. "I'd be a dead man before I got my hands on the money."

Thorpe changed the line of questioning. A man with nothing to lose was the most dangerous. "How much are you in for?"

"Seventy-five thousand." The phone rang and Morrow jerked up. The gun was pointed at Thorpe's head.

"Fifteen minutes, Ed," Thorpe reminded him calmly. "We arranged for me to check in every fifteen minutes, right?"

Someone pushed a cup of coffee into Liv's hand. She never tasted it. Thorpe's voice came suddenly, low and calm, from behind her through the machines in the van. Jolting, she dropped the cup. Coffee splashed warm around her ankles. *You can't stand here and do nothing,* she told herself, steadying. Do your job. Turning, she went back to her crew to send out the next live bulletin.

Thirty minutes crawled into sixty. The office was stuffy. Thorpe knew he was dragging out the interview. All had been said. But his instincts told him Morrow wasn't ready yet. The man was slouched in his chair, his eyes filmy. There was a thin bead of sweat over his top lip, and a muscle twitched in his left cheek sporadically. But the gun was still in his hand.

"You're not married, are you, T.C.?"

"No." Carefully, Thorpe drew out a cigarette, offering one to Morrow.

Morrow shook his head. "Got a woman?"

"Yeah." Thorpe lit the cigarette and thought of Liv. Cool hands, cool voice. "Yeah, I've got a woman."

"I had a wife—kids too." The film in the eyes became tears. "She packed up and left last week. Ten years. She said ten years was long enough to wait for me to keep my promises. I swore to her I wouldn't gamble anymore." Tears rolled down to mix with the sweat. He wiped neither away. "I always swore I wouldn't gamble anymore. But I needed to get even. You know what they do to you when you can't get even." He shuddered.

"There are people who can help you, Ed. Why don't we go outside. I know some people."

"Help?" Morrow sighed on the word. Thorpe didn't like the sound of it. "No help now, T.C. I crossed the line." He looked up and stared into Thorpe's eyes. "A man should know what's going to happen when he crosses the line." He raised the gun again, and Thorpe felt his heart stop. "You make sure," Morrow sobbed, "I get my airtime." Before Thorpe could move, Morrow had turned the gun on himself.

One shot. Just one. Liv felt her legs buckle, saw the granite-faced building fade. Someone gripped her arm as she swayed.

"Liv, come on. You'd better sit down." It was Bob's voice in her ear, his hand on her arm.

"No." She shook him off. She wasn't going to faint. She wasn't going to give in. Fiercely, she began to push her way through the crowd again. She was going to be standing up when he came through the doors. When he came through them, she would be there for him.

Don't let him be hurt. Oh, God, don't let him be. . . . The fear was rising in her throat. No hysterics, she warned herself as she pushed a print reporter and two cameramen out of her way. Soon he'll be striding across the street. We've got a whole lifetime to start together. Today. Risks? We'll take hundreds of risks. Together, damn you, Thorpe. Together. She shoved her way clear.

Then she saw him. Alive, whole, walking toward her.

She was running, past the barricades, away from the crowd.

"Oh, damn you, Thorpe. Damn you!" Weeping, she clung to him. The more she shuddered, the more she cursed him, the tighter he held her.

Suddenly, she was laughing. It was, after all, a beautiful day. Taking his hair in her hands, Liv pulled his head back to see his face. "You bastard, you're going to beat me on the air with this, aren't you? Oh, *Thorpe!*" She pressed her mouth to his and tightened her hold. Neither of them took any note of the cameras whirling and clicking around them.

He drew her away and the grin was back, though she could see traces of horror in his eyes from whatever had happened inside. "Do you love me?" he demanded.

"Yes, damn you. Yes."

When she tried to pull him back to her, he held her off, lifting a brow. "Going to marry me?"

"The minute we get a license. We're not going to waste any time."

Briefly, his mouth touched hers. They linked arms. "By the way, Carmichael," he said, as they strolled away from the building, "you owe me two hundred dollars."